DAYS GONE BY

A SAM POPE NOVEL

ROBERT ENRIGHT

GW00497816

For my girls,

CHAPTER ONE

TWELVE YEARS AGO…

The Paris skyline was always a magnificent sight, with the Eiffel Tower a totem to the majesty of the capital city. Swathes of tourists would pay extortionate prices just to revel in its beauty and ride the elevator all the way to the top for their posed pictures and fond memories. The surrounding vendors, hawking 'I Love Paris' T-shirts would be rubbing their hands at the footfall, and even as the sun began to set, the bright lights of the city would only enhance the visage of culture that Paris had cultivated.

It made Pierre Ducard proud.

As he walked across the viewing platform of the tower, he weaved between the groups of hysterical tourists, all of them giddy from their trip to the magnificent structure. Music was playing through the speakers, and the good vibe of the city was etched across the face of every smiling visitor. Ducard made his way to the edge where the tall, thick glass panels kept the tower safe from potential jumpers, and he peered out at the city before him.

His city.

Below was the Jardin de la Tour Eiffel, the magnificent gardens

1

that surrounded the iconic tower, where street artists beguiled tourists with their talents and food vendors served delicious meals for extortionate prices. A city alive beneath his feet.

He then turned and watched as the tourists gathered for photos and returned any gaze that fell upon him with a handsome smile. Ducard was the quintessential French gentleman. His dark hair was speckled with grey flecks and flowed in thick waves behind his ears, immaculately combed into a side parting. His strong jaw was clean-shaven, and his muscular frame was enhanced in a tailormade, perfectly fitted pinstripe suit. He looked a decade younger than his forty-eight years of age, and he was proud of that fact.

To the passers-by, he was just a handsome man waiting for his guest to arrive. They had no idea he was one of the most powerful and influential men in the country.

The Chef d'État-Major des Armées.

As the military head of the French armed forces, Ducard was responsible for the safety of his country and their international military position. As one of the most powerful countries and armed forces in the world, it was a position he held with ferocious pride, and every step along his thirty-year career within the military had been towards this position. The notion of a family life had never been a factor, and while Ducard was never shy of attention, he had always kept a serious relationship at arm's length. As cliché as it was, he had been married to his job from the moment he put on his uniform over three decades ago, and there wasn't a woman or a thought of fatherhood that would lure him from it.

It was why he was perfect for the job.

And why he was on the verge of a dangerous move.

Protecting his country wasn't just about sending the well-trained soldiers of the French military into battle. While his career as a soldier was highly respected within the government, it was Ducard's ability to play the political game that drew him the most plaudits. Although he knew that his morals would need to be malleable, Ducard had served numerous presidents with loyalty and respect. If there was a favour to be gained or leverage to secure, Ducard would seek it ruthlessly and over the years, he had amassed such power that those in higher positions would still sit up when he walked into the room.

It was power that couldn't be bought, but it was a power that could be stripped, and that was why the next few days were so important.

It was why his morals were going from malleable to missing.

Three days prior, two French diplomats, on an official visit to Peru, had been abducted during transit from the French embassy to the airport.

Simone Rabiot and Didier Chavet.

The media was a melting pot of conspiracy theories, all of them running sensationalist stories on what could have happened to the two captives and why it had happened. Thankfully for Ducard, the public seemed to have accepted the very real fact that abduction and ransom was rife in the country, and that his proposal on seeking help from allied countries was the best course of action. There was no need for any escalation between united countries, and as the Chef d'État-Major des Armées, *he knew he needed to have the coolest head to prevail.*

He also needed to ensure that everything was put in place for the breadcrumb trail to stop before it arrived at his doorstep. The only thing the world needed to be able to prove was that he had done every-thing within his power to ensure the safe retrieval of the two French diplomats, even if he was unsuccessful.

Even when he knew they had been killed.

That he had given the order.

Ducard knew how to play the political game, and while every step of his military career had led him to his current seat at the top table, every move he made while in it was engineered to one final move.

The day he became Président de la République Française.

For many, the idea would be a pipe dream, but he knew, as he looked out over the stunning city which he called his home, that for him, it was inevitable. He already had enough stock with the other powerful players within the government, as well as a groundswell of

3

support from the public. As skilled as he was a military tactician, politically, he was looking five moves ahead.

It would be at least a decade before he made his move to the political sphere and by then, the country would be united behind the notion of his leadership. Rabiot and Chavet would be long lost in the memory and even if they were remembered, Ducard was about to ensure that his involvement was nothing more than trying to bring them back.

As he looked out at the city of Paris as the sun finally set, he marvelled at its beauty as the big city lights began to explode to life, welcoming its inhabitants and visitors to a night of endless opportunity. Despite the sick feeling in the pit of his stomach, Ducard knew he had no other choice.

Despite the footfall on the Tower's public platform, he could tell his visitor had arrived, as the thumping footsteps grew nearer, walking with the efficiency of a man who wielded just as much power as he did.

They came to a stop next to him, and the hulking figure looked out over the city, his hands clasped at the base of his spine.

'Ducard,' the man's gravelly voice boomed. 'This really is a beautiful city, isn't it?'

'It is.' Ducard sighed. 'Thank you for coming.'

'Well, this is a matter of international security.' General Ervin Wallace turned; his round face distorted in a cruel grin. 'Besides, what's a little favour among friends?'

'Right this way, sir.'

The head concierge flashed her immaculate smile at Pierre Ducard and then stepped out from behind the marble counter that ran the length of the reception. The St Pancras Renaissance Hotel was a stunning building, steeped in gothic architecture, where it loomed up in the London sky with pointed towers and a grand clock affixed to the end of the structure. The brown brick was symmetrically separated by tall, curved windows and stood out from the rest of the surrounding buildings with ease. A stone's throw from St Pancras International Train Station, the expensive hotel was set back from the busy Euston Road by a black iron gate that ran the length of the building. With numerous, high-end guests, the hotel was equipped to not only offer complete discretion, but also the required security that Ducard had requested.

Along with the stunning décor and rich, vibrant history, the hotel was his only choice for his visit to the UK.

The head concierge walked purposefully towards the lift, motioning to a member of her staff to collect Ducard's bags. As she led Ducard to the express elevator to the top floor, her subordinate headed towards the employee-exclusive lift. Surrounding Ducard was his private security, all of them having followed him out of the military and into a higher paid role. Men that he had served with for years, all of whom were fiercely loyal to him and men in whom he had the utmost faith. The head of his security, Laurent Cissé, was the most dangerous man he had ever met and had the military record and rock-solid physique to go with it.

As they waited patiently for the doors to open, Ducard peered towards the luxurious bar that was positioned on the other side of the foyer, with the glass doors closed but offering a sneak peek at the array of drinks on offer. The doors slid open, and Cissé stepped in front of Ducard, appraised the safety of the lift and then gave a curt nod with his bald head. Although his parents had been born in Senegal, Cissé was as French as Ducard and had served both his country and Ducard with ferocious commitment.

'*Merci, Laurent.*' Ducard offered a smile and then followed the woman into the lift. Cissé nodded, and then began barking orders in his native tongue to the rest of the eight-man security detail, who all marched off to do their preliminary checks.

'He's very intense.' The Head Concierge smiled.

'He is a very good man,' Ducard replied in perfect English, with every word slathered in his seductive French accent. 'One of the best.'

'You must be very busy at the moment.' The woman shook her head. 'Sorry, we get a lot of famous people stay here, but rarely do we get a world leader.'

'I am not President of France yet.' Ducard flashed his charming smile.

'Well, it's only a matter of time. Two weeks, isn't it?'

'You follow French politics?' Ducard asked, as the lift slowly came to a stop on the top floor.

'Well, when I saw that you were staying, I thought I would brush up on my knowledge.' The woman suddenly shook her head. 'Sorry, this way.'

Ducard chuckled to himself as he followed the woman down the pristine corridor, admiring the black dress that clung to her shapely frame. Although he was on the verge of his sixtieth birthday, Ducard still boasted a full head of neatly cut hair, which had now turned a dashing grey. With the military man still deeply embedded within, he was a fitness addict and was fitter than most men half his age. The French press joked that he had aged better than their vintage wines, and although a lifelong bachelor, he found that his sexual appetite hadn't decreased as he had aged. As the woman approached his hotel door, he decided then and there that he found her very attractive.

'You have been most helpful…' Ducard motioned to the woman.

'Emily.' She blushed. Although twenty years his junior, her attraction to him was obvious.

'Emily.' He over-egged his accent. 'Such a beautiful

name. I trust my stay here will be even more wonderful than I had imagined. So, thank you.'

As he lifted her hand and planted a delicate kiss on the back of it, Cissé emerged from the stairwell. Despite clambering three floors swiftly, he wasn't one iota out of breath. With a stern expression on his face, he approached the duo at the doorway.

'Please, call reception if you need anything,' Emily said, anxiously looking at Cissé. 'It will be my personal pleasure to help.'

'Do not worry about him.' Ducard gestured to Cissé. 'I have never seen him smile, and I have known him for twenty-five years.'

Emily giggled, said her goodbye, and then headed back down the hallway, glancing back at Ducard who kept his eyes on her and a smile on his face. Although they were there for three days of business, he was always open to the idea of a little pleasure and he was certain that if he sent an invitation for her to join him for a drink later, then he'd certainly have an enjoyable evening ahead. The penthouse suite was in line with the cost of the room, with lavish furnishings and enough space to hold a conference. As Ducard slid his jacket from his shoulders, he peered out of the window to the busy street below. The early May evening was a warm and welcome one, and he could see numerous locals swarming around the smoking areas of the bars across the street.

A city alive with activity.

Just like his darling Paris.

'*They will close the restaurant between seven thirty and nine for you,*' Cissé spoke, refusing to waver from his native tongue. '*I trust you will eat alone?*'

'*Perhaps.*' Ducard showed Cissé the respect he deserved by speaking French. '*However, I may ask that lovely lady to join me. I trust all security is in place?*'

'*Oui.*' Cissé nodded.

'*And any further word on Olivier?*' Ducard's brow furrowed, and the usual charm in his voice was replaced with anger.

'*My men are still looking into it. If he is foolish enough to go through with it, we will find him.*'

Cissé stroked the neatly trimmed greying beard on his chin. At over six feet tall and with the build of a heavy-weight boxer, he was certainly an intimidating presence. While most would quiver in fear at just the sight of the man, Ducard knew exactly what the man had done and was capable of. If people knew that, they'd run the second Cissé entered the room.

After a few more moments gazing out of the window, Ducard turned and faced his long-time ally and gave him a stern nod.

'*Oh, I know.*' Ducard turned back to the view of the city of London, afforded to him by the grand window of his room. '*You've never let me down.*'

Cissé nodded and then turned and left the room, leaving the future President of France to his own thoughts, and determined to once again kill for his future leader.

CHAPTER TWO

As another cool evening began to ascend over the city of London, Sam looked up to the sky and breathed in. With spring fully underway, the bitter cold of the winter had subsided, and the welcoming evening meant London was alive with activity. Every bench outside every pub was crammed full of eager co-workers, all of them knocking back their drinks and sharing cigarettes, desperate to make the most of the relationships they were forced into. He had found it fascinating how a job could determine your social circle, and how the few people he could call friends were mainly people he had served alongside during his time in the military.

London Bridge offered a multitude of watering holes, and despite approaching three years without a drop of alcohol, the allure of a cold beer on a warm evening still held a significant appeal.

But Sam wouldn't waver.

He had lost too much in his life to allow his walls to be torn down by a tidal wave of booze, and he knew that sobriety was one of the key pillars of dealing with his grief. In just a few months' time, it would be the six-year anniversary of his son's death, and despite accepting that Jamie was gone, Sam still felt that absence with every waking minute of the day. There was a time when it had driven him to drink.

To the brink of suicide.

It was a feeling he could never explain to anyone. The persistent nagging at his heart, as if there was a small opening in the muscle itself and it was slowly flooding. And as the years went by and the pain subsided, the grief and the guilt would still fill up within his heart and threaten to stop it from beating.

It was why he had been desperate for something to nullify the pain.

To make Jamie's loss mean something more than just the end of his happiness.

At first, he had channelled it into punishing criminals who had beaten the system, but that only got him so far. It was fate and the corruption of those sworn to protect that put him on the path to salvation.

That gave him even the slimmest offering of peace.

Jamie's mother, Lucy, had moved on. Re-married and with a new family, she had been able to process the loss of their son, but not Sam's grief. As quickly as Jamie had been snapped from existence by a drunk driver, Sam had cut off the world, with her included.

A lifelong soldier, the only way back for Sam was to find a new purpose and protecting the innocent from the corrupt and powerful had been his only recourse. Whether it was saving an innocent therapist from a corrupt police inspector, a teenage girl from sex traffickers or most recently, bringing a billionaire sex offender to justice, Sam had managed to find a path that meant Jamie didn't die for nothing.

His death had propelled Sam to fight back, and since he began his one-man war on crime over four years ago, some of the most dangerous and powerful criminals in the country had been put down.

To the authorities, he was public enemy number one.

To the public themselves, he was becoming a necessity.

He'd seen as much with his interactions with the good people of the country, with the likes of Martin McGinn, who had offered him employment in Scotland, taking Sam in when he was injured. The good people, those who put their faith in the law, were starting to put their faith in him.

He didn't do it for money.

Sam certainly didn't do it for ego.

He fought back, because he could.

Because someone had to.

As he rested his arms on the metal barrier than ran the length of London Bridge, he looked out over the Thames and marvelled at the sight of the city. The gentle breeze ruffled through his dark hair, which had grown out into a messy side parting. Like his thick beard, it was losing its battle with age, as the grey tinges were becoming more prominent. Although he felt a little unkempt, it at least provided him with somewhat of a disguise from the public, who had seen his clean-cut army photos in the press.

The sun, as it began to set, still glistened across the myriad of glass buildings before sending a shimmering wave across the water. The bridge itself was in the midst of one of its hourly traffic jams, with black cabs and buses inching their way across, as cyclists weaved in and out with reckless abandon.

Sam had been under heavy fire in Afghanistan, gone toe to toe with an arms dealer in a burning building and faced off with a Mexican cartel and an American motorcycle gang at the same time. Despite all that, he couldn't think of anything more terrifying than trying to navigate London by bicycle during rush hour.

At a leisurely pace, Sam strolled down the walkway, his

hands tucked into the pockets of his jeans, his muscular arms tucked against his sturdy frame. Keeping up a regimented fitness regime was another pillar of his coping. Replacing the chance of a depressing drunken stupor by dedicating himself to his physical health had worked wonders for his mental wellbeing. It kept his mind and his body sharp, and when facing the barrel of the gun or the long reach of the law, it meant he had a chance of survival.

And that's what he did.

Survived.

Weaving through a crowd of commuters, Sam walked past a few more busy pubs and felt a twang of sadness as he witnessed friends greet each other with a loving hug.

There were those who hadn't survived.

Those he had lost along the way.

His best friend, Theo Walker, had been killed while protecting an innocent woman, put in the firing line by Sam's actions. His mentor, Sergeant Carl Marsden, had been murdered in an underground facility just outside of Rome, for trying to expose the truth of what Sam had been subjected to.

Paul Etheridge, a good man who had found purpose in supporting Sam's campaign, had sacrificed his wealthy life and freedom, and had been on the run for three years without so much as a word.

They were good people.

Some of the best.

But now, they were absent from Sam's life because of him.

There were others too, like Adrian Pearce and Amara Singh, both of whom found their morals questioned and their lives changed inconceivably by their association with Sam. While Singh had been out of his life for three years, Sam still found himself thinking of her from time to time, and the life they could have had under a different series of events. Wherever she was, Sam hoped she was safe, as he understood, better than most, the grimy grey area that secretive government agencies operate in. Heartbreakingly, Pearce's absence in his life was of his own doing, and Sam knew that he had broken the trust with Pearce by asking him for a gun when he knew the man stood for peaceful resolution. The work the former detective had done for the underprivileged in the wake of Theo's death was astonishing, and while he had offered Sam a few years of solace, Pearce had made it clear that Sam wasn't welcome in his world anymore.

Then there was Mel.

The woman who Sam thought about every day and found his thumb hovering over the *send* button of a message he yearned to send her.

But he knew he couldn't.

For the six months they were together, Sam had forgotten about the mission. Forgotten all about the destruction he had left in his wake and had even forgotten about the numbing pain of Jamie's absence.

But he had put her at risk. More importantly, he had put her teenage daughter, Cassie, at risk, too.

While he was better off with them, they were better off without him, and in the four months since he had said goodbye to them at the station, he had come to terms with that fact.

He was, for the first time in a long time, completely alone.

The press had gone a little cold on him, too. An egotistical man would have been offended, but Sam had found the lack of interest in his movements to be rather comforting. From time to time, there was the odd quote from the Commissioner of the Metropolitan Police, Bruce McEwen, who would remind the country that Sam was a dangerous man who needed to be brought to justice.

But Sam knew that was for show.

He had saved McEwen's life when a dangerous son of a billionaire had him and a young woman at gunpoint, and while Jasper Munroe was serving years behind bars, McEwen had clearly done his best to steer the Met's focus away from Sam and onto the powerful players in the city in which Sam stood.

It wasn't permission, per se. But Sam knew that McEwen had given him enough rope to continue his mission. It's what had brought Sam to London Bridge, and more specifically, the alleyway that ran down the side of the Golden Bell, a generic pub that was packed with patrons, all of them ramping up for a boozy night on the town. The outside of the establishment was rife with punters, and a thick, heavy cloud of cigarette smoke clung to them all like a deep fog. The smell was sickening, and Sam was grateful for the bench on the other side of the road, where he could observe the alleyway, without the poisonous fumes swirling around him.

He was there for Pete Gideon.

Gideon was the landlord of the Golden Bell, which made him a popular man with some of the locals. Having grown up in the East End of London, Gideon fancied himself as a gangster, and when he wasn't charming his customers with his cockney charm, he was dabbling in all sorts of stolen goods. Not enough to really bother the police, and certainly not enough to warrant Sam's attention.

That was until Gideon's name came up when Sam had questioned a known sex offender about the contents of his laptop. Staying in a bedsit in Maida Vale, Sam had seen the local fliers, warning parents of a known sex offender seen loitering near the school. Ever the good Samaritan, Sam checked it out, and it took two days for him to clock Azeem Ahmad and follow him home. While the man showed no intention of acting on whatever urge he may have been suppressing, Sam watched as the man leered at the children, before making a brisk exit when a group of Dads marched towards the gate.

Sam followed.

Just as Azeem was entering the stairwell to his block of flats, Sam had pounced, slamming the man through the door, and easily overpowering him. He'd marched Azeem up the stairs to the man's flat, and once inside, he had hurled the pervert to the mat. The plan was to threaten the man enough to keep him away from the school, but when he saw the thumbnails on the screen of the man's computer, he felt the red mist ascend.

Images of kids.

It had turned Sam's stomach, and after a few jaw rattling haymakers, Azeem had given the name of Gideon.

He was the man who was distributing the material.

Sam had left, but not before breaking both Azeem's laptop and right arm, and now, as he sat watching the Golden Bell, he knew the man profiting from such atrocities was inside, mugging for the customers who found him so endearing.

Sam waited.

And waited.

As last orders was sounded with the clang of a bell, Sam lifted himself from the bench and made his way through the remaining drunks loudly putting the world to rights as they chain-smoked, and he entered the bar.

It was dim.

It was grimy.

In the fair corner, a few men sat alone, not looking at each other, but keeping an eye on the rest of the pub. Their awkwardness was apparent, and Sam wondered if they were customers for more than just the overpriced alcohol. Sam kept his eye on them as he approached the bar.

'Cutting it fine, ain't ya?' Gideon flashed Sam a grin as he leant across the bar, his gold tooth prominently displayed. 'What can I get ya?'

'Just a Diet Coke.'

'Ooo, watch out. We've got a wild one, ere.' Gideon chuckled as he obliged. 'Don't drink that too fast, now.'

Sam offered the portly landlord a wry smile.

'I won't.'

Sam took his drink and made his way to a table at the far side of the pub, opposite the awkward men who refused to make eye contact. Gideon stared at Sam as he took his seat, and Sam knew the man was weighing up whether Sam was a different sort of customer.

Someone who was after something else.

Chuckling to himself, Sam couldn't help but think how right Gideon was.

Sam was there for something else.

Justice.

CHAPTER THREE

With long, deep breaths, Olivier Chavet stepped onto the Northern Line train that had arrived at Highgate Station. It wasn't his first trip to the United Kingdom, and as a man of twenty-nine years of age, he had taken in the capital city numerous times on various city breaks. Having grown up in Bordeaux, Olivier had been accustomed to the busy city life, writhe with art exhibitions, museums, and a love of alcohol. While he wouldn't compare the British love for beer to his nation's affinity for wine, he did appreciate the vast number of galleries and museums that were open to the public, and during his maturity into an adult, he had enjoyed visiting them.

This visit was under very different circumstances.

As he boarded the train, his eyes flicked from side to side, peering through the lenses of his glasses at every other commuter. Although he had no concrete evidence, he was certain that Pierre Ducard would be searching for him, and the slightest movement from a fellow passenger caused Olivier to squirm. Ever since his father, Didier Chavet, was abducted and subsequently killed in the Amazon over a decade ago, Olivier had placed the blame squarely at the feet of the former *Chef d'État-Major des Armées*. Despite all the pandering to the media, and the reparations that were sent to Olivier's family, Ducard had never seemed completely shellshocked at the murder of two of his own.

Didier, along with his colleague, Simone Rabiot, had been diplomats for the French government, and as far as Olivier had researched, had served their country with pride and honour. While their names weren't well known to the public, within the inner workings of international relations, Olivier knew that his father was a highly respected and beloved figure. When the news filtered through that the two of them had been captured while on a routine, peace-keeping meeting in South America, he had expected an immediate response from Ducard. But the French military ran through a laundry list of excuses as to why they couldn't react swiftly, with Ducard himself laying into the bureaucracy and political moves of those in government.

Olivier didn't buy it.

Not because Ducard's eventual move into politics highlighted him as a hypocrite, but because Olivier was certain that Ducard had sanctioned the murder of both Olivier's father and Simone Rabiot himself.

He'd spent the last decade digging for information, yet whenever he highlighted any red flags to the various French authorities, he was shot down or ignored completely. It was clear to him that the path was being cleared for Ducard, who in the decade since, had become one of the most popular political figures in the country to ascend to the presidency. Whenever the slick, well-groomed man appeared on his television, spewing out virtuous nonsense about the good of the country, Olivier felt his stomach turn. He began protesting as loudly as he could, through internet forums, social media, and a few relatively successful protests outside government buildings.

It had drawn the ire of his sister, Michelle, who he hadn't spoken to in over five years as his campaign for the truth became all-consuming. Their mother, Annette, passed away two years ago from cancer, her heart broken by the mysterious nature of her husband's death and the fractured relationship between her children.

Olivier was alone.

Alone in the world.

Alone in knowing that the man with the handsome grin and the heroic military record was nothing more than a murderer and a traitor.

But now, someone was willing to listen.

Morgana Daily wasn't a name he had ever come across during his research, and when an email from her landed in the inbox of his campaign, he almost dismissed it. He was used to scam emails, trying their level best to extort his cause for their own gains by offering him support and a few dodgy links for him to click. The reason he opened the email was when he noticed the email address.

British News Network.

BNN were a known, respectable media outlet in the United Kingdom, one which he had watched on lazy mornings on a hotel bed. Swiftly, he researched the station, navigated to the reporter profile page, and sure enough, he found Morgana's profile. The woman was striking, her light brown skin and jet-black hair only adding to her beauty. Below, it listed her academic and professional achievements and it then highlighted how she had been promoted into the international relations team.

Olivier returned to her email, where she outlined her interest in hearing his theories surrounding the past of the likely future French Prime Minister, especially as he was due in London for a few days.

She pitched it as an opportunity for both of them.

An opportunity he was happy to take.

In his home country, Olivier had received an avalanche of backlash for theories that many felt 'threatened the safety of the country's illustrious future'. It saddened him that the public would rather celebrate a man like Ducard than hold him accountable for his actions. While history is littered with many doing what was 'necessary' for the safety of their country, the brutal murder of two diplomats didn't fit the criteria.

All Olivier knew was that his father and his colleague died alone and afraid, and somewhere, there was a dot that he couldn't quite connect. That final straw to place on the pile that would break the camel's back. Perhaps, by highlighting the discrepancies in Ducard's past on international TV, he could drum up enough interest for someone to look further. For people to take him seriously.

As the train sped through the dark tunnels beneath the city, every twitch of a commuter's hand, or tilt of the head, drew Olivier's attention. He was certain he'd been followed for the past few months, undoubtedly by dangerous men who were loyal to Ducard and his cause. Olivier knew he was a nuisance to the squeaky-clean reputation of the man and looking over his shoulder was something he'd become accustomed to. If he were to be killed in France, the news would swarm over it, almost solidifying his claims.

But if he was to die abroad? That might just be easier for Ducard to sweep under the rug.

It was why he had booked his lodgings and travel tickets under a friend's name and bank card. He'd repaid them in cash, but it was enough to sneak into the UK at the same time as Ducard did. He'd also scheduled in social media posts to appear across his various timelines for the duration of his trip, to falsify his location.

Despite all that due diligence, every person on the train was a potential threat, and the interview he was heading towards could well be a trap.

But he had to take the chance.

For his father.

And for the truth.

He stepped off the train at Charing Cross and checked his watch. It was seven thirty, yet the street was packed with commuters, all rushing to get to work or sneak in that morning coffee. He was meeting Morgana at a 'rent a space' office on the Strand, which meant he had thirty minutes to grab a coffee and scope the place out.

Taking a breath deeper than the one he did before he boarded the train, Olivier set his course for the high street, knowing that the day ahead could change everything.

'You've got this.'

Morgana Daily stared at herself in the mirror of the small dressing unit that was crammed against the wall of her bedroom. Her unmade bed took up most of the room and was littered with different outfits and underwear. She'd settled on a black pencil skirt and black blazer, with a white, collarless shirt. It was the smartest she could look while still maintain an element of glamour, which she hoped would only increase her appeal.

She'd been working at BNN for six years, starting straight out of university with her journalist degree and a naïve assumption she'd be in front of the camera in no time. It had been a startling revelation when she was offered the role of an office runner and was given the menial tasks of fetching coffee and printing. For a long time, she wanted to quit. The flat she shared with two of her friends was extortionately priced, and her paltry salary barely covered her share. But they had wanted to live in Clapham, and although they had to scrimp and save on some things, they were still able to enjoy the booming social life of the area. Eventually, Morgana had worked her way up to a research assistant, and was entrusted with writing a few articles from time to time.

It took four years for her to eventually be brought onto one of the reporting teams, and now, with her feet under the table and a little respect against her name, she had been promoted as an actual journalist for the BNN International Relations team.

She even had a runner of her *own*.

But now, as she sat on the edge of her bed in her small, modest room of the flat share, she stared at herself and blew out her cheeks.

This was her moment.

When the announcement came through that Pierre Ducard was visiting the city and the Prime Minister, her editor, Danny Bull, had tasked the team with finding interesting pieces they could run on the man. With a history as decorated and public as Ducard's, it wouldn't be hard, but Danny had been disappointed with the ideas that were pitched. It was all powder pieces on how great the man was, and what his ascension to presidency would mean for relations with the United Kingdom.

Morgana had ventured down a different route, looking for a controversy that could drum up conversation, and when she stumbled across Olivier's story and the decade long crusade he had raged against the man, she dug deeper.

There was something to the man's story. She could feel it.

Danny often referred to it as 'the hunch', which he said separated the taught journalist from the natural ones. When Danny sighed and asked if anyone had anything else, Morgana pitched Olivier's story, including the details of the dead diplomats, the potential links to the now deceased, disgraced Ervin Wallace and how no true reason was ever found for the death of Didier Chavet and Simone Rabiot.

Danny had snapped his fingers, told her to get working on it, and when she revealed to him that Olivier was willing to do a face-to-face interview, her boss was thrilled.

This was her moment.

It was her first television appearance for the network, and she had a gripping and relevant story. Olivier, while dismissed as a conspiracy theorist, had spoken eloquently over the video call they had, and he was also easy enough on the eye for the casual viewer. The man had a studious appeal, with his round lens glasses and sweeping brown hair but was classically handsome with a strong jaw.

Paired with Morgana on a TV screen, she was certain it would prove to be a hit.

She gave herself one squirt of perfume and then stood, cramming her feet into her most expensive but most uncomfortable heels, and then headed to the door. The spring morning welcomed her with a warm glow of sun and a gentle breeze, and as she scurried towards Clapham North station, her mind was racing with the possibilities the day would hold.

National television.

A critically acclaimed piece of journalism.

Her career skyrocketing.

Throughout all the excitement, she hadn't even thought about what the repercussions of publishing such a story would be, and, in truth, she didn't care. This was her chance to get where she wanted to be, and if it took upsetting the French government to put her on the map, then so be it.

She was an investigative journalist.

It was her job to present her findings to the public.

And it was what she had been working towards for nearly a decade of her life.

As she approached the station steps to the platform, the train screeched to a halt, and she bounded up the stairs two at a time. The doors beeped chaotically and just before they slammed shut she slithered into the carriage and drew a few grins from the other early risers. The train set off on its tracks, and Morgana slipped her ear buds into her ears, played her favourite song and looked out of the window as the city of London began to speed by.

'You've got this.' She told herself once more. 'You've got this.'

CHAPTER FOUR

'So, what you're saying is not only was there no satisfactory reason given for your father's disappearance, but that your own government was behind it?'

Morgana sat forward in her chair, motioning with her hand as she spoke. The room itself was nondescript, but the lighting that her team had configured had illuminated both her and Olivier in a bathing glow. They were the focus, and it also kept the location unidentifiable. Olivier, as he had been throughout the interview, kept his jaw stern and nodded before he replied.

'Correct.' Olivier reached into his jacket and pulled out a number of papers. 'This is the original statement, sent to me by the Gouverne-ment Francais, explaining the details of my father's death. It is signed by Pierre Ducard. Two years later, upon an internal investigation about the securities for our international diplomats, he signed this document, where he admits to failures within the Forces Armées Françaises, contradicting the previous statement—'

'So you're saying it's a cover up?' Morgana interrupted, her eyes twinkling with excitement.

'I'm saying there are inconsistencies,' Olivier continued without skipping a beat, his impeccable English only enhanced by his alluring

French accent. 'As the Chef d'État-Major des Armées, I appreciate he needs to make hard decisions. Decisions to protect our country and work in hand with many countries. But these decisions, they did not protect my father. Didier Chavet served his country proudly, and he was allowed to die alone in the middle of the Amazon jungle. The documents I have here, they may not prove Ducard was responsible for my father's death, but they raise enough questions as to what Ducard has claimed happened is not the truth.'

Olivier sat back in his chair and took a sip of water from the glass on his side table. The magnitude of what he was doing wasn't lost on him, and he returned the glass with a shaky hand.

'And you've been championing this for a while?'

'For over a decade. When my father died…' Olivier took a moment to quell his pain. 'When he was killed, I remember the government was so kind to my me and my mother. But as I began to question and demand, they pulled back. Ducard put his name to a story that doesn't line up and ever since then, I have pulled up numerous discrepancies with his control of the military, but every time, they have been pushed back. I've been threatened. I've been followed. I've been in hiding for a while because it could hurt his campaign.'

'To become the President of France?'

'Exactly.' Olivier nodded curtly. 'Pierre Ducard may not have pulled the trigger that put a bullet through my father's skull, but he has blood on his hands. My country is doing its best to keep that hidden, because it wants him as the next leader. They see him as a return to the stronger, more direct country we used to be. But before that happens, and before your country welcomes him with open arms as an ally, just know that he got there by treading on the lives of inno-cent people. That he did it by killing his own people.'

'Olivier, thank you for your time. I appreciate how difficult it must be to talk about what has happened to you and your family.'

'Thank you. I will keep fighting until my father and Simone Rabiot get the justice their deaths deserve.'

The flat screen television that stretched across the wall of the kitchen continued onto the next segment of the British News Networks continuous news channel, but Ducard hit mute on the remote. With ever-building frustration, he slammed the remote down on the glass dining table, causing the cutlery to clang against the glass.

'*Fuck.*'

Like an irritating fly at a picnic, Olivier Chavet had been orbiting his rise up the political ladder over the past decade. Whenever Ducard made strides towards the overall leadership of the country, the young man would be in the press, crying out wild theories about the death of his father and the underhand deals that Ducard had made with other countries to ensure his path to the top was kept clear. There were numerous other countries, who, like Ducard, had believed that the entire world had gone soft, and they looked forward to his rule over one of the most powerful countries in the world. Their leaders were not concerned about the ramblings of an activist, especially as they had all done heinous things for the prosperity of their own nations.

The issue with Olivier was the court of public opinion.

While Ducard was tracking to be further ahead than his rival in the polls, the last thing he needed was for people to start asking questions. It was unlikely to have an impact on him making it to the top chair, but it could cause issues for his presidency. A number of leftist publications had already given credence to Olivier's claims, and despite pressure from Cissé, they were unlikely to stop.

There were those who didn't want Ducard, with his iron fist and his battle-hardened military background to take the reins in France.

And if they could prove that he had sanctioned the murder of two of their own diplomats, and the reasons behind it, then it would be the end of his political career.

And his liberty.

Despite every effort that was made by colluding with the former head of the UK Armed Forces, Ervin Wallace, there was still a slim chance that the truth would come out. That four soldiers were sent into the Amazon at the command of Wallace, only to be pulverised by a waiting army and a deadly sniper.

The Bolivian.

Ducard never knew exactly what happened in the centre of that jungle, as the rain and bullets rained down on the quartet, but he knew that blood was shed to keep his record intact.

To hide the truth.

One of the soldiers had made it out alive, but Wallace had assured him that the man wouldn't be a problem. Ducard had no information about the survivor, not even a name, and as the mission was as off the books as they could keep it, there would be no record of it. At least, not one that Ducard would have access to.

Olivier's interview with the British reporter had turned Ducard's stomach, and he pushed away the uneaten half of his breakfast. As always, the food at the St Pancras Renaissance was of the highest quality, and he felt a tremor of anger at not wanting to finish it. As he slumped back in his chair, he reached for his coffee and took a sip, trying his best to configure answers to the likely questions he would be asked at the publicity event later that day. The Prime Minister, a snake of a man who nodded obediently to anyone who offered him a whiff of friendship, would do his best to protect Ducard, but there would be some journalists who would be sensing a possible scoop.

They wouldn't get the truth, but they could get themselves a little more notoriety by being the one who confronted the next French President with a dangerous accusation.

Ducard sipped his coffee and then placed the cup down on the table and sighed. Like the fly at the picnic, Olivier needed to be swatted aside.

The longer he lived, the longer the threat to his power hung above his head.

As if he could read Ducard's mind, Cissé barged through the door to the magnificent presidential suite, his eyes locked on his boss as he strode with purpose.

'Good morning, Laurent.' Ducard offered with disinterest.

'*I trust you have seen the news,*' Cissé responded, clearly offended that Ducard spoke in English.

'*I have.*' Ducard rubbed his temples in frustration, massaging his fingers through the grey hairs. '*It is a headache you have yet to get rid of.*'

'*Permission to use whatever force necessary, sir.*'

'*As in?*' Ducard turned and faced the head of his security team. Cissé was a terrifying man that looked like he was made of concrete. His dark skin only emphasises the sheer whiteness of his eyes, and his bald head gleamed under the lights above. His powerful jaw was covered in a neat, greying beard that was styled into a point at the chin. He filled out the black jacket and grey jeans that were stretched across his powerful frame, and concealed under his muscular arm was a firearm.

'*I may need to upset a few people to find him,*' Cissé said diplomatically. '*I trust you can keep the local authorities off my back.*'

Ducard sighed stood. Usually, his stays at the Renaissance were most enjoyable, but this one had been a disappointment. After their flirtatious back and forth on arrival, Ducard had invited Emily for a drink in the hotel bar. She accepted, but promptly rejected his proposal to return to his room with him on account of being happily married. Despite politely accepting her decision, Ducard had already contacted the hotel manager to have her dismissed.

From one setback to another.

Ducard pulled open the curtains and looked out at the busy streets below, as Kings Cross was brought to a stand-still by the traffic. Somewhere out in this vast city was the one person who could uncover the things he had done. The only reason Ducard was worried was because Olivier had no political agenda.

This wasn't an empty threat to his presidency, or an ill-advised play for his position.

This was personal.

Olivier *knew* that Ducard had a hand in the death of his father and had already proven he was willing to risk his life to tell as many people as possible.

He *had* to be stopped.

Even if that meant Ducard had to clean up Cissé's mess.

'Do what you have to,' Ducard said without looking back. *'Tear this god damn city apart if you have to.'*

'Oui, sir.' Cissé turned on his heel and marched back towards the door. As he yanked it open, he stopped, as Ducard's voice called after him.

'Make sure he doesn't make it back home.'

Cissé nodded, stepped into the hallway with murderous intent, and shut the door behind him.

———

Despite being one of the most famous and iconic places in London, Bruce McEwen always felt that Downing Street existed in a different world entirely. It was always eerily quiet, shut off from the public, and although the police officers showed him the respect he commanded as he approached, he always felt a little apprehension when approaching the famous door with the number ten emblazoned on it. As the Commissioner of the Metropolitan Police, McEwen was a serious ally for not just the prime minister, but his entire cabinet, and although he had ruffled feathers over the past few months, he felt aggrieved at the lack of progress he had seen in tackling elite level corruption. It had been four months since McEwen had exploded at the press conference that had shaken the city of London. Rallying back against the power of the rich, McEwen had stated that Jasper Munroe would be the first of many to fall in line. Whether it was the adrenaline of having survived being shot in the hip or having seen Sam provide justice he hadn't been able to, but McEwen had visions of bringing the entire city to its knees.

It had been slow progress.

While many found his newfound commitment to the law commendable, there were too many people in high places that wanted to protect their own interests. Not just those who had amassed eye-watering fortunes, but those who they had colluded with to get there.

Politicians.

Government officials.

The list was endless.

Despite being ordered to take time off to recover from the gunshot wound, McEwen still worked tirelessly from his own office. He hated being away from the action, but he did enjoy being looked after by his doting wife, Leanne, who had thrown her full support behind his new stance against the powerful. It would likely end with him being forced from his position, but she had told him she'd rather see him go out on his sword, than hand in hand with the corrupt. He was eager to ensure the new direction didn't run out of steam, but such was the power of his position, he was required elsewhere. Now, sitting in a meeting room within the political epicentre that was 10 Downing Street, McEwen had lowered his tall, gangly frame into a hardback chair at the meeting table. Opposite him sat Admiral Nicholas Wainwright, the Chief of Defence Staff who had worked diligently in the past three years to undo the damage that his predecessor had done.

General Ervin Wallace.

Alongside him was Dipti Patel, the current Mayor of London, who had become a popular figurehead since she defeated, disgraced candidate Mark Harris nearly four years ago. Although she had won by a landslide after Harris's connections to the Kovalenkos had been uncovered, she had proven herself a force to be reckoned with and many had earmarked her for a bigger role in British politics in the years to come. All three of them had their eyes fixed on Dianna Mulgrave, the Foreign Secretary, who was finishing her briefing on the upcoming meeting between the Prime Minister and the potential new president of France. Mulgrave was a bullish, fierce woman, who had a reputation for treading on anyone she could for praise. Her eyes were always on the next goal, and while she was a perfectly competent talker to the media, behind closed doors, she was seen as a snake.

All three of the important people around the table knew it, but such was their commitment to their jobs and their country. They knew they needed to let her take the lead.

'Just to clarify, Admiral, we have no reason to worry about any terror attacks?'

'No, ma'am,' Wainwright said with a proud nod. His wrinkled face was framed by thinning white hair and a thick, grey beard. 'We envisage no problems.'

'Good.' Mulgrave didn't look up from her paperwork. 'And, Bruce, no further concerns your end?'

'I mean, it's a publicity stunt, isn't it?' McEwen shrugged and drew a scowl from the Foreign Secretary. 'If this was of any true importance, then I'd have a few more concerns but no. My only issue has been how standoffish Ducard's private security have been with a few of my officers, but beyond that, we should be good to go.'

'Great,' Mulgrave said insincerely, as she popped the lid on her pen and began to gather her paperwork. 'I'll brief you all tomorrow at eight.'

'What about the interview?' Patel cut in, looking around the room with her eyebrows raised.

'What about it?' Mulgrave sighed as she stood.

'Well, do we give it any credence?'

'She's got a point,' McEwen agreed, offering Patel a friendly nod.

'Look, this might come as a shock to you, Dipti, but very senior political figures get these sorts of threats all the time. I'm more disappointed in the fact that our own news networks thought it was worth putting on live TV. This Olivier Chavet, he may be upset over his father's death, but he's just looking at somewhere to point the finger of blame. We shouldn't be encouraging it, and we most certainly won't be giving it any consideration.'

'If I may, ma'am…' McEwen stood, buttoning his resplendent police tunic. 'We should at least consider the possibility that there may be a few people who'll be angered by his celebration.'

'If you want to dedicate your time and resources to it, Bruce, then be my guest.' Mulgrave snapped. 'But Admiral Wainwright has seen minimal threat or issue, and I will take his word on international military affairs over yours. Now, if that's everything?'

McEwen nodded and watched the Foreign Secretary leave, shaking his head in disappointment. Admiral Wainwright stood and shook both McEwen's and Patel's hand before making his exit, marching with the authority of an experienced soldier. McEwen reached for his hat and winced, the stiffness in his hip reminding him of his limitations.

'Here.' Patel reached over and handed it to him.

'Thank you, my dear,' McEwen said in his charming Glaswegian accent. 'This should be fun.'

'Yup. A real "event" for our city to savour.' Patel rolled her eyes and drew a chuckle from the Commissioner. Her expression changed, and she looked up at him. 'So, that attack at the Golden Bell…'

'I can't talk about ongoing investigations, Dipti. You know that.'

McEwen took a step back and signalled for her to lead the way. She headed to the door, with McEwen following close behind.

'Of course.' Patel sighed. 'I'm just wondering if… well…you know…'

McEwen nodded his thanks to the security within Downing Street and then stepped through the iconic door and onto the street. Further up the road, a member of the cabinet was playing up for the cameras as a small gaggle of reporters gathered around him. McEwen took the mayor to one side and offered her a warm smile.

'I know what you're wondering. A child pornography ring has been exposed, with the ringleader beaten to a pulp along with two of his customers. And also, the web domain and password written on a piece of paper that was then stapled to the man's chest.'

'Is it Sam?'

McEwen shrugged.

'Maybe. Probably.' He looked out to the street beyond the journalists and the city of London.

'Should I be concerned?'

The question caught McEwen off guard, and he

chuckled. What a strange order of events that had the Commissioner of the Metropolitan Police actively rooting for the country's most wanted man. He placed his hat on top of his head, offered the mayor a firm handshake and then offered her a softly spoken, vague response.

'We'll handle it.'

CHAPTER FIVE

When Sam woke that morning, he tried to remember the last time he had an interrupted night's sleep. For the first few years after Jamie's death, Sam would awaken multiple times in the night, the vision of his son's motionless body and open eyes jolting him upright. After a while, the dreams became irregular, and just when he thought he was over the worst of it, they would return tenfold.

The guilt he had of not stopping Miles Hillock, the drunk behind the wheel, would forever haunt him. Once his war on crime started, he began to be visited by those he had put in the ground, along with the charred remains of his best friend Theo, who had lost his life over four years ago. Sam understood what was happening. His subconscious was trying to guide him away from the path he had chosen, and by putting the carnage he had caused front and centre when he had no control of his thought process, it was a valiant attempt to get Sam to stop.

But he was beyond that.

There was no going back.

The few years he spent hidden away with Pearce in the youth centre seemed like a lifetime ago, and the war had escalated beyond a few dodgy criminals or a sex offender. He'd taken down billionaire businessmen, dangerous gun runners, and even faced off with some of the most dangerous hitmen in the world. As he lay on the bed, his exposed torso covered slightly by the sheet, he knew one day he'd come across someone he couldn't survive.

A situation he couldn't walk away from.

But until that day came, he'd keep fighting. For the people who couldn't fight back. It was that notion that kept his focus razor sharp, and as he pushed himself off the uncomfortable mattress, he thought about Hayley Baker, and how she had been denied justice by a system that favoured the rich and powerful. She'd been raped by Jasper Munroe, who had hidden behind his father's billions, to ensure he evaded the law.

Sam had set that right.

Although he'd never be able to give her back what Jasper had taken from her, Sam knew he had at least given her a reason not to give up on the world. And if he spent the rest of his life giving that back to the people the world had done wrong, then he'd gladly walk towards the loaded gun that would inevitably find him one day.

Stepping into the bathroom, he contemplated a shave. The thickening beard was becoming irritating, but it did provide him with a modicum of disguise. The grey flecks reminded him of his age, yet his rippling physique was impressive for a man in his early forties.

The scars that adorned it, however, told a tale of a man who was lucky to still be alive.

Third-degree burns. Knife wounds. The two white scars on his broad chest that peered through the thin layer of hair like open eyes courtesy of General Ervin Wallace.

Sam's body was a walking war zone and he grimaced as the pain of those events flashed through his mind. and he gritted his teeth and stepped away. The shower in the bedsit was nothing more than a lukewarm dribble, and Sam scrubbed himself for a few minutes and then gave up the ghost. With a towel wrapped around his waist, he re-entered the single room that he rented, and he switched on the small TV that only offered the basic channels and intermittent volume. Stretched across the far end of the grubby room was a sink and sideboard that had been advertised as a kitchen, and Sam flicked on the cheap, plastic kettle that began to rumble to life. As he waited for the water to boil, he looked over the knuckles of his right hand. All four of them were split. His overexuberance as he pummelled Pete Gideon to the horror of his despicable clientele had been driven by the depravity of his crimes.

The man was a child pornographer, and as he had begged Sam for mercy through his broken teeth, Sam had found none for the man. The bloodied and broken state he left the man in was a testament to the horrendous pain the man had inflicted on so many, and Sam ensured that the other two customers who had been waiting as the Golden Bell had closed for the night, were not let off lightly either. Once the last, drunken patrons had been shuffled out of the door, Gideon had transformed from the charming, cockney landlord to a sleazy salesman, greeting Sam and the other two men with a detestable grin as he had rubbed his hands together.

'Lets get down to business, shall we?' He had said with a glint of excitement in his eye. The other two men, both of them nondescript and feebly wandering through middle age, had shuffled uncomfortably. Sam had stood, barged past Gideon, and locked the door. As the three perverts congregated in fear, Sam slid his jacket off his impressive frame, cracked his knuckles, and stared at them all.

'Lets.'

Sam had then delivered the beating to Gideon, to the sheer horror of his depraved customers, and after Sam had dished them out a few hard blows, he had demanded that Gideon relay all the information pertaining to his website. Hidden behind multiple firewalls on the dark web, Sam had written down the instructions that the man had gurgled through the blood.

Once he finished, Sam called the police, told them he had found three men violently assaulted and then hung up. Then, with the very real threat that he'd come back and take Gideon apart, limb by limb, he stapled the details of the man's website to his chest, with Gideon squealing as the metal punctured his skin.

Sam made sure he was gone before the police arrived.

The kettle clicked and drew Sam back into the room, and he poured himself a cup of tea and turned his attention to the screen, which was on British News Networks scrolling, twenty-four-hour news channel.

He half expected to see his face plastered in the corner after another successful night's work, but that wasn't the case. They were discussing the meeting between the Prime Minister and the expected next President of France, Pierre Ducard. Sam sat on the edge of the bed and sipped his drink with mild interest, as an attractive young journalist spoke with enthusiasm at the interview she was introducing.

An interview that had taken place less than an hour ago at an unknown location with a man named Olivier Chavet.

Chavet.

Sam frowned. The name rang a bell and seemed to set off a pointless pursuit of the reason in his mind. The screen faded to the young journalist, sitting with a strong-jawed, stern-looking man, who peered through his glasses with conviction.

Then the interview began.

Minutes later, Sam was heading to the door, realising

within a few moments that he was on a hunt for a truth that had evaded him for over a decade, but also that the life of the only person who could provide it, was in inconceivable danger.

The reaction to the interview was beyond anything Morgana had expected. After wrapping up her interview with the charming, yet slightly eccentric Olivier, she had raced back to the BNN studios, eager to face the ensuing reaction. As soon as she had stepped onto the main floor, one of her fellow journalists, a political editor who Morgana viewed as a mentor, stood from her seat and began clapping her hands together. The sound rose as the applause echoed around the floor, and Morgana felt her eyes watering as she held up her hands in faux embarrassment.

It was the greatest moment of her life.

As she nodded her thanks to them all, she received a few pats on the back from the other journalists, all of them eager to help a young woman make her way in the business.

It also helped that the interview went fantastically well.

As soon as she got to her desk, she began to watch the footage back, pleased not only with how she looked and spoke, but the authority with which she held the interview together. Olivier was a bright and enthusiastic guest, but she gave herself credit for how she kept the whole thing on track.

The following call only re-emphasised how well she had done.

She was being invited up to the seventeenth floor to discuss the interview with the two anchors for the morning BNN channel. It was a huge deal, and she took a few deep breaths before she lifted herself from her chair and rushed to the bathroom. As quickly as she could, she made her way to make-up, where the busy artists buzzed around her with a frantic energy that made her uncomfortable.

'This way, Morgana.'

One of the runners offered her a warm smile as she ushered her through the door towards the famous crescent desk that was in front of two magnificent screens which displayed moving images of London. At their chairs were the famous faces of the morning news, and Morgana slid into the seat at the end of the desk, ready for their interrogation.

It went well.

Yet again, she found a poise she hadn't realised she possessed, and as they thanked her for her speculation on the impact such a hard-hitting interview would have on the French President in waiting, Morgana stood and smiled at them both. They were highly respected and, as BNN went to a commercial break, they both heaped more praise on her.

The greatest moment of her life was turning into the best day of her life.

The rest of the day seemed to pass like a blur, and she couldn't pull herself away from social media. Her followers on every platform were skyrocketing, with the likes tumbling in for every photo, along with the usual deluge of sexist and thirsty comments about how she looked.

She didn't care.

This was the day she had made her impact in the world of journalism, and there was no way that the British News Network wouldn't want to capitalise on it. Her chief editor had already put in two meetings for the week ahead, both of them indicating some juicy stories they wanted her to tackle.

Doors were opening.

Opportunity was waiting.

After picking through an uninteresting salad one of the work experience kids had picked up for her, Morgana found herself on a slight comedown as the afternoon progressed. Her interview with Olivier, which had been playing every hour, had already been reduced to a brief headline and a re-direction to the BNN website for the full video. She understood how quickly news tumbled down the pecking order, but it was a gut punch nonetheless, and as she began brainstorming her notes for her meeting with her editor, her mobile rang. Excitedly, she answered, and the voice on the other end of the phone was wrapped in a strong French accent. The man on the other end of the phone spoke excellent English and explained to Morgana that he was part of the French Security Authority working out of the French Embassy in Knightsbridge and had been tasked with assigning Olivier Chavet with a security detail. Using her journalistic instincts, Morgana ran a few checks on what the man was saying before continuing the conversation.

All they needed was Chavet's location, so they could set up three security officers within the building to ensure his safety and return to France.

Olivier himself had been adamant that he was in danger, and Morgana had found herself liking the man for his relentless commitment to what he deemed the truth. The last thing she wanted was for him to come to any harm, and she shared the location of his hotel with the security officer. He thanked her and hung up the call.

Then her phone rang again.

Reception.

'Hello,' she answered cheerily.

'Miss Daily. There are some flowers in reception for you.'

'Oh, how lovely.' Morgana beamed. 'Can I collect them shortly?'

'I'm afraid they need a signature.'

'I'll be down shortly.'

The receptionist hung up the call, and Morgana stood from her desk and casually walked through the office, passing the desks of the other journalists who were all busy either rattling their keyboards or slouched in their chairs with their phones to their ears. It was a real epicentre of activity, and she basked in its electric atmosphere. As she waited for the lift, a few other co-workers walked past, congratulating her on a job well done and Ryan, who she had a crush on, told her he hoped to see her at the pub later to celebrate.

Morgana gave him a wry smile and then stepped through the opening doors, trying her best to play it cool. The young man watched her until the doors closed, and she clenched her fists with excitement as the greatest day of her life threatened to get even better. The lift stopped on a few other floors on the way down, and by the time it reached the ground floor, Morgana had been squashed to the back of the lift. She waited patiently for the others to exit before following, making her way through the security barrier and out into the main hall. The BNN hung proudly on the wall of the mighty reception desk, which had four separate counters for the receptionists who worked tirelessly behind them. On the one furthest from the lift and nearest to the door, she saw the large bouquet. Their bright colours burst through the wrapping paper.

Perhaps they were from Ryan?

Giddy, she scurried past a small queue of visitors and approached the counter where they stood. She made eye contact with the receptionist, who was on another call. The young lady was about Morgana's age, and she nodded towards the window, where a broad man was standing, gazing out onto the immaculate grounds that surrounded the building. Morgana approached him with a smile.

'Hi. I'm here to sign for the flowers.'

The man turned, his impressive physique filling out the black polo shirt that clung desperately to him. His face bore a few wrinkles and a scar through his right eyebrow, and his powerful jaw was covered by a thick, neatly trimmed beard speckled with flecks of grey. The black baseball cap was pulled down to his brow, but she knew she recognised him.

But she couldn't place him.

'Miss Daily?'

'That's me.' Morgana shifted uneasily, searching the man for a clipboard or electronic device. The man looked anxiously across to the security guards, who were distracted at the barriers before he took a step towards Morgana and lowered his voice to a firm whisper.

'My name is Sam Pope.' She took a step back in shock and he lifted his hands in surrender. 'Please don't make a scene. I just need two minutes of your time.'

'Jesus. It is you,' Morgana stammered, her eyes shooting towards the security guards.

'Please. Just two minutes.'

There was something instantly disarming about the man she had read about in the papers. Although there was no justification for the sheer level of violence that the man had used to tackle organised crime, she understood how people could find themselves on his side. For a man who had single-handedly killed over seventy people, she knew he wasn't there to hurt her.

He had no reason to.

But he had a reason for tracking her down, and while she knew that any other action other than calling the police would put her in a place she didn't want to be, the journalist within her was curious.

The greatest day of her life had just become the most interesting.

'Tell me what it's about.'

'Olivier Chavet.'

Morgana's eyes narrowed in confusion.

'What about him?'

Sam grimaced as the memories filtered to the forefront of his mind.

'He's telling the truth.'

CHAPTER SIX

Sam knew he was taking a risk.

In the four years since his war on crime had started, he knew that his actions had split the journalistic world right down the middle. There were many who had lambasted him for taking the law into his own hands, labelling him more dangerous to the country than the criminals he targeted. While Sam knew he was breaking the law, there was never any doubt in his mind that he was doing the right thing. The law had let too many people down for the public to maintain its faith within its structure, and Sam had experienced it first-hand. Miles Hillock, the man who had killed his son, had received a short sentence for death by dangerous driving, but was released early on a technicality.

That was the first time that Sam had seen the broken system for what it was, and in the years since, as criminal after criminal fell by his hand, he peeled back further layers that justified his actions.

But the press didn't always see it that way, and approaching a journalist without knowing where she stood on his actions was a move of desperation.

But that's what Sam was.

Desperate.

There had been reporters who had come round to his way of thinking. Lynsey Beckett, now one of the most popular reporters at the BBC had helped him track down Hayley Baker after she had tried to take Jasper Munroe to task over his sexual assault charges. Their history was intertwined with their relationship to Sean Wiseman, who had suffered a life-threatening beating at the hands of a vile criminal, at the behest of another powerful enemy that Beckett had made.

Helal Miah had lost his life, hanged to death by Ahmad Farukh for scratching too far beneath the surface.

As he waited for Morgana to decide, Sam wondered how she regarded him.

When the interview had played out on his small, cheap television, he felt his fists clench with fury and his eyes water with anguish. Over a decade ago, he had been part of a four strong squadron who had been lifted into the Amazon jungle, with the sole purpose of bringing back two French diplomats. All of them had been operating under the name Project Hailstorm, which was under the Blackridge umbrella, run by the iron fist of General Ervin Wallace. As always with those missions, there were no details.

Just names and locations.

Over the years, Sam would discover that they were no more than highly skilled hitmen, used by General Wallace to become one of the most powerful figures in the political world. But back then, he had still believed in the good of the world, and that he fought for the freedom of it.

That they were helping people.

The extraction mission was simple enough, and while they had expected some resistance, they didn't have any qualms about putting suspected terrorists in the ground.

But that hadn't been the case.

The diplomats, who were being held in an abandoned outpost deep within the jungle itself, were already dead. As soon as Sam and his squadron had discovered the bodies, they were set upon by the local militia, who laid siege to the outpost that Sam and his fellow soldiers had for cover. To turn the tide, a sniper, whom Sam had confronted in the aftermath, had them pinned, and picked some of them off with the cold efficiency of one of the best. One of his fellow soldiers, Vargas, had sacrificed himself for Sam's freedom, drawing the crosshairs of the rifle to his forehead to let Sam make a break for the trees.

There had never been a reason for the betrayal, and it had gnawed at Sam for years. Four people had been sent into the jungle to die, yet he had emerged, and never heard another whisper of it. He'd shed blood to return home, and all he got for it was silence from Wallace, and another mission when he had recovered from his injuries.

But Olivier Chavet offered answers. The truth.

And more than that, he offered Sam the chance to honour the three people who had died valiantly by his side on that fateful afternoon under the torrential rainfall.

Morgana had agreed to give Sam a few minutes of her time, and he had followed her out of the BNN building and down a backstreet to an independent coffee shop. As if it had been ordered out of the catalogue, the shop was a display of distressed wood and cliched wall art, sprouting eye-rolling sayings like *But first, coffee* and *Live, laugh, coffee*. The shelves on the bare brick walls were lined with traditionally classic novels to give off the impression of sophistication. Behind the till, a tall, gangly man stood, his forearms covered in random tattoos and his thin face framed by a wispy beard and topped with a tight topknot. Sam had ordered them both a coffee and then, once they'd been made, he carried them over to the corner table where Morgana sat, anxiously picking off her nail polish.

'Here you go,' Sam said with a smile, handing her the coffee.

'This is crazy,' Morgana said. 'I could get in so much trouble.'

'I know,' Sam agreed. 'But I just need to know where he is.'

'Who? Olivier?' Morgana shook her head. 'No chance.'

'Morgana, it's important.'

'He's a wanted man, and let's face it, you hardly have a great track record with people who are wanted by the law.'

'Wait, you think I want to kill him?' Sam sat back in shock and Morgana raised her eyebrows. For a woman who was clearly shaken, she was doing a good job at hiding it. 'You've got it wrong.'

'Enlighten me.' Morgana sipped her coffee and regarded Sam with scrutiny. Sam sighed, and then relayed her the highlights of what had happened all those years ago, from arriving at the compound and finding the bodies, to when he shot a bullet at the sniper who had killed his squadron and sent her tumbling down the cliff face. As the story progressed, Morgana's jaw fell more slack and as Sam finished, she sat quietly, staring at her coffee.

'Morgana, Olivier is in danger.'

Shooting upright in her seat, she frowned at him.

'He's in hiding.'

'You've advertised to Ducard that he's in London.' Sam shrugged. 'Do you not think he'll have his men tearing this city apart to find him?'

'Surely they wouldn't be allowed to. Not in a different country.' Morgana bit her bottom lip in anxiety. 'Besides, he's already been assigned a security detail.'

Sam frowned in confusion.

'I thought he flew in under the radar?'

'Yeah, but the French Security Authority called me this afternoon to assign a security detail to Olivier...' Morgana's words trailed off as the panic on Sam's face confirmed her worst fears. 'Shit.'

'Look, it's not your fault. But I need to know where he is right now.'

'He's staying in the Premier Inn in Highgate, but under a different name.'

'Thank you.' Sam stood, his eyes glancing at the doorway. 'Just be careful, Morgana. These are not good people.'

The young journalist looked up at Sam with tearful eyes and a sense of undeserved guilt stricken across her pretty, youthful face.

'What are you going to do?'

Sam slid his powerful arms into his jacket and then placed his baseball cap on his head. He gave her one last reassuring smile before he answered.

'Whatever I have to.'

Olivier had spent the entire afternoon attached to his laptop, which was set on the small desk that the cheap hotel offered. With the uncomfortable chair causing a stiffness at the base of his spine, he would often stand, stretch it out and gaze out of the window at the busy city below. He was on the top floor of the eight-storey hotel and was at least offered a view that stretched beyond the first few buildings. The empty wrappers of the supermarket meal deal surrounded his chair, and his laptop was framed by three empty coffee cups and a bottle of water. He stood once more, his spine thanking him for the respite, when he looked once more at the screen.

The BNN official YouTube channel was open on his screen, with the thumbnail of the video showing himself and Morgana Daily sitting opposite one another. The headline was pretty crude, but he could live with it.

Wild conspiracy about Pierre Ducard could actually be true.

It offered him just enough credibility while also keeping BNN at arm's length if it drew Ducard's attention. They were a news outlet after all, so reporting on the French President-elect was their job, especially with his much-publicised visit to their country. What Olivier was most excited about was the number of views.

The video had been available for just over five hours, and already, it had over two million views. Not only that, the number of people who had liked the video far outweighed the negative responses and the comments beneath were heart-warming.

OIivier seems so genuine. I hope he gets justice for his father.

Ducard is a snake. Please don't elect him.

#justiceforchavet.

I could listen to Olivier all day. And look at him, too.

If France is looking for an honest and noble president, then look no further than that man right there.

Ducard is a criminal.

Although the comment section of a YouTube video would never register as anything meaningful, it at least gave Olivier the vindication that people were listening. They were hearing what he had to say, which meant there would at least be an element of doubt about people's perception of Ducard. The man's image was slicker than oil and his career as the *Chef d'État-Major des Armées* had made him a living legend to a number of people.

All Olivier wanted was justice, not only for his father and his family, but for the people of France. Their soon-to-be-leader was a murderer of his own people and the country had a right to know.

It was approaching the evening, as the sun set over the skyline afforded to Olivier by his open window and the temperature was dropping. The warm, spring day had made way to a cooler evening and although he was loath to leave the safety of his hotel, the rumble of his stomach reminded him that it had been hours since he had eaten. The 'room service' was a fancy brochure of poor food and, although his paranoia screamed at him to stay put, he craved some fresh air.

He slung his blazer over his arms and headed through the dull corridor to the lift, which he rode down to the ground floor. As he descended through the building, he rolled himself a cigarette, licking the back of the paper and putting the finishing touches on it as the doors opened. He nodded politely to the receptionist as he passed through the white and purple lobby and emerged through the automatic door. The fresh air hit him with a firm hug, and he took a minute, with his eyes closed, to breathe it in. The day had been an emotional rollercoaster, as discussing his father's death without letting himself lose control took a toll on him physically. All he needed now was a cigarette, something substantial to eat, and then a good night's sleep.

Then he could go home.

Olivier cupped his hand from the gentle breeze and flicked his lighter, bringing the cigarette to life with a plume of smoke. He began his stroll through Highgate towards the busy high street, weaving in and out of the other civilians as they made their way home from another hard day's work. With the busy city slithering around him, and the nicotine pumping through his body, Olivier took a few moments to enjoy the calm, knowing he was likely heading home to a shit storm that his interview would have created.

For years, he was certain that authorities were after him, at the behest of Ducard himself, but for those few peaceful moments, he pushed the thought out of his mind. In doing so, he was oblivious to the suited man who was following from the other side of the street.

'He's at a place called the Premier Inn in Highgate.'

Francois Lascelles hung up the phone and swivelled in his chair, looking up at Cissé who loomed over him like a tidal wave. With his fluency in five languages and impeccable programming skills, Lascelles was one of Ducard's most valuable assets, a role which Cissé respected and understood. While Cissé was more adept with a gun in his rather than a wireless mouse, he appreciated that to operate as the most effective security force; they needed the right skills in the right seats, and Lascelles was a much valued cog in the machine.

It didn't mean Cissé had to like him, and he made no effort to hide his disdain. Lascelles had never seen combat in his life, and the money that was spent on his education by his wealthy parents could have built schools and hospitals in Cissé's homeland. Despite being a passionate French nationalist, Cissé still held love for Senegal, and seeing a smug, rich kid like Lascelles coast through life while many were impoverished, turned his stomach.

But Cissé took his orders from Ducard, and those orders were to work with Lascelles when necessary.

'Is he alone?' Cissé asked, stroking the grey beard that clung to his chin.

'Oui.' Lascelles nodded, respectfully speaking to Cissé in their mother tongue. *'She said he was staying under the name of a friend, but a quick search of his known accomplices should be easy enough.'*

Lascelles spun on his chair and faced his laptop, his fingers dancing across the keyboard with an efficiency that

Cissé found impressive. Although it was alien to him, Cissé found 'Lascelles's knowledge and capabilities with a computer enviable. His own methods were a little more medieval, but when it came to getting what he wanted, he was just as ruthlessly efficient.

Only his hands usually ended up covered with a little more blood.

'Give me the address of the hotel,' Cissé ordered firmly. *'I will have one of my men watch it until Ducard gives the order to move.'*

'A please would be nice,' Lascelles responded with a cocky grin. Seconds later, he felt the pressure on the back of his head as the wood of the desk rushed up to meet him. His nose crunched against the solid oak as Cissé slammed his head brutally against it, shattering the cartilage and spraying blood down his face. Lascelles howled in agony as he rocked back into his chair, tears flowing down his cheeks and disappearing into the blood.

Cissé lowered himself down to Lascelles's eye level and glared at him with a demonic pleasure.

'Please.'

Cissé patronisingly patted Lascelles on his bloodied cheek and then wiped his hand on the man's blood-stained shirt. As ever, his reputation would precede him, and Cissé enjoyed the terror that erupted whenever he entered the room. Lascelles blinked through his tears and scribbled down the address with a shaking hand. He passed it to Cissé, who snatched it, turned and headed to the door.

Ducard would likely reprimand him for the assault on the analyst, but all would be forgiven by the end of the day.

When he killed Olivier Chavet.

CHAPTER SEVEN

'With all due respect, sir, this is bullshit!' McEwen remonstrated loudly, his fist slamming onto his desk, rattling a few of the adorning objects. With his phone pressed to his ear, McEwen winced as his anger had caused the pain in his hip to return.

'You would do well to watch your tone, Commissioner.' Admiral Wainwright spoke with authority. *'We need to ensure smooth international relations with France, now more than ever.'*

'But this should be handled by us. This is London, sir, and the last I checked, that meant the Metropolitan Police Service were the ones who upheld the law.'

'You are. And I expect you to keep doing that.' Wainwright took a sip of a drink, angering McEwen further. *'But this is a matter of international safety, and the Foreign Secretary has made it clear that we are to support Ducard's request.'*

McEwen rubbed the bridge of his nose with frustration. There were many plates that the Commissioner of the Met needed to spin, and the political back scratching was the one he hated the most. The Foreign Secretary was as shifty as they came, and he didn't trust her one bit. But Admiral Wainwright was a man of superior rank and had been advising the Prime Minister on all safety measures pertaining to Ducard's visit. As Chief of Defence Staff, Admiral Wainwright wielded significant power and respect, which he was well aware of. McEwen's enraged silence drew Wainwright to speak up.

'It's a simple enough request, Bruce.'

'Like I said, it's bullshit.'

'Well, your objections are noted. But in the eyes of the French authorities, Olivier Chavet is a wanted man for his threats to the public.'

'Threats?' McEwen chuckled.

'I know. It seems excessive, but here we are. They will arrest him this evening at the hotel they have acquired through their intel. Legally, I might add.'

'Tell me something, Admiral. Why are Ducard's men in charge of this arrest and not the French Police? I'd be happy to liaise with them, make the arrest myself and then handle the transfer. Properly.' McEwen overemphasised the final word and knew instantly he'd poked the bear.

'Let me give you some advice, Bruce. As a friend. Your little stunt after the Munroe fiasco may have made you a popular figure with the public, but behind many closed doors, you're on thin ice. Far be it from me to threaten the Commissioner of the Metropolitan Police Service, but as a friendly warning, you're already running out of rope. So why don't you just fall in line on this one, eh?'

McEwen felt his fists clench and his blood boil. His hip hummed with a dull agony, but his rage pushed it aside. This was exactly the sort of thing he found so disillusioning. It was why he had found himself not so far as agreeing with Sam Pope's methods, but at least understanding them.

There should be no grey area with right and wrong, yet he felt like every decision he had to make, or every meeting he had to attend, was smeared with the colour. After a few more moments of contemplation, he sighed.

'Fine.'

'You know it makes sense.'

'Goodbye, Admiral.'

McEwen slammed down the phone before the admiral could respond, a petty victory that he immediately regretted. Like himself, the admiral was just following his orders and doing his job. With the UK's rocky relationship with the EU, palling up to one of its leaders was a smart move. McEwen knew that, and deep down, he understood it, too. The Foreign Secretary was probably under immense pressure to ensure the red carpet was rolled out for Ducard, who had already made encouraging promises to the Prime Minister.

Looking the other way while he dealt with a problem wasn't the most egregious request, yet McEwen felt dirty obliging him.

After taking a few minutes to calm down and wrap his head around the situation, McEwen popped a couple of paracetamols, pushed himself out of his chair and marched from his office to inform those who needed to know about what he had agreed to. As he walked through the corridors of the New Scotland Yard building, he cursed the amount of grey paint that had been used in the building.

It felt like he couldn't escape it.

Posing for the photos was always a highlight of her job that Dianna Mulgrave adored, and she beamed her best smile towards the lenses. Dressed in her best blazer and skirt, she knew she looked powerful, and she wanted that to emanate through the image as she forcefully clutched Ducard's hand. Her dark hair was cut into a short bob, and her glasses sat on the sharp nose that matched the rest of her face. While everything about her persona seemed forced,

Ducard was the complete opposite. The charming smile and staged handshake came naturally to him, and as the flashes of the cameras erupted before them, he held Mulgrave's hand with as much force as she did.

'I trust my request has been accepted.' Ducard spoke through the smile, just loud enough for the Foreign Secretary to hear.

'Absolutely,' Mulgrave responded desperately.

'Thank you,' Ducard said, withdrawing his hand and placing a friendly hand on her shoulder. 'The PM is lucky to have you.'

Ducard turned and began his charm offensive on the rest of the room, leaving Mulgrave to cherish his words and undoubtedly now firmly in his pocket. He thanked the journalists who had been there for the event for their time and honesty and even made a smart remark about the scandalous interview that BNN had aired earlier that day.

'I thought I was watching one of your terrible soaps.'

It had drawn a loud chuckle from the crowd and instantly undercut Chavet's credibility. He made his way through the room, shaking hands with everyone who had lined up to meet the French President in waiting, and he gave all of them equal time and attention. It was a tiring part of his campaign, but a worthwhile one. Considering they would all be writing their editorials that evening, leaving them with a great and personal impression would certainly influence their opinion. He was a man of many talents, and commanding people to his will had been one of them.

At the far end of the room, Cissé stood, resplendent in a black suit and black polo-neck jumper. Wrapped around his ear was his radio, and it coiled down to the back of his blazer. As Ducard made eye contact, Cissé gave a stern nod and Ducard hurried through the last of his pleasantries and approached.

'You have him?'

'Oui.'

A smile spread across Ducard's clean-shaven face and Cissé scanned a careful eye over the corridor and then hurried his boss towards the back exit. The black 4x4 was waiting, the engine running, and the windows tinted. The journey back from Westminster to Kings Cross wasn't particularly far, but with the evening traffic, it offered Cissé plenty of opportunities to brief Ducard on the plan. Emile Domi, Cissé's second in command, had identified Chavet leaving the hotel and had tailed him to a steak restaurant ten minutes from the hotel. With eyes on their target, Cissé had sent the seven other men from the security detail to meet Domi, who would lead the extraction. Ducard knew that Cissé trusted Domi as he trusted Cissé, with the two men both coming from impoverished villages in Senegal. Two years younger than Cissé, Domi had earnt Cissé's trust and respect, which were two things he held in the highest regard.

Ducard trusted his judgement.

There would be a scene, as the other guests were likely to cause alarm at the sight of an armed tactical team sweeping through the building and covering the exits, but Ducard had already had assurances from the weak, British Foreign Secretary that the police would not interfere, as long as it was a swift operation and minimal footprint left behind.

'Domi can deliver?' Ducard asked as their car pulled through the grand iron gates of the Renaissance hotel. The driver rolled the car to a stop, stepped out, and then opened the door for him.

'He can,' Cissé said with confidence.

Ducard felt a twinge of excitement shudder through his body. Chavet had become an irritant that had the potential to become a problem. By having Cissé's team extract him from the hotel and then stage a mugging gone wrong in a back alley in London would be enough to keep the public off his back. As far as he was aware, only three people knew of the operation beyond his team, and he had assurances from them of permission.

Having Britain by the balls gave him great satisfaction indeed.

Cissé led the way to the suite, opening the door to reveal Lascelles, sitting at the gorgeous dining table, with a laptop open before him. He turned to Ducard, who startled at the broken state of the young man's face.

'Good lord, what happened?' Ducard asked with genuine concern. Lascelles shot a glance at Cissé, who didn't even give him the courtesy of eye contact.

'I fell,' he muttered unconvincingly.

Ducard tutted, seeing through the lie and making a mental note to reprimand Cissé in private. With the long day of political performance behind him, he removed his jacket and stretched out his back. It was rare that he felt his age, but now and then, his body would remind him. He took his seat at the table as Lascelles walked through the technical setup.

Domi and his team had all been fitted with body cameras affixed to their chests, which, when turned on, would provide a live feed of their raid of the hotel. It would allow them to capture any potential witnesses, as well as give Ducard the assurance that Chavet was in their custody. Cissé had insisted on leading the assault himself, but Ducard made the valid point that he had been by his side through his entire campaign.

He could easily be identified.

Cissé was a hard man to forget, and despite being a man of few words, he left a devastating impression. Through the four decades of his stellar military career,

Ducard had met plenty of men and women who commanded respect.

Very few of them commanded fear.

Disgruntled, Cissé had accepted the order and now, as Lascelles finished the explanation, his head of security stood behind his chair, his muscular arms folded across his chest and his piercing eyes locked on the black screen.

'They are ready when you are,' Lascelles said, before sheepishly scurrying from the room. Ducard nodded his appreciation and then placed the headset onto his grey hair and then motioned to Cissé for a drink. Moments later, Cissé returned with a glass of red wine and placed it next to the laptop and then returned to his position. Ducard took a pre-victory sip, approved of the quality, and then switched his microphone on.

'Let's do this quickly,' he uttered into the mic, and within seconds, the eight boxes on his screen burst into life, all of them showing soldiers adjusting their cameras.

'Oui, Monsieur Président.' Domi's voice cackled through the headset, sporting a thicker African accent than Cissé.

'Not yet.' Ducard chuckled. *'But soon.'*

———

In the tactical van, the security team switched on their cameras at Domi's order. He had a direct line to Ducard and Cissé, and the entire squadron were terrified of both men equally. Although it was a routine extraction, with their civilian target alone and unarmed, the ramifications of getting it wrong were enormous. All of them had a PAMAS G1 automatic pistol strapped to their hips. The French-made copy of the Beretta 92 that was standard issue for the French Military. All of them had served at varying levels under Ducard and their loyalty to their country was only beaten by their loyalty to the man themselves. Decked out fully in black tactical wear and boots, each man slipped a balaclava over their head as Domi gave the order for them to move. The back of the van burst open, and they hopped out, two at a time, and stormed to the front of the hotel, sending a current of panic through the passing civilians who all rushed for cover in a rising panic.

Calls would be made to the police.

Alarms would soon be rung.

Domi knew Ducard had received assurances that there would be no interference, but that would already be on a countdown.

They needed to be quick, and they needed to be efficient.

As two of the team raced through the doors of the hotel to threaten the reception staff, two more would stand 'point' on the door. Domi sent two men to cover the rear exits, while the final one would be with him on point, as he rushed through the automatic door to the sound of terrified pleading from the hotel staff and the unfortunate young Swedish couple who were checking in.

Ordering two of his men to guard the lifts, Domi rushed to the stairwell, followed closely by three of his men. As they began their ascent, the two he had sent to guard the exits took up their positions, guarding the two visible exits with violent menace.

Everyone was in position.

Little did they know that a ninth person had entered the building five minutes before.

CHAPTER EIGHT

It hadn't been hard for Sam to be proven right.

He'd left Morgana at the coffee shop and made his way from the BNN studios across London, traversing the city through the incredible underground network of trains. With the rush hour in full effect, every train was crammed from door to door, and he managed to squeeze onto one of the frequent trains. The metal cannister shot through the tunnels, humming with warmth and the odour of a full day's work.

He was happy it was a short journey.

After leaving the train station, Sam typed the name of the hotel into the map on his smartphone and followed the little blue line as it guided him through the streets. Weaving in and out of the London foot traffic, he finally came upon the Premier Inn, reaching up into the darkening sky. Its well-known sign was hanging above the automatic door, and Sam looked around the street for a viable place to scope it out. He'd run into numerous 'no win' situations over the years, and had multiple scars to show for it. If Ducard had initiated anything, it would have been on the news by now, and the last thing Sam wanted to do was to spook the man into thinking there was anything else going on. But he wanted to make sure he had at least cast his eye over the situation before rushing blindly towards a possible death.

Sam crossed the street and entered the local pub, which was quickly filling up with the local workers, all of whom had piled out of the surrounding offices, gasping for the alcoholic release of another day on the grindstone. From time to time, Sam missed drinking, and remembered how easily he was able to slip away from his guilt when the inebriation took control.

But it would also lead him to darker places, and had it not been for the timely intervention of Sgt Carl Marsden all those years ago, he would have taken his own life.

The drink may have washed away the guilt, but in doing so, it opened a tidal wave of pain that he never wanted to visit again. To an ignorant scoff from the suited man next to him, Sam ordered a Diet Coke. He paid for it, eyeballed the man until he looked the other way, and then made his way to the vacant table near the window.

He would wait.

As the sun set and the streetlights burst into life, Sam finally had his confirmation. Looking slightly dishevelled and in need of a good sleep, Olivier Chavet emerged through the automatic door and onto the street. Sam recognised him from the interview that had been plastered across the morning news. His brown hair was a mess, swept to the side by an agitated hand. The Frenchman pulled his jacket tight, then cupped his hands around a cigarette and sparked it into action. Then he set off, strolling away from the hotel, leaving a trail of smoke behind him.

A man followed.

It was almost instant, and just discreet enough that Olivier wouldn't notice. But Sam did.

He noticed everything.

The blue Mercedes parked just down the street.

The young couple sitting outside a restaurant, in the midst of an argument.

The small details were the difference between life and death and had saved his life on many a mission. The man was clearly military by his build and the way he marched with a regimented pattern. Sam quickly finished his drink and followed, sticking to the other side of the street and his eyes firmly on the man following Chavet on the other side of the road. The three of them walked in their respective positions until Olivier turned onto the high street. He'd finished his cigarette and now his attention had turned to the menus that were slapped against the front windows of multiple restaurants until he finally decided to venture into a local steakhouse. It also confirmed Sam's suspicions of the tail. As soon as Olivier entered the restaurant, the other man crossed the road and ducked into a bar. He didn't notice Sam then, and he didn't notice when he emerged out of the front into the smoking area, where he lit up and locked his eyes on the restaurant.

Waiting.

Sam contemplated following Olivier into the restaurant, but it was too risky. If Olivier was spooked, he would run, and that would set off a chain of events that would likely get both men killed or imprisoned. Sam pulled his baseball cap down a little lower and walked past the French soldier, who didn't even register him. Two doors down was a Starbucks, and Sam stepped in, ordered a coffee, and then took a seat by the window.

He couldn't see the tail, but he could see the door to the restaurant, and if the man had been assigned to follow Olivier, he would only move when his target did.

So they waited.

After an hour, Olivier emerged, a hand-rolled cigarette

hanging out of the side of his mouth, and he drew his hands up to light it. As he stood in the doorway, the smoke trickling out of the side of his mouth; he seemed to be lost in a moment of contemplation. Sam could understand that. The man had effectively called his future president a murderer on television and, judging by the dangerous-looking man on his tail, Olivier was right about being targeted. As Olivier turned and meandered back towards his hotel and enjoyed his cigarette, Sam quickly rushed to the door of the Starbucks.

Sure enough, the military man was leaving the bar a few doors down and once again fell into step behind Olivier.

They were keeping tabs on him, most likely to ensure he would be in the hotel when they made their inevitable move. All three men moved briskly down the street, various distances apart, and each one none the wiser they were being followed. Eventually, Olivier flicked his cigarette and entered a bar and ordered himself a drink. To Sam's surprise, the man decked out in black followed, and Sam watched from the window as the tail ordered himself a drink and then took a seat near the back of the establishment.

In the reflection of the window, Sam could see the street behind him, and he noticed the blue Mercedes he had spotted earlier that evening. It was slowly edging down the road, keeping its headlights off and its movement minimal.

Who else was watching?

With his attention drawn to the vehicle, Sam almost missed Olivier as he stepped back out onto the street and strode straight past him, heading with purpose back to the hotel. Thinking on his feet, Sam then decided to enter the bar itself, pulling open the door just as the tail came bounding through, the two men almost colliding. The man grunted at Sam, who stepped to the side and apologised and then waited a few seconds and then turned back to the street, falling in step with the two men ahead of him. Olivier disappeared through the automatic doors and the man following him swiftly raised a mobile phone to his ear.

They had him.

Sam stood, his mind racing, and then he shot a glance back towards the blue Mercedes. The woman behind the wheel noticed him, quickly drew the engine to life and sped off down the street, confirming Sam's suspicions and adding another layer of danger to an already escalating situation. Whoever was in that car had enough of a vested interest to be watching, and Sam was under no illusion that the man who had been following Olivier wasn't just a fan of the interview.

The young man had been brave enough to tell the world about what he had discovered about the death of his father and in doing so, had painted a bullseye on his back. Sam knew how men like Ducard operated.

They would eradicate problems such as Olivier for the *greater good* and the world would pat them on the back for making the bold calls.

But for twelve years, the deaths of his fellow soldiers, as they were pinned down in the abandoned outpost under the torrential rain of the Amazon, had clung to the periphery of his mind.

Good people had died.

Murdered.

And while Sam's one-man war on crime had always been for the greater good, this time, it was personal.

He needed to know the truth.

Not just for himself, but for the three soldiers who died so he could live.

Weighing up his next move, Sam noticed as a large, black van sped down the road and pulled up a few doors down from the hotel. The windows were tinted, and if Sam needed any further confirmation that time was running out, the man who had followed Olivier jogged to the back of the van, slammed his fist against the door and it swiftly flew open. He hopped in and it slammed shut.

'Fuck,' Sam uttered under his breath, and then stuffed his hands in his pockets and marched down the street before stepping through the automatic door. The reception of the Premier Inn was as nondescript as the rest of the hotel, with a high, wooden counter that shielded the staff from their guests and the logo emblazoned on the wall behind. A half stocked vending machine stood on the far wall, alongside two leather chairs and a potted plant that had seen better days. The young woman behind the counter was just tall enough to see over it, and she offered Sam a smile as he approached. When Morgana had informed Sam about where Olivier was staying, she told him that Olivier had bragged about booking things under the name of an old friend to evade detection. Sam approached the desk with a sheepish smile and told the woman he had lost his key card. As he apologised, she shrugged and then asked for his name, which Sam gave.

Daniel Modeste.

The woman clicked her fingers across the keyboard, gazed for a few moments at the screen, and then turned to Sam with a smile. She activated another key card and handed it over the counter, offering Sam another flirtatious smile as she did. He nodded his thanks and then approached the elevator, which was thankfully waiting on the ground floor. He took it all the way to the eighth floor, and then, after checking the signage, headed down the long corridor that was draped in the company's brand colours. The hotel suddenly felt a lot bigger than Sam had anticipated, with the rooms wrapping all the way around the building, and Sam turned the corner and eventually came to Olivier's door.

He took a deep breath, pressed the card to the lock and then entered, ready for the truth and whatever mayhem was to follow.

Olivier couldn't help but think he was being followed. Although his better instincts had told him not to leave the hotel, he needed to eat, and the craving for nicotine had been building all afternoon. The reaction to his interview had been phenomenal, and as he had strolled down the streets, he'd cast his eyes in every direction to see if he was being followed.

He never spotted anyone, but he couldn't shake the nagging feeling there were eyes on him. The entire duration of his dinner was spent half expecting a bullet to the back of the skull, and every time someone entered the restaurant, he had felt his entire body stiffen with fear. He'd brought it on himself, he knew that, but the paranoia was worth it if it meant his father's death would be acknowledged for what it was.

Cold-blooded murder.

And Olivier had discovered why. It was the Hail Mary he would play if things ever came to an inevitable conclusion. His entire campaign against Ducard had been predicated on the fact that the former *Chef d'État-Major des Armées* hadn't done enough to bring his father back alive. But when the time was right, he was going to drop the anvil on Ducard.

He had proof of why he killed his father.

Spreading that across an interview in the UK wouldn't have the impact he wanted, but he had done enough, he hoped, to start getting more prominent journalists or public figures to start asking questions. As dangerous as it was, Olivier was elevating himself from irritant to serious problem.

With his stomach full and his nicotine craving satisfied, he had returned to his hotel room, and he gazed out upon the city of London, wondering if he was ever likely to return. His interview was already trending online in France, and when he returned to the country in the morning, would he be likely to face incarceration?

Perhaps…but Ducard wouldn't want to make a martyr out of him, nor add credibility to his claims by silencing him.

It was a dangerous game Olivier was playing, but he felt he was playing it just right.

As he contemplated a shower and an early night, Olivier's entire body began to shake as the distinctive beep of a key card against his door echoed out, followed by the mechanical whirring of the lock opening.

The door flew open, and in marched a man he vaguely recognised but immediately feared.

'*Putain qui es-tu?*' Olivier barked, stepping around to the other side of his bed. Suddenly, his hotel room felt tiny, with the man stood in the narrow walkway between the bathroom and the in-built wardrobe. The man's muscular frame filled up the space, yet he stepped in with his hands raised and his face etched with an embarrassed look.

'I don't speak French,' Sam said calmly. 'I saw your interview, so let's keep this English, shall we?'

Olivier's brow furrowed; his hands balled into unthreatening fists.

'Okay,' Olivier stammered. 'What the hell are you doing here?'

'We don't have a lot of time,' Sam said, his eyes flicking around the room. 'We need to go. I'll tell you on the way.'

'I'm not going anywhere with you.'

'Seriously?' Sam shrugged. 'There is an easy way and a much harder way of doing this, so please, let's just go.'

'Who are you?'

'My name is Sam Pope. I've watched for the last few hours while Ducard's men have been tracking your every movement. There is van of them outside on the street ready to burst in here at any minute and I'm going to hazard a guess that it's not to pat you on the back for your interview.'

'Oh god. Oh god.' Olivier was beginning to panic.

'So we need to go *now*!'

'We need to call the police…'

Sam stepped out of the small, cramped alcove and into the room. He shook his head and Olivier flinched with fear.

'Listen to me, Olivier. If they've got men on the ground out there, then you can guarantee they have clearance to take you. Rightly or wrongly, if they've made you out to be a threat, then the police won't stop them. So we need to go…'

Olivier anxiously looked around the room, wasting valuable seconds.

'Why should I even believe you?'

Sam sighed.

'Because I was there, Olivier. I was one of the men sent to die to make it look like Ducard tried to save your dad. I don't know why he was killed, but what I do know is three soldiers were also killed, and I want to fucking know why.'

Before Olivier could answer, a rising commotion was heard on the other side of the hotel door. Sam held a finger up for quiet and then he silently approached the door, his ear cocked. He turned back to Olivier and raised a hand.

'Get down,' Sam said through gritted teeth and then squeezed himself into the small nook between the door frame and the wardrobe. Olivier looked on in terror, but then threw himself to the ground as the door burst open and a man, clad in black swarmed into the room, followed swiftly by another. As they entered into the room, one of them started to bark angrily at Olivier, instructing him to his feet in French. Through the crack where the door hung on its hinges, Sam could see the final man about to enter, and as he did, Sam threw his entire bodyweight into the door. The heavy wooden door crushed the man against the frame, causing him to groan with pain, and as he dropped to the ground, his two associates spun around. The one nearest to the doorway was met immediately with a thunderous right hook, which sent him spiralling onto the bed with his brain spinning. The first through the door sized Sam up, his eyes bulging with fury through his balaclava. His hand swiftly moved to the PAMAS G1 handgun strapped to his waist, and as he brought it up, Sam drove his fist down into the man's forearm. The gun fell to the floor, but the man blocked Sam's next intended blow and then lunged forward, driving the two of them back into the desk that buckled under their weight. Among the wreckage, Sam was able to drive his boot into the man's chest, sending him sprawling backwards and by the time the man got to his feet, Sam was standing and he swung a vicious elbow that sent the man crashing headfirst into the wall, and then crumple to the ground beneath. The man that Sam had sent onto the bed was woozily getting to his feet, and Sam sent him sprawling once more with a sickening drill of his knee to the man's face.

'Holy shit,' Olivier murmured as he slowly stood, his eyes darting around the carnage that dominated his hotel room. Sam stretched out the pain in the back and then bent down and lifted the PAMAS G1 that had fallen to the ground. He gave it a quick check and then nodded his approval.

'Believe me now?'

Before Olivier could answer, the door slammed open again, and the man Sam had crushed stumbled forward, his fists raised and in one of them, a serrated blade. Olivier gasped, but Sam pulled the trigger, sending a bullet shattering through the man's shin. The gunshot echoed throughout the hotel, stirring the entire building into a panic, and Olivier turned pale as the man fell to the carpet among his unconscious team, howling in agony as blood gushed from the wound. Sam calmly stepped over him towards the door. Olivier stood over the man, his jaw open and his body shaking.

'You shot him?'

Sam got to the door, then, with the gun held tightly, ducked his head out. He looked up and down the hallway.

It was clear. For now.

He turned back to Olivier, who stood helplessly, his face stricken with terror among the fallen men. Two of them were beginning to stir. One of them was radioing for support.

They didn't have long.

Sam stepped back into the room and extended his hand.

'We need to go. Now.'

CHAPTER NINE

Ducard's excitement turned to horror within seconds.

Sitting at the table of his presidential suite, he had casually sipped at his glass of wine until near empty, where, without prompting, Cissé had generously topped it up again. Ducard watched with enthusiasm as Domi and his team prepped in the van, all of them holstering their weapons and listening intently as Domi's authority came to the fore. His command of his men was exemplary, and Ducard turned to Cissé and nodded with approval.

Domi was ordering his men to ensure they covered every viable exit from the building and that they needed to leave as little a footprint as possible. Although Ducard had squared it with the admiral and the foreign secretary, he had been informed that the police commissioner wasn't thrilled at the idea of the snatch and grab happening within his jurisdiction, but he would toe the line where required.

But they needed to be efficient.

All eight segments of the screen began to move, with various angles of their entry into the building being transmitted in real time, and Ducard kept his eyes squarely on the camera affixed to Domi's chest. With considerable authority, he threatened the receptionist, before barking his orders at his men to cover the exits. Ducard nodded his agreement and watched as some of the cameras moved from the reception to their various stations, covering the automatic entrance, the back doors and the lifts. With four men left on the ground, Domi burst through the door to the stairwell and with impressive stamina, the four men took the stairs two at a time, racing up the flights to the top of the building, evading any of the guests and keeping their presence to a minimum.

At last, they emerged onto the eighth floor, and with the knowledge obtained by reception, Domi led two of the men down the corridor to Chavet's room. Ducard could see from one of the cameras that one of the man was left guarding the door, ensuring a smooth exit once they had their target.

It was running like clockwork.

During his long tenure as *Chef d'État-Major des Armées*, Ducard had overseen numerous extraction missions, and if he was walking through the tactical playbook, Domi was running this one to the letter. It was most impressive, and Ducard gave a wry smile of pride at the resources he had available to him. That, and the fact that a growing irritant was about to put to bed.

Watching the camera of one of Domi's soldiers, Ducard could see Domi pressed against the wall beside Chavet's door, and after a silent countdown, he instructed the soldier to enter. A boot shot up onto the screen and connected with the door, sending it flying open and Domi burst into the room, swiftly followed by the human battering ram. With his eyes locked on Domi's camera, Ducard felt his fists clench as Chavet was shown on the screen, his arms raised in terror on the other side of the modest room, which paled in comparison with the luxury with which Ducard was accustomed. The second camera followed in, swiftly followed by the third.

But then something happened.

Out of nowhere, the camera on the third soldier was blindsided by what appeared to be the door, and the impact was enough for Ducard to wince. The impact scrambled the camera's feed, and Ducard's eyes flicked to the two other cameras in the room. The second soldier in spun around, and as he did, the figure of a person was seen briefly, before the soldier went spinning into oblivion and clearly came to a stop on his back.

The impact of the blow had been sickening, and Ducard slammed his fist onto the table in frustration. Domi turned to face the attacker, and the image of the man was clear as day. Ducard felt a small twinge of recognition, but not enough to place him. Domi lifted his weapon in front of the camera, but the intruder smacked it from his hand, before the two of them tumbled backwards into the wall, obliterating the desk, before the man drove his boot into Domi's chest, scrambling the feed so only the audio was clear.

By the sounds of it, the man swiftly eliminated Domi from proceedings, just as the camera of the second soldier was beginning to rise up, the man trying to enter the fight. A swift image of a knee shooting up and a gut-wrenching crunch of bone sent the camera zipping backwards again.

Ducard turned his mic on.

'This is Ducard. Chavet is not alone. I repeat, Chavet is not alone.' Ducard flashed an angry glance at Cissé. 'Domi and his team are down. Do not let these men escape. Shoot on sight.'

Ducard slumped back in his chair, just in time to see the fuzzy image of whoever Chavet's saviour was directing a gun at him.

The gunshot was deafening.

The soldier dropped to the ground, howling in pain,

and the final images that Ducard saw were of Chavet and the mystery man stepping over the camera and off into the hotel.

The gunshot would draw attention, which meant the authorities would be called.

Their window was closing.

Furious, Ducard hurled his empty wineglass across the room, where it exploded against the wall. As the fragments clattered to the ground, he spun to Cissé, who seemed unmoved.

'I want to know who that man is. Now.'

Cissé nodded and left the room. Lascelles would be down the hall, no doubt watching the same feed, and despite being an irritation Cissé would love to remove, he'd be able to run a facial scan through his system.

Whoever was helping Chavet, they would know soon enough. Heading down the hallway, Cissé hoped that the rest of the mission would provide a better viewing experience for his boss.

———

Sam had only taken eight steps down the corridor before another black-clad man appeared round the corner, obviously drawn by the gunshot. Like the others, he was decked out in black combat boots and trousers, a black jacket that encased a bullet-proof vest, with a camera strapped to the front of it. Around his face, he wore a balaclava, but through the eyeholes, Sam could see the rage in the man's glare. With a gloved hand, the man reached for his own handgun, but Sam lifted his up, drew it to his expert eyeline, and gently squeezed the trigger.

The gunshot echoed throughout the hotel, drawing screams from the occupants of other rooms, followed by the howl of agony as the man dropped to the ground, his kneecap shattered. The gun spilled from his hand, and he scrambled to try to reach it. Sam set off, sprinting to make up the space between them, and just as the man was about to clasp his hand around the weapon, Sam swung his boot and connected with the man's jaw. It sent the man spinning, driving the consciousness from his body, and he slumped backwards into the blood that had already pumped from his leg.

'*Merde.*' Olivier uttered, and Sam bent down and picked up the other PAMAS G1. He looked at Olivier, saw the fear in the man's eyes, and decided it would be best to keep hold of both weapons. The downed soldier had been guarding the stairwell, and Sam looked across the hallway to the elevators.

One of them was swiftly rising through the building, no doubt some reinforcements to even the odds.

'In here,' Sam demanded, pushing open the stairwell door. Olivier followed, and Sam swung his arm across Olivier's chest and pinned him to the wall behind the door. As the Frenchman went to remonstrate, Sam lifted his hand to stop him, just as the elevator doors pinged open.

Two men rushed out. Their panic in seeing their fallen friend apparent in a deluge of French expletives.

Sam waited.

The door to the stairwell burst open, and with it being the top floor, the first man immediately began to bound down the stairs. As the second one pushed through, Sam reached out and grabbed the man by the back of his jacket and jerked him backwards. Caught off balance, the man yelled with surprise, and Sam drove the hard butt of the gun into the back of the man's skull. As he flopped forward, Sam held onto him, lifted the gun, and unloaded two bullets at the soldier who was halfway down the first staircase.

Two more leg shots.

The soldiers collapsed down the last few steps, dropping the gun he had drawn, and he screamed in agony. Sam quickly spun the woozy soldier around and drove his elbow into the side of the man's skull, sending him flopping into the door of the stairwell and wedging it shut.

Sam turned to Olivier, who was as white as a sheet.

'Let's keep moving.'

Sam didn't wait a second, and he bound down the stairs, kicking away the fallen weapon that the crippled soldier was lamely trying to reach for. Olivier followed, keeping as close to Sam as he possibly could, and as they passed the sign for floor four, Sam stopped and leant back against the wall. Olivier copied, and Sam lifted a finger to his lips. Below them, the sound of footsteps barrelling up the stairs echoed, growing louder with each passing second. Sam lifted the guns up, taking a few deep breaths, and just as the footsteps threatened to round the corner of the stairs, he pushed off the wall and leant over the banister.

A few panicked words echoed in French.

Sam pulled the trigger.

He hit the first man in the thigh, snapping his leg out behind him, and the man hit the step ahead of him with a worrying crunch. The second shot hit the man behind him in the shoulder, sending him spinning and tumbling back down the staircase from which he had climbed. Without a shed of emotion, Sam turned to Olivier and nodded, and the young Frenchman followed in horror.

He knew he had caused some problems along the way, but now the reality of the situation was becoming clear. Everything he had dug up on Ducard, and every accusation he had levelled at the future president had been true, and now, they were trying to use an opportune moment to eradicate him. He had counted eight men that Sam Pope had taken out, all of them armed, all of them clad in black to disguise their identities.

All of them were there for him.

To rip him out of his reality and scrub his intrusion into Ducard's ascension from the world.

Sam leapt down the final few steps, and as he hit the ground floor, the door to the stairwell flew open, and another gun was pointed at his face. The man pulled the trigger, but Sam instinctively dropped his gun and clasped the man's wrist, driving his arms upward and sending the bullet into the stone of the staircase above. The final soldier was heavyset, his stocky frame outweighing Sam considerably, and with a grunt of fury, he barrelled forward, driving his shoulder into Sam and sending him crashing back into the wall. Sam hit the wall hard but used the impact to bounce forward and he drove a knee into the man's gut. The man absorbed the blow admirably before he grabbed Sam by the scruff of his jacket, and with all his might, he turned and lifted Sam off his feet and hurled him into the door to the stairwell.

The impact took the door clean off its hinges, and Sam clattered into the reception among an avalanche of wooden splinters and screams. The receptionist, who had the phone to her ear, howled in terror, and a young couple were huddled in the far corner, their eyes wide in astonishment. Sam pushed himself up a little, but the stomping boots of his attacker approached, and he felt the full force of them as the man drove one into Sam's ribs, lifting him off the broken door and sending him slamming into the vending machine. The protective screen shattered, reigning down shards of glass onto Sam's back.

The boots crunched across the debris, and as one of them lifted, no doubt aiming for the back of Sam's skull, Sam's instinct kicked in. He wrapped his hand around one of the jagged shards, and ignoring the damage to his palm, lifted it and drove it into the back of the man's calf. The pain struck the soldier like a bolt of lightning, and as he collapsed into the reception desk, Sam stood, rushed forward, and drove his elbow into the side of the man's head with all his might. The blow sent the man snapping into the wood, the edge of the desk driving into the side of his neck, followed by the sickening crunch of bone.

The man flopped to the ground, his eyes wide open as his life left him. Taking a few deep breaths, Sam held his hand up apologetically to the civilians in the room. His eyes flicked to the elevator, which had shunted into motion.

Whoever he had left on the top floor was heading down to find them. Olivier stepped through, noticed the urgency in Sam's eyes, and handed him his guns.

'Thanks.' Sam laboured, the air still battling to return to his lungs. His back was throbbing, and he was sure that one of his poor ribs had been broken again.

As they stepped out of the hotel, a curious crowd, drawn by the commotion, dispersed in panic, especially as Sam lifted one of the guns and aimed it at the driver's door of the black van parked outside the hotel. The door opened, and the driver, also clad in a balaclava, was armed.

Sam opened fire.

The bullets embedded in the door, and another shattered the window, causing the screams to spread throughout the street. Beyond them, the familiar wail of sirens, which was Sam's usual hint to get going.

A black cab barrelled down the street and Sam stepped in front of it, the other gun drawn, and this time, he aimed it directly at the driver. The driver hit the brakes and lifted his hands in the air, and Sam pointed the gun at the sky and pulled the trigger.

The gunshot roared the driver into action as he opened the door and rolled onto the ground, scrambling away as

Sam guided Olivier to the abandoned vehicle. The driver of the van had snuck around to the other side of the van, and he spun out, erratically firing at the two of them as they ducked into the cab. Sam leant out of the driver's seat and stood, swinging his arm over the door, and he unloaded two more shots in retaliation.

One of them connected.

As the driver hit the pavement, the onlookers, now all running for cover, squealed in terror at the very real capabilities of a loaded firearm. The man was groaning in agony, and as Sam slammed his door shut and put the cab into first gear, he glanced back at the hotel.

The leader of the squadron was racing towards the door, his eyes wide with anger and in his hand, he had a gun.

Sam slammed his foot down, and the cab screeched forward, as two bullets blew out the back window. Next to him, Olivier was hunched forward, the events of the past few minutes resonating with him in a terrified shake.

As Sam approached the end of the road, he could see sirens in the distance.

He could also see the few soldiers still standing boarding the black van in a hope of pursuit.

Among it all, the blue Mercedes also stirred to life to join the action.

CHAPTER TEN

Commissioner McEwen's phone was ringing off the hook, and he sat at his desk, his eyes locked on the screen of his laptop and the nagging sense of dread hanging over him. Turning the other way while Ducard's private security handled the Chavet problem hadn't sat well with him, and since it had escalated to a shootout, he was battling the need to send the foreign secretary a big, fat *I told you so*.

But then he had seen the CCTV footage from the hotel where it had happened.

He would express his anger at the tactics that had been used by Ducard's men, especially the intimidation of the staff and civilians, but they had been as swift as possible with no collateral damage. The ski masks and black attire sent a message of danger, which again, he disapproved, but up until they had burst through the door of Chavet's room, they hadn't done enough to warrant his wrath. It was when he saw the third man to enter Chavet's room take the brunt of the door to the chest, followed by a few moments later being sent to the floor with an apparent bullet to the leg that McEwen's heart caught in his chest.

Someone was fighting back.

Moments later, through the surprisingly decent video footage, Sam Pope emerged through the door, holding a gun and with Chavet following in panic, did he realise the gravity of the situation. Suddenly, his rod to beat the Foreign Secretary with had been turned against him, as his perceived lack of investment in Sam Pope's capture would now be linked to an international incident. As he followed the rest of the CCTV footage, he caught snippets of Sam's valiant fight through the rest of Ducard's crew, culminating in a pretty nasty looking brawl in the reception, which ended with Sam breaking the man's neck on the wooden desk.

A further sweep of the building found four more men with gunshot wounds, all non-lethal, along with another, who appeared to be the driver of their van.

It was chaos.

But through it all, there was one thing that was buzzing around McEwen's mind like an errant fly.

Why had Sam Pope involved himself?

There were many things that McEwen didn't agree with when it came to Sam's idea of justice, but there was one thing he was crystal clear on.

Sam Pope may well have been a criminal, but he wasn't a bad man. As excruciating as it was for him to admit it, McEwen knew there was a justification for every person that Sam had killed. As deadly as he was, Sam had a strict moral code, and although he seemed to have a habit of looking for trouble, it wasn't a coincidence that he always looked in the right places.

Which meant Sam had a reason.

Whether it was just Sam being a good Samaritan and seeing the inevitable coming once Olivier had revealed his presence in London, or something more sinister, there would be a reason.

A justification.

As his phone buzzed once more on his desk, McEwen paused the footage on his laptop and sighed.

It was Dianna Mulgrave.

He had already ignored multiple calls from the foreign secretary and knew that he was running out of rope. He squeezed the bridge of his hooked nose with frustration, lifted the phone, and put his Glaswegian charm to work.

'Ma'am.'

'What the hell is Sam Pope doing?'

McEwen looked back at the screen. The image he had paused on was of Sam himself, marching towards the exit of the Premier Inn, gun in hand, followed by Chavet and a trail of chaos behind him. Ever since he went off script at the press conference four months ago, McEwen knew the knives were sharpening.

He made too many powerful people nervous.

There were rumours of collusion.

Undoubtedly, they would be ramped up, and Mulgrave wasn't someone he'd label an ally. This was her decision, to allow Ducard to conduct such a shady operation on UK soil, but it would now be McEwen's inability to rein in Sam Pope that would be the dominant issue. Whether his tenure as commissioner would survive the fallout, he didn't know, but he'd be damned if a politician as ignorant as Mulgrave was the one to push him.

Straightening his back and stiffening his lip, he replied,

'It looks like he's stopping a crime that you sanctioned.'

'Excuse me?'

'Whatever the reason, and there will be one, Sam has stopped an innocent man from being abducted.'

'Innocent?'

'With all due respect, Dianna, it's hard to see the bigger picture when your nose is planted firmly in Ducard's arse.' McEwen heard her gasp in shock. 'I have a situation to get under control, so thank you for your call.'

'You need to get Sam Pope under…'

McEwen disconnected the call and tossed the phone back onto his desk. There would be repercussions for his insult, but he didn't care. He wielded enough power to bite back, and right now, he needed to get a handle on an incident that was spiralling out of control. As he stood, he stretched out the dull ache in his hip. Then, he lifted his hat from its hook, tucked it under his arm, and made his way to the door of his plush office, where no doubt, he'd be in high demand. Just as he rested his hand on the door handle, he glanced back once more at the laptop, and shook his head and chuckled to himself.

'For fuck's sake, Sam.'

The rush hour traffic had subsided enough to give Sam a clear road, and although there were still narrow roads and multiple buses to navigate, Sam managed to rip through the first seven or eight streets away from the Premier Inn at top speed, working up through the gears until he was barrelling down a main road at over seventy miles an hour. Lining the pavements were onlookers, all shocked at the ferocious speed of the black cab shooting by, followed closely by a black van with windows tinted. Behind them by a street or two, the wailing of sirens and the blue lights affixed to the top of the white cars soon shot by.

Sam had no plan.

Olivier was strapped in the back of the cab, his eyes closed and muttering a silent prayer in French as he clung to the belt that was looped across his chest. The brisk spring evening was rushing in through the blown out back window, and Sam swerved around another car, then ran a red light, drawing a cacophony of car horns and angry outbursts.

The van followed suit.

Sam had already woven his way towards Muswell Hill, the residential streets all looking identical and most likely exceedingly overpriced. Interspersed among the houses was the odd shop or fast-food outlet, and Sam kept his eyes on the road as he sped through. Speed cameras flashed and car horns roared into the night as he whipped through, speeding down Fortis Green as the sound of a gunshot echoed behind him. The bullet hit the back of the car, causing little damage, and Sam took a sharp right onto the road that would lead him to the North Circular and then west towards the M1.

He wanted to get out of the city centre.

The longer he was enclosed in the labyrinth of identical, narrow streets, the greater the likelihood of being blocked off. The sirens that followed their pursuit were growing in visibility, as more police cars joined the chase, and he was under no illusion that he was the priority. The French security detail who had laid siege to a hotel would be swept under the rug, as Sam would be the bigger prize. He'd taken a hell of a risk, but if he could get himself and Olivier to safety, then he'd be one step closer to the truth.

To finding out why good soldiers were killed.

As he pulled onto the high road, he cursed under his breath at the obstruction ahead. A temporary set of traffic lights had been constructed, filing the traffic into three separate rotations that would weave around the lengthy road works. A sign stood on the side of the road, informing of ongoing works to replace a gas pipe, but it meant that the road had come to a standstill.

Sam approached it at fifty miles per hour, with the pursuing van only a metre or so behind him.

'Hold on,' he yelled over his shoulder to the terrified Olivier, and Sam turned the wheel to the left, swerving the car into the curb where it rocked up onto the pavement.

Screams of horror filled the road, and the civilians dived out of the way, as Sam struggled with the wheel, keeping the black cab straight as it piled down the pavement, obliterating the store signs and any outside seating for the few bars on the high street. Sam checked his rear-view mirror and saw the van struggling to follow, and just as Sam rounded the road works and re-joined the road, he saw the van speeding down the pavement through the wreckage he'd left behind.

'Shit,' Sam uttered under his breath, before he finally joined the North Circular, weaving onto the dual carriageway and putting his foot down. Seconds later, the van burst into view behind him, eating up the yards between the two vehicles before its bumper slammed into the back of the cab.

The entire vehicle shunted forward, and Olivier yelped in fear. Sam reached across the driver's cab to the other seat and lifted his PAMAS G1. With one hand on the steering wheel, he took a few quick glances at the road ahead, which was clear, and then turned to the plastic divider between him and Olivier.

'Get down,' Sam yelled, and then slid his arm through into the back of the cab, grasping the gun with expert fingers. Olivier threw himself across the seats, his hands over his ears. Trying to keep the car straight, Sam did his best to draw the gun somewhat into his eyeline.

He squeezed the trigger.

The gunshot shook the entire car, causing Sam to struggle blindly with the wheel to keep it straight. The shot didn't hit, but did draw a retaliation, as another bullet slammed into the back of the cab. Beyond the van, a wave of flashing blue lights was approaching.

Sam turned back to the road to steady the car, and noticed a few more blue lights up ahead, as he hurtled towards a police blockade. Everything was moving at such a speed that Sam took one brief moment to clear his mind.

There had been shots he had taken that had been life or death. From when he raided a Taliban camp a few miles outside of a small, Afghanistan town called Chakiri, to the bullet that eventually killed Andrei Kovalenko and saved Amara Singh's life.

Sam took a breath.

He straightened his arm again, drew the gun level with his eye, and then fired. The bullet whipped through the shattered window and flew through the air before burrowing into the rubber of the front right tyre of the van. Instantly, the van collapsed to the side; the metal scraping across the tarmac in an incredible trail of sparks, as the driver tried his best to course-correct.

It was too late.

Sam turned back to the steering wheel and gazed up at the rear-view mirror, just in time to see the van spin out to the side before flipping over entirely, the gigantic vehicle spinning a few times before landing in an explosion of metal shrapnel and broken bodies. As the carnage spread across the dual carriageway, the army of police cars following broke sharply to a stop, with a few of them colliding into each other and causing a small pileup behind the wrecked van. Sam pressed on, and Olivier slowly lifted himself from the seat and peered out of the shattered rear windscreen and gasped.

'Jesus,' he exclaimed, as the road ground to a halt behind the chaos that Sam had left in his wake. 'You're a madman.'

'Maybe. But you might want to hang onto something.'

Olivier frowned with confusion, but then looked ahead, as the two police cars blocking the exit of the dual carriageway rushed towards them, as Sam pressed his foot down on the accelerator.

'Shit,' Olivier yelled, once again gripping his seat belt and shutting his eyes.

Sam could see the penny drop for the few police officers stood by the cars, and in a blur of high vis, they dashed to the sides of the road as Sam guided the taxi towards the small gap between the two police cars. The impact was substantial, causing his head to snap back with guaranteed whiplash, but he held firm on the steering wheel, and the cab hurtled through, the front lights completely obliterated as the two police cars spun out of the way. There would likely be another blockade before he hit the M1 itself, and he looked back in the rear-view mirror to ensure the police officers weren't hurt. They were scurrying around the damaged panda cars, their hands locked on their radios.

'We need to get off the road,' Olivier offered from the back, clearly shaken by the collision.

'You're not wrong,' Sam responded, before taking the next exit off of the North Circular, before a sharp turn took him towards Brent Cross. The famous shopping centre loomed large on the horizon, and Sam kept to the back streets as they made their approach towards it. Although the shops would likely be closing, the car park and centre itself would be alive with activity, due to the restaurants and recreational offerings such as the cinema and bowling alley. It was a place, at least, to dump the car and make their way on foot to the train station. There were direct, overground trains that would take them right out of London, and Sam wanted them out of the city as soon as possible. As they weaved through the final few streets, he saw a signpost for Hendon, and guilt shook his body worse than the collision had.

They were only a few miles from the Hendon Police College, where the Met's newest recruits would be trained.

Where he himself, after his career in the military ended, had trained to become a police officer.

Near to where he lost his son, and his life changed forever.

Sam pulled himself back from the brink of a painful rabbit hole and focused on the road, guiding the busted cab into the shopping centre car park and following the spiral up to the fifth floor. Carefully, he cruised to the far corner of the car park and killed the engine.

Neither man spoke for a few moments, as the adrenaline of the high-speed pursuit through London began to die down. As Sam ruminated on their next move, Olivier unbuckled his belt and leant across to the partition.

'What now?' he asked, in hope more than anything.

'I need a cup of tea.'

Sam's answer caught Olivier by surprise and drew a wry smile, and Sam pushed open the door to the cab and stepped out. He tried to stretch out the whiplash, but his neck felt like it was bolted to a wooden plank. His spine still ached from the reception brawl and he was certain he'd broken a rib. Olivier stepped out, clearly shaken, and he looked back at the cab and shook his head.

'Worst cab journey I've ever had.'

Sam smiled, and before he could respond, the roar of an engine bounced through the fifth floor of the car park and the headlights of a car flooded their vision. Sam pulled his gun as the blue Mercedes sped towards them, before it screeched to a stop and two people quickly stepped out, their weapons drawn.

'Drop your weapons.'

Sam couldn't make out the person through the blinding full beam of the headlights, but he could tell it was a woman's voice. The silhouettes told him he was outnumbered, which meant a shootout was a suicide run.

He didn't lower his weapon, but he did take his finger from the trigger.

'Who the fuck are you?' Sam yelled into the blinding light.

'Agent Renée Corbin. DSGE,' the voice bellowed back in impressive English. 'Drop your weapon.'

'Jesus fucking Christ,' Olivier blurted from behind Sam. 'It's the French Secret Service.'

Sam frowned, lowered his weapon slowly, and stood in the bright lights and imminent threat of death, wondering what the hell was going on.

CHAPTER ELEVEN

In the decades that he'd worked with Laurent Cissé, Ducard had never once questioned the man's judgement. Sure, there had been times when the man's extreme measures may have pushed the boundaries a little too far, and the man's commitment to efficiency could sometimes be a little overbearing, but his judgement had never been in doubt. It was an alien feeling, and it sat like a god between the two of them as they locked eyes across the table of the presidential suite. At the far end of the table, with his busted face glued to the screen of his laptop, Lascelles was diligently clicking away on the keyboard, digging for answers.

'*What a mess.*' Ducard sighed, looking over his glass of wine at Cissé, who remained emotionless. '*I asked you to handle this for me, Laurent. You gave me your word that this would be taken care of. And now, we have three dead, several wounded, and the rumours of a secret military operation carried out by the French on UK soil. Like I said, you gave me your word, and for the first time in my life, I am wondering what weight does that actually carry.*'

Cissé shuffled slightly, his muscular frame absorbing his

side of the table. His knuckles whitened as he clenched his fists, which were resting on the table.

'I will fix this.'

Ducard chuckled and shook his head.

'There is no fixing this, Laurent. There are too many layers to peel back. Too many people involved. No, this isn't something you can fix with bullets, my friend.'

'He killed Emile. I want his head.'

Cautiously, Ducard leant forward, looking his long-term ally in the eyes. If there were tears shed for Emile Domi, Ducard couldn't see any evidence. He knew of the close bond between Domi and Cissé, forged in battle of the years.

'We need to play this carefully. It won't take long for some idiot reporter like that Daily woman to try to connect the dots. I mean, there aren't many dots to connect are there? My security team laying siege to the building that Chavet was staying at. Jesus. I may as well just say we did it.'

The awkward pockets of silence between the two men were interrupted by Lascelles's incessant clicking. After a few more moments, Cissé turned to the analyst and erupted.

'Will you stop with the fucking typing!'

'Sorry,' Lascelles replied insincerely. He looked past Cissé to Ducard and spun the screen around. *'I found him.'*

Instantly, both Ducard and Cissé pushed themselves out of their chairs and marched across the room to the laptop. As soon as the unknown man had interrupted the extraction, Cissé had threatened Lascelles with extreme violence if he didn't identify the man in question. With access to a number of databases, a facial recognition scan would do the trick. The issue was the imagery of the cameras, as the man moved with such speed and precision that the unfortunate wearer was down before a clear image could be taken. Lascelles, already privy to the damage

Cissé could cause, ventured down a different path, and broke a few data privacy laws by hacking into CCTV of the hotel in question, and pulling up the clearest image he could of the man who had dismantled Ducard's team.

Ducard's eyes flickered from side to side as he read through the report.

'Sam Pope,' he said with a vague recollection.

'He's wanted by pretty much every law enforcement agency in the UK. Responsible for nearly seventy kills over the last four years, targeting organised crime and corrupt officials. Basically, he's a one-man firing squad.'

'What is his known address?' Cissé interrupted; his intentions clear.

'There isn't any. The guy's a ghost. Last known sighting was in Glasgow, Scotland, at the back end of last year. Left a string of dead bodies in his wake as he brought down a son of a billionaire who had escaped jail.'

'What a hero,' Ducard said dryly.

'So that's who we are looking for?' Lascelles seemed to grow with confidence. 'I did some more digging. There were mentions of a military background in some of the reports, and so I ran the name through some more discreet channels. Highly decorated sniper, with several tours of some of the most dangerous places on God's green earth. Then suddenly, his military record went blank. Nothing for years. Then, he's discharged after taking two in the chest and returned to civilian life.'

'What do you mean blank?' Cissé barked; his fist clenched once more.

'Wallace.'

Ducard's voice cut through the rising tension of his trusted team, and both Cissé and Ducard turned their heads to their leader. Shaking his head, Ducard meandered back to his seat, lifted his wineglass and took a long sip.

'The General?' Cissé enquired, familiar with the former military leader. Ducard nodded.

'Wallace was the man who promised me this problem would go away. I didn't want to send more French people to die, and that vulture saw an opportunity and reeled me in.' Ducard shook his head once more, this time with disgust. 'One man survived that onslaught that day, and Wallace assured me that the man didn't know anything. Would never ask questions. The best of the best.'

'And you think Sam Pope is this man?' Cissé asked, hands on his hips, vengeance in his eyes.

'If so, then we have a serious problem.'

Cissé snapped his attention back to Lascelles, who shuffled uncomfortably.

'I can do some more digging. See if we can find where they are headed. Perhaps, sir, you can ask if I can work alongside the police to—'

'We need more than that.' Ducard cut Lascelles off. After a few more moments, he blew out his cheeks in resignation. 'Call the Bolivian.'

Cissé spun in fury.

'No, he is mine to kill.'

'I'm not asking.'

'He killed my brother.'

Ducard stood, and for a split second, the fire and fury of the ruthless *Chef d'État-Major des Armées* from days gone by was evident. He squared up to Cissé, who was a cocktail of blind rage and heartbreak.

'You have failed me, Laurent,' Ducard snarled through gritted teeth. 'It is regrettable, but I cannot accept failure. Call the Bolivian.'

A few seconds ticked past, with the loyal duo nose to nose and the tension in the air palpable. Eventually, Cissé took a step back, remembered his rank and stood straight and proud.

'Yes, sir.'

Ducard took another sip of his wine and then took a few steps towards the window. Unsurprisingly, the city of

London didn't offer him as much beauty or reverence as it had twenty-four hours ago.

Now, it offered nothing but a headache and a very real threat to his future.

To everything he had worked for.

Without looking back at his men, Ducard gave one final order as he contemplated a first cigarette in over a decade.

'This situation needs to be handled. Whatever the cost.'

The entire car journey was played out in silence. Sam sat behind the driver's seat, kept his eyes on the two DSGE agents in the front. The driver, a broad man with thinning, dark hair and a strong jaw, kept his eyes firmly on the road ahead, guiding the Mercedes through the traffic and away from the noise of the carnage Sam had left in his wake. In the passenger seat, the woman who had introduced herself as Agent Renée Corbin was looking out of her window, her brow furrowed and the severity of the situation etched across her face. She was attractive, Sam had to admit, with her short, brown hair pulled back from her face in a loose ponytail, and her nose curving up slightly at the tip. While she was dwarfed by her burly partner, Sam could see that she was a bundle of lean muscle and dedicated purpose. In some ways, she reminded him of Amara Singh, and he had to scold himself for allowing his mind to wander to her while effectively under capture by the *Direction Générale de la Sécurité Extérieure.*

Translated as the General-Directorate for External Security, the DGSE had been established for over forty years, but had roots of origin that could be traced back to nearly a hundred. Designed to enhance France's intelligence gathering and overseas security, it soon branched out into more clandestine operations such as espionage, sabotages, assassinations and extractions. While Sam inherently distrusted secret government agencies after his experiences with General Wallace and Blackridge, he understood their necessity to the superpowers of the world, and there was one thing he was certain of.

He was in a whole heap of trouble.

The DGSE were licensed by the French government to act as necessary to ensure the safety and security of the nation overseas, with the DGSI assigned to internal matters such as counterterrorism. As they rode in silence, Sam glanced across to Olivier, who was leaning against the window, a look of resignation across his face as he anxiously gnawed at his fingernails.

Sam wanted answers, but the few times he had begun to interrogate the agents, his questions were shut down. He'd have to wait, and as they drove through the nondescript, dark country roads, he saw a sign for Hatfield. They were somewhere in Hertfordshire, miles away from London and the threat of police intervention. Wherever they were heading, it was off the grid, and although that had been Sam's residence for over four years, he felt uneasy.

Eventually, the car pulled off the road and onto a gravel path; the wheels crunching over stones as it approached a derelict cottage that had seen better days. It rolled to a stop, and the driver killed the engine. He nodded to Agent Corbin and then stepped out, and the female agent turned back to Sam with a scowl.

'I take it I don't need to tell you not to try anything funny?'

Her English was immaculate and was laced with an alluring French accent. Sam shrugged.

'I've been working on a few knock-knock jokes…'

The blank stare told him the joke hadn't landed, and he shook his head. Corbin nodded, then turned to Olivier.

'Both of you. Out.'

Corbin exited the car and Olivier shot a terrified glance at Sam, who nodded his approval. Together, they both stepped out of the car and Sam stretched his spine. His entire chord felt like it was hanging by a thread. The burly driver had already entered the cottage, flicking the lights on, and Corbin stood a few feet from the two of them, her hand resting on the weapon on her hip, and directed them towards the door. Both men obliged, and Olivier trudged behind Sam, who powered into the house with his shoulders straight and no fear.

He'd been in worse situations, and even if this was the end of the road, there was only one way he knew how to go out.

And that was fighting to the bitter end.

Corbin closed the door, and then, much to Sam's surprise, caught him off guard with a smile.

'Tea?'

Olivier looked at Sam with confusion, and Sam sized up the agent. She removed her jacket and confirmed Sam's suspicions as her arms bulged with lean muscle. Behind her, the sound of a kettle being activated crept from the kitchen, as her partner riffled through cupboards, looking for mugs. Sam raised an eyebrow in bewilderment.

'Excuse me?'

'You Englishmen. You're obsessed with tea, right?' Corbin turned and marched to the kitchen, and Sam shot Olivier a curious glance and followed. The cottage was quaint enough, with low ceilings that were held up by thick wooden beams. A rusty hob sat atop a cooker in the corner of the kitchen, along with a small fridge and one long worktop, where the driver was organising their drinks. Corbin casually sat at the table, stretching back in her chair and regarding Sam with a nonchalance that betrayed the severity of the situation.

'Okay, what the hell is going on here?' Sam finally asked.

'Take a seat,' the driver said, plonking a mug of tea down on the table. Sam tentatively obliged and sat opposite Corbin, who gratefully accepted her mug of coffee. Olivier had ventured into the room, and the driver shoved a mug into his hand before he returned to the far side of the kitchen. He crossed his arms across his chest and stared at Sam with a pointless display of intimidation. Sam rolled his eyes and returned his gaze to Corbin.

'Like I said, I'm Agent Corbin. That there is Agent Martin Agard. We are DGSE.'

'What do you want with me?' Sam asked, before sipping his tea.

'You?' Corbin chuckled. 'We aren't here for you. We're here for him.'

All eyes fixed on Olivier, who sheepishly recoiled.

'Am I in trouble?' he eventually stuttered.

'Very much so.' Corbin waved it off. 'But not with us. You see, we have been building a case against Ducard for years based on his international dealings. The DGSI, they've been monitoring his actions back home—'

'DGSI?' Sam interrupted.

'*Direction Générale de la Sécurité Intérieure.* Basically, internal investigations on home soil. There is a lot of stuff that the man has done wrong, but not enough to nail him to a cross with.'

Olivier stepped forward.

'And you think I'm right?'

'Mr Chavet, I know you're right. We have proof of an operation within the Amazon, with tentative links to Ducard. Nothing concrete, but enough to keep digging.

Problem is, we haven't found enough to substantiate the claims you've been making.'

'That man killed my father.'

'And we believe you. But the reason we are here is that we had intel that a move would be made against your life during this visit and we needed to get you out alive. Believe it or not, Mr Chavet, you've got a lot of people asking questions and while Ducard might look like he's floating nicely towards the presidency, he's thrashing about wildly beneath the water to shut you up.' Corbin took a sip of coffee and then turned to Sam. 'But that doesn't explain what the hell you're doing here.'

Sam shuffled uncomfortably and began to respond.

'My name is—'

'Sam Pope. Ex-military. Wanted fugitive.' Corbin bore a hole through him. 'We have access, Mr Pope. But it doesn't explain why you had seemingly beat us to the punch today.'

'You weren't exactly knocking on his door.'

'No, our plan was to intercept Ducard's men on their exit from the hotel. See this badge?' Corbin slammed her badge on the table. 'Might mean little to you, but to Ducard and his men, this trumps whatever they think they are doing. We weren't planning on shooting up a hotel and bringing the whole Metropolitan Police down on the whole thing.'

'I saved him, didn't I?' Sam turned to Olivier, who nodded eagerly.

'Be that as it may, I want to know why?'

'I have my reasons.' Sam's attention was drawn to Agard, who cracked his knuckles. 'Seriously, buddy. If you think you "have ways of making me talk", save yourself the hassle.'

'You're in a lot of trouble, Mr Pope,' Corbin threatened. 'We could just hand you over to the authorities…'

'That would be a mistake,' Sam said calmly, finishing his tea.

'And why is that?'

'Because I was there. I don't know what intel you have about what happened to Olivier's father, but one of us made it out of that jungle alive.'

Corbin's eyes lit up, and she looked at her partner with excitement. He grunted, suspicious of Sam's claim, before Corbin stood.

'So, you know what happened?'

Sam shook his head. Then his eyes met hers and, in that moment, they seemed to make a silent pact.

'Not exactly. But I'm willing to go to war to find out.'

CHAPTER TWELVE

As the singer brought her immaculate voice to a rousing crescendo, the entire audience stood to their feet and applauded. Rows upon rows of elegantly dressed opera lovers were in awe, showering the woman with adulation as the curtain swept across the stage and drew the first half of the show to a close. The Teatro Real was an historic building in the world of opera, situated in the heart of Madrid. The wealthy elite of the Spanish capital was out in force, and as the house lights came on to signify the interval, they all shuffled in their droves to the collection of expensive bars that were situated around the iconic opera house.

Waiters weaved through the groups of tuxedos and gowns, handing out glasses of champagne as compliments were thrown around for the performance and important conversations were had. As Eva Marie Rojas made her way through the crowd towards the bar, all eyes fell on her.

She was stunning.

Wearing a tight black dress that clung to her athletic frame, she strode confidently in the heels that she found as uncomfortable as impractical. However, wearing her preferred combat boots would have drawn attention for the wrong reason.

Her dark hair flowed in rich waves down to her uncovered shoulders, and as she approached the bar, she wasn't shy on offers of a drink. Politely, she declined all the leering men who tried to impress her with their wealth, with several of them sizing each other up as if she was a prize for them to fight over.

She was unattainable, but it amused her to watch pathetic men peacock. She ordered a sparkling water from the bar and then gazed into the wall-length mirror that reflected the entire room behind her. Avoiding the lustful eyes of the surrounding men, she focused on herself.

Despite her discomfort in her attire, she had to admit that she scrubbed up well. Her dark eyes and tanned skin were passed down to her from her father, Luis, who had raised her on his own from such a young age. She was only five years old when she lost her mother, and Luis, who had run a successful cocoa farm in their native Bolivia, raised Eva to the best of his abilities. He was a kind and generous man, who spent as much time providing a steady income for his workforce as he did in instilling those notions within Eva. As she had ventured into her teens, she excelled at school, startling her uneducated father with her aptitude for maths and she soon helped him build the business.

Simpler times.

Happier times.

With no siblings, Eva's only family was her father, and when he was killed in a car accident not long after her eighteenth birthday, everything changed. She lost her focus, allowing the business to fall into the hands of a conglomerate that soon reduced it to ash. As drink and drugs became her world, she found herself at her lowest ebb one night, when a mysterious sexual conquest thought she was a prostitute. That had been the most sobering moment of her downfall, and led her to joining the Ejército de Bolivia, where she not only blossomed into one of the finest markswomen the army had ever seen, but she also made a solemn promise to her father never to drop her guard like that again.

The only memento she had of her parents was her mother's wedding ring, which she still wore on a chain around her neck, exactly as her father had done in the thirteen years he was widowed. She liked to think that they had reconnected in the afterlife, but the years of looking through a sniper scope had made her lose faith in there being anything after the fact.

Death was simply death.

It was what she dealt in, and revelling in its finality had made sending so many people to the ground a lot easier. She originally thought she would have struggled with the idea of ending a life, but having had her parents snatched from her had hardened her to a world that gave little regard to those who inhabited it. For seven years she had served as a *Teniente*, before she walked away from her tags and ranks when she realised that she and her comrades were nothing more than sacrificial pawns in a political game played by stuffed shirts in hidden-away offices.

She became a gun for hire, amassing such a deadly reputation that she soon found herself in the employ of some of the most powerful people in the world, but on her terms. There were no orders anymore.

Just contracts.

The money was eye watering, and while she ensured she enjoyed the finer things in life, the majority of it was sent back to her village of Coroico. She may have become a cold-blooded killer, but some of the goodness instilled by her father still remained.

Now, as she approached her thirty-eighth birthday, the

only time she ever thought about her father was when it rained.

'There is no sound more beautiful than the rain falling on the leaves.'

It was something he used to say whenever the heavens opened, and although Madrid was a concrete jungle, whenever the rain did make an appearance, it would pull together the fading memories she had of the man.

The waiter handed her the glass of sparkling water and she thanked him before turning back to the reception area. A few men tried to lock eyes with her, but she ignored them, taking a delicate sip of her drink before she confidently strode across the room to the open glass doors that led to the balcony. The thick, heavy smell of smoke welcomed her, and she swiftly placed a cigarette between her painted lip.

'May I?'

A hand held up a lighter and courteously, Eva accepted. She leant into the flame, sparked her cigarette to life and then inhaled the welcome hit of nicotine. She blew the smoke out and turned to the man.

'Thank you.'

Fluent in over five languages, Eva was always thrilled when she worked in Spain and got to use her native tongue. The gentleman offered a dashing smile, his greying hair slicked back neatly, and his strong jaw was clean shaven. Of a man fast approaching middle age, he certainly looked after himself, and the tuxedo he wore told Eva he was worth a small fortune.

'Are you enjoying the show?' he asked, taking a rich puff on his cigar.

'It is beautiful.'

'I imagine that is something you are very familiar with.'

Eva turned away with a coy smile. For a chat-up line, it was a good one, and she seductively walked away from the man towards the white stone that sealed off the balcony. The city of Madrid was basking in the spring evening, with the streets filled with locals and tourists alike. The roads were filled with cars and there were queues forming outside some of the local bars. She placed her drink down on the stone, along with her clutch bag, and then rested an elbow next to it, puffing firmly on her thin cigarette.

'Beautiful view.'

The man's voice emanated behind her, and she nodded her head.

'It is an amazing city.'

'The city isn't bad either.'

She turned to him with a frown, telling him that his follow up hadn't landed, and he playfully held up his hands in defeat. A half empty glass of champagne was in one of them, his cigar in the other.

'Give me a break. It's been a while since I've spoken to a woman such as yourself.'

'Oh, I doubt that.'

' It's true.'

She flicked him a devilish grin.

'There are no women like me.'

The comment worked a charm, and she could see from his body language that he was eager. With an undeserved confidence, he took a swig of his champagne, downing the last of it and then set it on the wall beside her own. He took a puff of his cigar, the thick smoke dominating the air between them.

'My name is Hector Almero.' He offered her his best practised smile. *'Of the—'*

'Almero Aerospace,' Eva interrupted. *'I know who you are.'*

'Really? And how's that?'

'You're a familiar face.' Eva shrugged. *'You don't own one of the biggest private companies in the country and live under the radar.'*

'I guess not.' Hector smiled, clearly enjoying the interaction. *'And your name?'*

'Eva.' She held out her hand. He leant in and kissed the back of it, not knowing it had been responsible for over a hundred deaths.

'No, last name?'

'Not one I want to share.'

Hector's eyebrows raised, as if accepting a challenge. Behind them, the speakers informed the crowd that the opera would be restarting in ten minutes and for them to return to the auditorium. Like sheep being herded, the faceless number of the Spanish elite began to head back inside.

'Shall we?' Hector offered his arm.

'I might stay out here,' Eva suggested. *'I enjoy the quieter moments of the evening.'*

'Perhaps another drink?'

'Perhaps.'

That was all the invitation Hector needed, and he hurried back towards the open doors to the bar. Eva turned and watched, observing as he defiantly waved away his personal security. Clearly, he thought he was on for a good evening, and as they continued remonstrating in the bar, she saw him clearly dismiss the man who shrugged, turned on his heel, and then headed towards the door.

His name was Bernardo Navas.

Eva had read all about him when she had begun her investigation into Hector Almero, which was usually her first port of call upon accepting a contract.

Where the target lived, where they socialised, who they knew, who they had on staff. The usual calibre of name sent her way was wealthy enough to afford private security, and she knew all about Bernardo and the potential issues he could have caused. Somehow, she didn't feel like reducing such a beautiful building into a war zone, so the path of least resistance was to have Hector believe he had struck lucky.

Men were a pathetic species, who instantly lowered their guard in the face of a pretty woman and the possibility of a sexual awakening.

Besides, Hector had previous, with two expensive divorces behind him due to his infidelity.

For a man who owned the dominant aircraft manufacturer in the country, he wasn't as smart or as dedicated when it came to the fairer sex. As he returned through the doors with two glasses of champagne and a goofy grin on his face, Eva almost felt sorry for him. She opened her clutch bag and lifted out her phone.

She had two notifications.

One was a text message from an unknown number, which she would check momentarily.

The other was confirmation from her offshore bank account that a seven-figure deposit had been received.

Confirmation of what was about to happen.

She smiled politely as Hector handed her the glass and they clinked them gently together. As he sipped his, she turned and gazed out over the beautiful Plaze de Oriente, with the stunning Monument to Felipe IV standing proudly in the middle. Beyond the gardens that surrounded the statue was the Palacio Real de Madrid, lit up spectacularly in the warmth of the evening.

There were worse places to spend your final moments and Eva could at least offer Hector that small mercy. She never questioned why someone was wanted dead, as long as the money was paid and there were no moral complications like the death of a child in play. For all she cared, it was just a rival businessman who wanted Hector's slice of the pie and there was little doubt that Hector himself had trodden on many to amass his fortune.

There was no such thing as a decent billionaire, and

although his death would make the news and there would be many civilians who would strangely mourn the death of a famous name that they had never met, her conscience was clean.

They were both exceptional businesspeople.

Only she dealt in death.

After downing his champagne glass, Hector slid his hand to the base of her spine. It was a forward move, one that made her shudder, and she reached into her purse and withdrew the needle. She turned to him, smiled seductively, and then in the minimal space between their bodies, she plunged the needle into the space between his ribs, piercing his lung.

A gasp of shock left Hector's lips before his body froze, his eyes wide with fear as the paralysing agent kicked in, and instantly went to work in shutting off the air supply to his body, along with systematically shutting down his vital organs.

It would take roughly two minutes for him to collapse, and for those one hundred and twenty seconds, he would be conscious enough to know that he'd been murdered. On the CCTV cameras, they would see her walking away, nothing more than a rejection of his advances. It will only be once the autopsy was complete that they would discover he had been murdered, and by then, she would be gone.

A ghost in the wind.

She withdrew the syringe once the entire tube had been emptied into his body and stuffed it back into her bag. She leant forward onto her tiptoes and gently kissed his cheek.

'Enjoy the view. Take it with you.'

With that, she marched back towards the bar and then down the lavishly decorated stairwell to the ground floor. By the time she was out of the front door and heading into the immaculate gardens of the Plaza de Oriente, Hector was already dead.

Without looking back, she lost herself in the crowd of tourists that had converged in the famous grounds.

She checked her phone.

It was a message from Laurent Cissé, a terrifying man who worked closely with one of her most dedicated clients.

She lifted the phone to her ear to discuss the job, and she lost herself in the majesty of the Madrid evening.

CHAPTER THIRTEEN

'Go on, say it.'

Mulgrave stared across the desk at McEwen with a degree of resignation in her eye. McEwen rocked back in his chair and shrugged, not wanting to be goaded into a childish argument by the Foreign Secretary.

'I don't think it's appropriate,' he offered with a forced smile.

'Well, if you do feel the need to throw an "I told you so" in my face, then the opportunity has passed you by.' Mulgrave waved her hand dismissively. 'We now need to focus on how we get this under control. As you can imagine, Mr Ducard isn't pleased about what happened.'

A few murmurs echoed around the table, with Mulgrave's team of executives began discussing possible ideas. Among them, Dipti Patel shook her head in slight disillusionment and when McEwen locked eyes with the Mayor of London, he could practically read her mind.

They were on the same page.

Simply clearing his throat, McEwen drew the entire room into silence, and he felt his authority re-enforced.

'With all due respect, Dianna, Ducard isn't top of our

priority list.'

The foreign secretary turned to McEwen, her eyes wide with fury, and she clenched her jaw. She regarded the tall commissioner with disdain and then stood from her seat.

'Can we have the room, please?'

Instantly, her entire team began scrambling up their papers and pads before scuttling from the room like teenagers late for the school bus. Once the door was closed behind them, Mulgrave turned, her hands clasped behind her back, trying her best to control the room.

'Forgive me if I sound patronising, Bruce, but do you know how much trouble this country is in?' She shot a glance at Patel, as if expecting an agreeing nod. 'Have you any clue on how much shit we have to wade through?'

'Forgive *me*, Dianna, but weren't most of those decisions agreed upon by *your* government?' McEwen held himself up straight. A pillar of control. 'I appreciate your job is a complex one but let me uncomplicate things for you. I wasn't comfortable with the permission *you* gave Ducard to carry out his operation in our city, and now it's blown up in his face.'

'Which wouldn't have been a problem if you had just done your job?' Mulgrave slammed her hands on the meeting table, shaking the remaining objects.

'I did do my job,' McEwen responded, unwavering. 'I proposed extra security detail on Chavet, but you shut it down. Why? Because you and the admiral had an agreement in place with Ducard for him to try this bullshit. Imagine my surprise when I get told to give them leeway. Permission granted to send armed men into a London building to take someone hostage…'

'A terrorist threat,' Mulgrave offered.

'Oh, fuck off. A terrorist? The man is looking for justice for his dad's death, and instead of helping him get to the truth, you're more interested in staying in Ducard's good books. I get it. When he's president, he has a big sway on how this country is treated in Europe, but don't for a second try to shift the blame away from him. We shouldn't be helping the man. We should be investigating him.'

Mulgrave glared at McEwen before taking her seat. She sighed, the toll of the past few hours hanging heavy on the bags under her eyes, and she needed a good night's sleep. But everything had gone wrong.

The biggest vigilante in UK history had interjected himself in an international incident, and now her and the UK's relationship with the future French President was hanging by a thread. The PM had made it crystal clear to her that her career depended on building that bridge, and right now, desperation was the only thing she had. Dipti Patel sat quietly, watching the argument play out. She raised her hand and Mulgrave motioned for her to speak.

'If I may. Perhaps we should think about a combined solution here? It's quite clear you are both opposed to the right way forward.'

'What do you suggest?' McEwen asked calmly.

'Bring him in.' Patel shrugged, looking at both of them. 'I've got plenty of people wondering what the hell is going on, just like you both. Now I appreciate, Dianna, that you've got your reasons, but I think Commissioner McEwen has a fair point. We can't be bullied by Ducard. So why don't we bring him in and ask him outright what is going on and how we can help him?'

'Can't hurt,' McEwen agreed. 'We'd be able to keep tabs on his team and at least look like we're trying to help.'

With the duo seemingly in agreement, they turned to Mulgrave, who was sitting with her head facing the table, and her face like thunder.

'How about this?' She rose her head to reveal her furious snarl. 'How about *you* find Sam Pope and bring him to justice? None of this would have happened if he was behind bars.'

McEwen stood and buttoned his tunic. With his tall, lean frame, he cut an intimidating presence and Mulgrave seemed to shrink a little beneath it.

'How about this? You tell Ducard that if he wants to go any further down this rabbit hole, then he needs to come and see me personally. If any of his men step out of line again, I will have them arrested and hold him accountable. Now...' McEwen looked at Patel, who was smiling. 'If that's everything, you know how to reach me.'

With a curt nod to the room, McEwen marched towards the door, as Mulgrave ran her tongue against the inside of her lip and then turned in her chair to watch him leave.

'You're already on thin ice, Bruce.'

'Well, it's a good job I can ice skate.' McEwen hauled open the door and then turned to face her. 'Just be careful, Dianna. There are some mistakes you can't come back from.'

McEwen slammed the door behind him, and as he walked towards the exit of Downing Street, he sighed deeply. A situation he wasn't comfortable with had just spiralled out of control, and as he stepped outside, he chuckled to himself.

'What the fuck are you doing, Sam?'

'She is on her way.'

Cissé hissed through gritted teeth, seemingly agitated at having the situation taken out of his hands. Despite being a man of immense pride, Cissé was a man of strict order and although he didn't agree with Ducard's decision, he would follow whatever orders the man gave. That was their relationship. Even though Ducard had transitioned from the military to politics, Cissé still saw him as the chief, and would action any and every request to the best of his ability.

But he wanted Sam Pope.

The man had killed his dearest friend for a reason they didn't know yet, but they were fast connecting the dots. Lascelles was working relentlessly to dig up more and more about the rogue vigilante who had obliterated their mission, and a few breadcrumbs were dropping to the ground.

He had clear links to Blackridge, all of which had been archived away by the British government since Wallace's death. The information was vague, but Ducard was confident enough that Pope was the lone survivor. The only one who could confirm Chavet's theories of his father and his colleague being dead on arrival, but it would still be hearsay. They would have hoped that Pope's history as a criminal would have removed any credibility, but the more Lascelles dug, the more worrying it became.

Pope wasn't a villain in the eyes of the public. If anything, he was seen as an anti-hero, someone who was willing to go beyond for the greater good. All of his targets were criminals, all of whom had the resources or capabilities of avoiding the law. Which meant, if the press got hold of what Pope had done, they were more likely to view his intervention as a good thing.

That, if Sam Pope was willing to fight for Chavet, then maybe his claims weren't so flagrant after all.

Cissé didn't question Ducard's insistence of innocence. It was unlikely, he knew that, but he would take the future French President at his word. There were big decisions that would have had to have been made over the years, and Ducard had the courage and the conviction to make them. It was a quality that Cissé admired and, as he informed

Ducard of Eva Marie Rojas' recruitment to the cause, he did so with the professionalism that was expected.

'*Thank you, Laurent,*' Ducard said glumly, sitting on the balcony of his presidential suite. The city of London was lit up, and with the hours that have passed since Sam's interference, Ducard had succumbed to his nicotine addiction. He puffed his cigarette, looking disappointed as he blew out the smoke. '*You know, you never really quit.*'

'*We all have vices, sir,*' Laurent replied with little emotion. '*I must ask, do you believe Rojas is a good idea?*'

'*She's the best there is,*' Ducard said through the smoke. '*No offence, Laurent. I trust you implicitly with my security at all times, and I know you have the background necessary to bring them in. But I need you with me. I need the world to see that nothing is wrong. If I let you off the leash and on a tear through this city, then it would only add more credibility to Olivier's claims.*'

'*I should have been there,*' Cissé said with a shake of the head.

'*You assured me that Domi could handle it.*' Ducard stubbed out the cigarette. '*I know he was a close friend, but he didn't deliver. It cost him his life, Laurent. Don't let it cost us our trust. I want you to collect Rojas when she arrives, give her whatever she needs, and stay out of her way. Do you understand?*'

'*Yes, sir.*'

Ducard regarded his right-hand man with a sorrowful look. Throughout their years together, the man had shown nothing but fierce loyalty. There had never been talk of a family or any ties that would ever get in the way of his orders, and Ducard knew he had taken Cissé's loyalty for granted over the years. It had only occurred to him, when Domi's death was confirmed and Cissé had to leave the room for a moment, that the man did have people he cared about. It was a frightening sight to see Cissé let loose on someone he didn't know or care about.

It was terrifying to think of what he would do to the

man who had killed his best friend.

Ducard lifted another cigarette from the packet and lit it with the embers of the previous one, cursing himself for chain smoking but doing little to abate it. As he took a long, hard drag, he looked up at the night sky. Within the next few hours, a private jet would be landing in Heathrow Airport, bringing in the deadliest assassin that Ducard had ever known. It had been over a decade since Rojas was first brought to his attention, when Wallace had handpicked her as a back-up plan for the mission gone wrong. Her reputation was exquisite, and in the years since she had escaped who he now knew to be Sam Pope, Ducard had paid her handsomely to handle international matters off the books.

The Bolivian.

It was a mysterious enough moniker to gain a legacy throughout the world of international espionage and having a direct line into her had been a valuable weapon in his arsenal. Although Cissé sometimes took it as a personal afront that he would look for alternatives outside of his own staff, Ducard had often done it with his loyal follower in mind. While Rojas was as dependable as she was lethal, she was also expendable.

There was never any paper trail.

Wired transfers pinging from offshore account to offshore account, running through so many shell companies it would tie anyone looking up in knots.

If she was caught, she would never talk. And if she did, she would have no way to prove it.

She was, in essence, the ultimate Hail Mary, as there would be no way of staging what she would do. She ghosted through cities, leaving no visible footprint, and through ways Ducard could never explain, she was able to find people who had worked extremely hard not to be found. And when she did, then they died.

The Bolivian had built her reputation.

Now, he was keen for her to enhance it.

They were too close to the seat now, and if Olivier and Pope were able in some way to prove what he had sanctioned all those years ago, then his campaign would be over.

His liberty would be over.

He'd spend the rest of his life behind bars, and whatever legacy he had built would be eradicated immediately. Ducard had come too far for that to happen, which was why hiring Rojas was a necessity.

But as he took a sip of the glass of scotch he had poured after he had run out of wine, he carefully drew his cigarette to his lips and looked at Cissé, who stood, as always, to attention and ready for an order. There was a clear sadness cloaking the man, who was mourning not just his friend, but also the opportunity to avenge him.

Ducard knew how dangerous Cissé was, and in that moment, as he felt the smoke hit the back of his throat, he thought of how much of a cluster fuck the evening had become. And that Sam Pope, a man who seemed to have a penchant for upsetting the apple cart, had once again found himself where he shouldn't.

Perhaps, Ducard thought, he should do a good thing for his loyal friend after all.

'Rojas is here to kill Olivier Chavet.'

Cissé nodded, and then, to Ducard's horror, smiled. It was a rare sight to behold, but as the edges of Cissé's mouth curled upwards for a few seconds, the message had been understood and the outcome would be biblical.

The Bolivian was there to make the Chavet problem go away.

As for Sam Pope, he was all Cissé's.

The leash had been loosened.

CHAPTER FOURTEEN

It was immediately apparent to Sam that he was dreaming, but everything felt so real. The smells of the damp leaves as the rain crashed over them. The sound of the spluttering engine as it tried to keep going, pushing the boat slowly down the Amazon. Sam looked around and everything felt familiar, but not exactly.

As if someone was colouring outside of the lines.

The random noises of the jungle echoed from the trees that lined the river, and Sam felt the humidity fall upon him like a cloak. Twelve years and he could still recall the rickety wooden floor of the speedboat as it waded through the waters of the Teles Pires. In the cabin ahead of him was Alberto, a local man who they had paid for the journey, but as the hands of time had passed, so had any distinguishable features of the man.

He wore a yellow shirt.

He had dark hair.

That was all that had been retained. Standing next to him was Sam's commanding officer, Sergeant Javier Vargas, whose world-weary face was shaded by the bill of his cap that was affixed to his bald head. In his arms was an SA80A2 assault rifle, which Sam could describe with his eyes closed. Although nearing fifty, Vargas's bare arms were rippling with muscles and veins, and he stood with complete authority. To Sam's left was Private Laurel Connell, a black bullet-proof vest strapped to her wiry frame and her dark ponytail poking from the back of her own baseball cap. Across from her was Private Jason Bennett, with his heavily tattooed arms and the cigarette clinging from his lips. There was some banter between them, stirring the clear sexual tension, but Sam couldn't remember what it was.

But they were there with them.

The vision quickly snapped forward, and Connell and Bennett were dropping over the side of the boat into the shin-deep water before they moved to the embankment, their guns up and their eyes alert.

'Are you a man of faith, Sam?'

Vargas's English was exceptional for a man who was born and bred in Argentina, and Sam had often found his mastery of the language better than the American duo who had already disembarked.

Sam knew his answer before he spoke it.

'I believe we know too much about the world to believe in divine intervention.'

The conversation leapt forward, his mind only remembering so much.

'What do you fight for?'

'I have orders, sir.'

'If you don't fight for something, then what are you willing to die for?'

'I don't intend to die, sir.'

Sam's recollection of Vargas was of a thoughtful man, who regarded Sam with a paternal gaze.

'Then what are you willing to live for?'

'My son.'

The answer now held a supreme guilt that Sam knew he had allowed his subconscious to place. When he had found himself in this conversation twelve years ago, he had hopes and dreams for Jamie and the life he would have. Now, revisiting it long after Jamie's death, Sam wondered why he fought so hard to survive.

'Then we will make sure you get back to them.'

As Sam stepped off the boat, it felt like the ground beneath him flipped, and he was now walking towards an abandoned outpost alongside the other three. Connell and Bennett were uttering concerns that didn't register, and all four of them entered the outpost.

At the time, the place had been a storage facility of all sorts of useless equipment, but now it was empty, as Sam's memory had etched out the finer details. All that was visible were the two bodies on the floor, the bullet wounds in their skulls as fresh as the moisture in the air.

Chavet and Rabiot.

Sam hadn't known the names at the time, but he remembered the feeling of betrayal, of knowing they had been set up and sent to die. The next few moments happened in flashes, as if someone was taking photos with a Polaroid camera.

Two Jeeps carrying sixteen militia approached.

Vargas taking position by the window.

Bennett rushing through the door to face them head on.

Then the sickening crack of a sniper rifle, a sound so familiar to Sam, that he recognised the deadly weapon before anyone else did.

The back of Bennett's skull, followed swiftly by the front, was obliterated by the bullet and as he slumped to a quick death, Sam recalled the grief-stricken scream of Connell. As Sam rushed to the upper floor to try to fight back, Connell pressed against the door frame and unloaded on the advancing soldiers. Beneath him, Sam knew Vargas was drawing most of the fire.

More flashes of guns and death, as Sam eliminated soldier after soldier from his position.

Then the sound of gunfire from the floor below, and as Sam turned, he looked down the barrel of a rifle and heard the gunshot echo. The intruder fell forward with blood pouring from his skull, as Connell rushed towards Sam.

Every footstep was in slow motion, and no matter how many times Sam replayed it in his head, he could never warn her quickly enough.

A bullet zipped through the glass, followed by the haunting clap of the sniper rifle, and Connell's spine was obliterated.

She died in Sam's arms.

'POPE. JUMP!'

Vargas's words rung out and Sam remembered flying from the first-floor window as the building erupted in a ball of fire and wooden splinters thanks to his superior grenade. Everything was hazy after that, as Sam fought the final few soldiers based on nothing more than muscle memory, as the fall had knocked him senseless. He remembered the sniper taking shots through smoke, trying their best to finish the job, and when it looked like Sam's time was up, Vargas managed to save his life.

The final moments of Vargas's life would stay with Sam forever. Already bullet riddled, the grenade had burnt half of his face, removed both his left arm and right foot and had sent a jagged piece of shrapnel into the man's thigh.

He asked Sam about Jamie. About Lucy.

As Sam held his only hand and obliged him, Vargas shed a tear and thanked him for his service.

'It's been an honour, sir.'

'Don't waste it. Now get back to your family.'

Sam was already running when he heard the sniper take their shot, as Vargas had used his final breath to haul himself above the jeep and draw their attention.

Then, Sam's memory grew hazy, and he recalled circling back round to the base of the mountain that had overlooked the outpost, where he found the sniper rifle.

And a woman.

They struggled.

Sam shot.

She fell.

Then, Sam collapsed to his knees, and unlike reality, the ground around him ran red with blood, and as it flowed past, so did the dead bodies of Vargas, Connell, and Bennett.

All of them dead.

Another echo of the sniper rifle rung in Sam's ear and shook him awake.

The dream startled Sam from his sleep and sat bolt upright, blinking his eyes to adjust them to his dark surroundings. The single bed he was lying in was drenched with sweat and, as he breathed his heart rate to a more natural pace, he swung his legs over the side of the bed and pushed himself off. The room he had been shown to by Agent Agard was a box room, with nothing more than the bed and a towel over the end of it. Sam used the towel to wipe the sweat from his shirtless torso before sliding his T-shirt over his scars. He opened the door and stepped out into the hallway of the rickety cottage and peered both ways. A few other doors were closed, presumably with Olivier and one of the agents getting a few hours' sleep before they figured out the next step. At the far end of the hallway was the staircase, with the faint blurring of light drawing him towards it. He made his way as softly as possible, but the tired floorboards gave him away and he gave up trying to be subtle. Halfway down the stairs, he could see the light coming from the kitchen, and then heard the sound of the kettle being set to boil.

He pushed open the door to the kitchen and entered.

'No sugar, right?'

Corbin was standing by the worktop, pulling two mugs from the sink and placing them beside the boiling kettle. She seemed a little less intense, probably due to exhaustion and Sam nodded and smiled.

'Please.'

'Can't sleep?'

'I did. But I got woken up.'

'Really?' Corbin raised a thin eyebrow as she pulled open the fridge and retrieved the milk. 'By what?'

'Just memories.' Sam blew out his cheeks and took a seat. His body ached. Before he'd gone to bed, he'd checked himself over in the mirror. His spine was stiff as a pole from where one of Ducard's men had sent him through the door, and judging from the bruising under his arm, his suspicions of a broken rib were pretty fair. 'You?'

'I'm on second watch.' She checked her watch. 'I'll give Agard a few more hours and then see.'

She poured in the water and then the milk, stirring briskly before dumping the tea bags into the nearby bin. The pokey kitchen was littered with a few ready-meal boxes, and Sam gratefully accepted the hot mug.

'Thanks.'

'So, tell me, Sam.' Corbin sipped her drink and then continued. 'What exactly is your plan?'

Sam took a sip of his tea and then sighed.

'I don't know. I'm sort of winging it.' He shrugged. 'As soon as I saw him on the TV, I just knew he was running out of time. Like I said, I worked for a man like Ducard for a long time. I know how they think. Olivier's a good kid, but he's naïve if he thinks he can keep running Ducard's name in the dirt and not expect any kickback. But I've spent a lot of sleepless nights wondering why the hell me and my crew were sent to die and their memory at least deserves the truth.'

'Pretty reckless. Especially now that you've got the whole of the UK looking for you.'

'Trust me. You get used to it.'

Corbin smiled. For a man who was described as the UK's most dangerous man, Sam Pope didn't seem like such a bad guy. His affable personality was at odds with the file she had pulled up on him. Multiple kills. Escapes from high security prisons. International incidents in Ukraine, Germany, Italy, and America, all within the last few years. But probably the most dangerous part of the man was his steadfast belief that he was in the right.

'Well, you know I can't just let you walk out the door,

right? We've spent too long building our case against Ducard to just let you loose on him.'

'Am I under arrest?'

'No, but you're in our protection. You and Olivier. Him, because he's a dead man on his own. You, well, I can't have a wildcard in play.'

Sam nodded his acceptance and took a big gulp of his drink. With her guard down, Corbin was quite likable. Although she was clearly an attractive woman, Sam's loyalty to Mel, however misguided, allowed him to see beyond that. Corbin clearly cared about her country and was seeking a truth that the majority wanted hidden. She'd put her own life on the line to hunt it, and the last thing Sam wanted to do was get in the way.

They both wanted the same thing.

Just for different reasons.

'Private Javier Vargas. Private Laurel Connell. Private Jason Bennett.'

It took Corbin only a second to realise she needed to note those names down.

'These were your comrades?'

'Yep,' Sam said coldly. 'They were all killed looking for your two diplomats. You probably won't find much on them, as Wallace had everything funnelled away behind so much security, you'd need the best hacker in the world to find it. Thing is, I know a guy, but I have no idea how to find him.'

'How come?'

'He's been on the run for three years. He helped me escape from prison. He's a good friend.'

'What's his name?' Corbin was scribbling away on her pad. 'Maybe I can track him down?'

'Trust me. You can't.' Sam smirked at the thought of Etheridge and then felt a sudden pain for their estrangement. 'But there is a way we can peg this on Ducard. A way to prove he gave the order. But I need something from you, too.'

Corbin dropped her pen and locked her eyes on Sam.

'I can't give you access to what we have…'

'I'm not asking for that.' Sam finished his tea and pushed the mug away. 'Look, I didn't get involved because I wanted to keep Olivier alive. I don't know the guy and from what I've heard, he's got a reputation for pissing people off. I didn't get involved due to the self-righteous reasons you think I did. I got involved, because I want to know why myself, Vargas, Connell and Bennett were sent to die that day. And seeing as how I'm the only one left standing, I owe it to them to find out why.'

Corbin stood and ran a hand through her dark hair. Clearly troubled with the line Sam was asking her to cross, she gripped the worktop that ran across the kitchen and sighed.

'I can't give a wanted man access to secure French files. I'll be arrested for treason.'

'I just want to know why those diplomats were killed. What was the reason for all of this…this pain?'

Corbin turned to Sam, reasserting her authority.

'You said you can prove Ducard gave the order?'

'I'm pretty certain.'

'Pretty certain or certain?'

Sam smiled.

'If I know my friend, I'm certain.' Sam stood and approached her. 'There was a USB stick that had *everything* General Wallace had ever done. Every mission. Every payment. Every deal. Every god damn death. It's not pretty reading, especially when my name was all over it. I traded the stick for the life of a police officer three years ago before I went to prison.'

'Where is it now?'

'Wallace destroyed it.' Before Corbin could respond,

Sam held up a hand. 'But…if I know my friend, then he'd make a copy. He's too smart not to.'

The sound of feet hitting the floor groaned from above them, and Corbin bit her bottom lip. Throughout her entire life, she had done things by the book. She took pride in her spotless record, and always lived by the notion that to deviate from the law was to betray it.

There were no grey areas. They simply didn't exist.

Agard was the same, and when he walked into the kitchen in the next few moments, there was no way this conversation would go any further. But she had spent years building this case, had sacrificed a marriage and a hope of family to keep her country safe. Ducard wasn't the hero the country believed, and she knew that to deal with the dirt, she had to get a little mucky.

Agard descended the stairs. Corbin leant in close to Sam.

'You find me that information, and I'll tell you everything you need to know. I promise.'

'Deal.'

The kitchen door opened, and Agard stepped in, his slick hair now a frayed mess, and he yawned into his fist.

'What's going on?' He grumbled.

Corbin spoke to him in French, clearly reassuring him that all was fine. As he dismissively waved them off and went on a search for the coffee, Corbin and Sam locked eyes across the kitchen and shared a brief but powerful nod.

They were in this together.

And together, they would get to the truth.

CHAPTER FIFTEEN

The following morning offered no respite. Ducard was awoken by a phone call from the desperate Foreign Secretary, trying her best to skirt around the shit storm that he had brought to her front doorstep. It was pitiable, to see a country so reduced to its knees that they were apologising to him that his off-the-books mission went south. If he wasn't so angry, he would have laughed, and when she made a thinly veiled threat for him to clear up his mess before the press caught wind of it, he unleashed a tirade of his own threats, all of which landed like a heavyweight haymaker.

By the end of the call, Mulgrave had given assurances that he was certain she wouldn't be able to keep.

She'd rein in the press where needed.

She'd talk to the Police Commissioner and smooth things over.

She'd handle it all.

The unfortunate thing was, that while all those things would be useful, he doubted Mulgrave had the clout to make them happen. He'd already zeroed in her as the weak link of the British Government, and considering the years of scandal it had faced, that was a serious indictment on her ability. But she was a useful way in, and by offering her a few strands of opportunity to help her career, he was able to manipulate her to his will.

Besides, he didn't need her to do too much. Keeping the wolves from his door for the next twenty-four hours would be enough, and he had already agreed with Cissé that once they had eliminated Chavet, then the trip was over. If Cisse needed more time to stay behind and deal with a personal matter, then that was something he would accommodate.

Ducard could only imagine what Cissé had in store for Sam Pope. He had witnessed firsthand the lengths the man would go to extract information, so he imagined Cissé's methods of revenge would make Satan himself squirm.

Ducard dressed in his expensive tailormade suit and made his way into the dining room of the suite, where a metal tray had been placed on the table. It was adorned with all sorts of fruits and pastries and a pot of freshly brewed coffee which sat in a cafetière. He pressed the top of it down slowly and as it offered a satisfying resistance, he could see the richness of the coffee bleeding through. Without looking up, he spoke.

'Would you like one?'

Nervously, Lascelles looked up from his laptop. The young man had been working non-stop throughout the night and the darkness around his eyes wasn't completely due to the injury that Cissé had inflicted.

'Thank you, sir.'

Ducard smiled firmly and poured them both a mug, before he marched around the wide table and placed it down beside the analyst. He felt sorry for the young man, who had proven himself time and time again that he was just as valuable as Cissé, only he didn't have command the same respect. With Chavet and Sam Pope on the run, and seemingly lost to the ether, Ducard was relying on the young man just as much as Cissé and now the Bolivian.

Only he doubted that pressure would be helpful.

'What do you have for me?' Ducard asked, sitting on the edge of the table beside Lascelles' laptop, and asserting his authority.

'Well, I don't know where they are. But I know who they are with.'

'With?' Ducard frowned. *'They have help?'*

'Well, I don't think you can quite call it that, sir. I ran through all the CCTV footage of the car chase and noticed this Mercedes following. Looking back over the twenty-four hours before, and the same car was sitting outside Olivier's hotel this entire time. See?' Lascelles pointed to the screen, and an impressed Ducard nodded.

'So who is it?'

'This is where it gets a little complicated.' Lascelles' fingers danced across the keyboard like a classical pianist. *'Officially, no one. The car doesn't exist. So that got me thinking that whoever it is wanted to cover their tracks. So I ran a search through a number of our own agencies, and wouldn't you know, I found who it belongs to.'*

Lascelles slapped the enter key on his keyboard, and the logo of the *Direction Générale de la Sécurité Extérieure* filled the screen. Ducard's eyes widened.

'DGSE?'

'Yup. They are tracking Chavet, but I can't find any information as to why. But I was able to snag this CCTV image and run their faces through the database.'

'And?'

'Agents Renée Corbin and Martin Agard.' He looked up at Ducard, who shrugged. *'Both senior agents. Both have a laundry list of accomplishments and are highly thought of within the organisation. Long story short, they would only send these two if it was a matter of extreme importance.'*

'And they have Chavet and Pope?'

Lascelles clicked the keyboard a few more times and pulled up the CCTV footage from what appeared to be the entrance to a shopping centre car park. As it played, a blue Mercedes eventually pulled out, and Lascelles stopped it in motion.

'It would appear so.'

'Fuck.' Ducard rubbed his stubbled chin and made a note to shave before his next media duty. *'I need to speak to the Director of the DSGE today.'*

'I'm on it.'

'Good work, Francois.' Ducard gave him a reassuring pat on the shoulder. *'Good work indeed.'*

A smile spread across his bruised face and Lascelles returned to his laptop. Ducard marched out onto the balcony, welcoming the cool spring morning with a large inhale. The city of London was already wide awake, with the daily commute already causing congestion across the roads and the pavements. Car horns erupted in frustration, and as he gazed across to the concourse outside of Kings Cross Underground Station, he saw a dull blur of people, all of whom had their heads down and their mind focused on getting to work. With a disappointed sigh, he reached for his cigarettes, and as he lit one, he immediately regretted it. But that was the feeling of every smoker, whether full-time or ex, and despite knowing the cancerous intentions of the smoke, they still willingly and knowingly inhaled.

The situation called for it.

With each puff, Ducard felt his nerves loosen, and by the time he was stubbing it out, he was reaching for another. The taste he once found vile had become rather welcome. He leant against the railing, his coffee in one hand and the cigarette in the other, and he tried to process the chain of events that had led to this moment.

The potential fallout.

The undoubted consequences.

What he did know, was that he needed to speak to the Director of DGSE as soon as possible, to work out what side of the coin he was on. If they were retaining Chavet due to him being a danger to the public, spouting ludicrous conspiracy theories, then Ducard was safe.

If it was because they had evidence to back up his claims, then the situation would become volatile. The DGSE was a powerful entity within the French government, but then so was he.

If he needed to bring the hammer down on them and their agents, then so be it.

A gentle tap at the glass balcony door stirred his attention, and Ducard turned, and a smile spread across his face. He hurriedly blew the smoke out of the side of his mouth and then stubbed the cigarette to a premature end. Then, with his most charming smile, he extended his hand.

'Eva.' He approached the woman as she stepped onto the balcony. 'Thank you for coming on such short notice.'

Eva Marie Rojas took his hand but didn't reciprocate the smile. Her hair was pulled back into a neat ponytail, and she wore a tight-fitting leather jacket, black trousers and boots.

'The urgency has doubled my fee,' she said coldly, looking Ducard straight in the eyes. 'I trust this is okay?'

'Of course.' Ducard waved his hand dismissively.

'Also, I do not wish to speak in French the entire time,' Eva said, drawing a scowl from Cissé.

'Forgive me, my Spanish is not so good.' Ducard shrugged. 'We can speak in English?'

'Very well.' Eva immediately switched to English, further impressing Ducard with her command of several languages. There was something about Eva that had always caught Ducard's eye, and it wasn't her traffic-stopping beauty. There was a coldness to her every move and word, underlying the true threat of what she was. She might have lacked the size and menace of Cissé, but the way she carried herself told Ducard what he already knew.

That she was the most dangerous person on this balcony.

'Can I get you a drink?'

'Coffee,' Eva replied quickly. Her love and appreciation for the drink always took her back to her childhood. To the happy memories with her father and a life free of bloodshed.

'Cissé,' Ducard ordered as he took his seat. '*Two coffees.*'

With a furious scowl, Cissé disappeared back into the suite to play waiter, and Ducard offered a seat to Eva with his hand. She obliged and once comfortable, stared straight into his soul.

'Who's the target?'

'Olivier Chavet.' He waited, but she gave no indication that she knew the name. 'Do you remember the first time we worked together? Well, I say worked together. You were put in place by Ervin Wallace.'

'I remember it well.' Eva leant forward and pulled her jacket open slightly, revealing the horrid scar of a bullet wound in her right shoulder. Ducard smiled nervously.

'Well, that was an unfortunate situation. Those four soldiers were sent by Wallace to die, and it seems one of them has a proclivity for survival. I wish that was by the by, but it appears he has reared his head once again.' He paused for a comment from Eva, but there was none forthcoming. 'His name is Sam Pope, but he is not why you are here. As I said earlier, Olivier Chavet is the man I want taken care of. His father was one of the men who was killed that day and…'

Eva raised her hand, her immaculate nails shimmering in the morning sun.

'I don't need to know your reasons, Pierre.' She emphasised his first name, an act of power. 'I just need to know where he is and I will, as you say, take care of it.'

'We don't know where he is.' Ducard, accepting her lack of respect as permission to drop his, once again lit a cigarette. Cissé emerged with the two mugs of coffee and set them down on the table. As Eva gratefully lifted hers to her lips, Ducard continued. 'But we do know he is with Pope, which is why Cissé will accompany you.'

'I work alone,' Eva stated firmly.

'Be that as it may, you are not the one paying the money. Pope owes my dear friend a personal debt, and he would like to collect it himself.'

Eva looked up at Cissé, who met her glare with his own piercing stare. Ducard watched with fascination, wondering to himself who would survive such a show-down. Eventually, she returned her gaze to Ducard.

'Fine. He can be on the ground. Draw Chavet out. Whatever he wants to do about Pope is his business.'

'Thank you.' Ducard turned to Cissé and nodded, seemingly drawing an approval from the man. 'There is another thing. They are currently off the grid and in the possession of the DGSE.'

Eva leant forward, unmoved by the news.

'How many agents?'

'Two.'

'Expendable?'

The abandon to human life was unnerving, and Ducard shook his head firmly.

'I'd rather you didn't kill any French law enforcement.' Ducard puffed his cigarette. 'It would make things…complicated.'

'So, before I go, the target is in possession of a man he has to kill.' She pointed at Cissé. 'Also, two agents from the

French Secret Service and you have no idea where they are.'

'I'd say that sums it up.' Ducard leant forward with a smile. 'I trust you can handle it.'

'It's what I do.'

With the conversation seemingly approaching its end, Ducard stubbed out the cigarette and stood. Eva followed, and she extended her hand and shook his firmly. There was plenty of work to do, and with time running out before their problem became an international incident, Ducard knew that bringing the Bolivian into the situation was akin to pouring petrol on a bonfire.

There would be no extraction.

He'd just sentenced Olivier Chavet to death.

Before any of them could move, Lascelles came bounding through the door onto the balcony, drawing a raised eyebrow from Eva and a death scowl from Cissé. Ducard stepped in front of his right-hand man before he could react and approached the analyst.

'What is it?'

Lascelles smiled at the trio, his gaze lingering on Eva a little longer causing her to roll her eyes. He turned back to his boss, his damaged face beaming with pride.

'Sir, I just found a way to get to them.'

CHAPTER SIXTEEN

As they entered the derelict flat, Sam felt like he was stepping back in time.

It had been nearly three years since he had last been in the building, and nothing had changed within the apartment itself apart from the thick layer of dust and the clear infestation of rats. The entire building was a shell of a property, with the funding running out as soon as Etheridge had gone to ground, and now it stood, uncompleted. A concrete reminder that the austerity within the city of London wasn't as alive as many thought. A dank smell hung in the air, and Sam stepped across the naked floorboards to the window and with considerable effort, jarred it open. Outside, the traffic was sparse, with the majority of the London traffic heading into the city centre. The abandoned building had once been offering the promise of luxury apartments in the popular Richmond area. Now, it stood as a symbol of over-ambition. For the first time in years, fresh air infiltrated the room, and Sam stood, hands on his hips, and thought back to the time they'd spent here.

It was just after Etheridge had sprung him from a

police convoy, taking him to another prison after he had broken out of 'The Grid'. Officially known as Ashcroft Maximum Security Prison, 'The Grid' was as off the books as Project Hailstorm, and after Sam had sacrificed his freedom for Amara Singh's career, that was where he ended up. The then Deputy Commissioner, Ruth Ashton, had revelled in the idea of Sam rotting away in an underground construction that housed the worst criminals the country had ever known. Only she failed to uncover that Sam had been put there by design. Through Etheridge's unrivalled knowledge of digital security, he and Sam had instigated Sam's transfer to the Grid to get closer to Harry Chapman, the man that controlled the majority of organised crime in the country. Once Sam had killed Chapman, which he did with a box cutter across the throat, Sam had escaped.

It was only the call of duty to stop his old comrade, Matthew McLaughlin, from blowing up a hospital that saw Sam back in chains. After turning down the opportunity to join another shady government operation, Sam was expected to continue the life sentence dished out prior. Etheridge intercepted, and for a week, the two of them had shared the flat. The two camp beds they had rested on were still set up, with the mattresses wrecked by whatever vermin had taken a shine to them.

Sam realised, in that moment, how much he missed Etheridge.

The man had given up everything for Sam's cause, finding a purpose in supporting Sam's fight that he never could in a business career that had made him millions. Once he had gone on the run with Sam, Etheridge had disappeared, and he had the skills and resources not to drop off the grid but create an entirely new one to hide behind. He'd left Sam at the airport, with a bulletproof fake identity and a seven-figure war chest, and simply stepped off the radar.

Almost three years since he'd even spoken to the man, and now, casting his eyes over where they had sat and chatted over cold beers, he felt his absence.

Corbin appeared in the doorway; her face scrunched up in disgust as she stepped over rat droppings.

'I thought you said this man had money.'

'He does.' Sam shrugged. 'I guess when he pulled his money from the development, so did the other investors.'

'There are homeless people in the flat down the hall,' Agard mentioned as he stepped in, his brow furrowed.

'You okay?' Sam asked. 'You look worried?'

Agard waved him off.

'It's just the smell.'

Sam gave Agard a curious look as the man stepped further into the room, pulling back the large dust sheets, exposing the brickwork. Olivier stood by the door, his hand over his nose and mouth and a look of pure disgust on his face.

'You slept here?'

'For a week.' Sam smiled. 'I've slept in worse places.'

'Me too,' Corbin joked. 'Hey, we all make mistakes.'

Sam chuckled. After their honest and open conversation in the middle of the night, a bond was building between the two of them. It was rare that Sam found someone so tied to their convictions that they were willing to upset the likely President of their country, but Corbin was genuine. She and Agard had been working on the case for years, and while her partner was a harder book to read, Sam could see the conviction in every move she made. After a few moments of rifling through the scraps of newspapers on one of the few boxes in the room, Sam blew out his cheeks in bemusement. Corbin stepped beside him with her arms folded.

'So what are we looking for?' she asked, her eyes darting around the room.

'I don't know.' Sam responded as he shifted the box to the side and began running his fingers across the ridges of the floorboards. 'Paul was a clever man, and he told me before he left that he'd stored everything away for me.'

'What for?'

'I don't know. Leverage, I guess.' Sam didn't look up. 'You have to understand, this USB stick didn't just have Ducard on it. It had everything on it. Every deal. Every mission. There's enough on that stick to start World War Three.'

'So why haven't you destroyed it?' Agard cut in from across the room.

'Because a dear friend of mine died to give it to me.' Sam said curtly, ending the conversation. Corbin glared at Agard, who continued looking through the dust sheets and the corners of the room, while she began running her hands against the exposed bricks on the far wall. After a few minutes of frustration, Olivier lit a cigarette, drawing a scowl from the irritable Agard. Sheepishly, he lowered his head and scurried across the room towards the open window and in doing so, he tripped over Sam's trailing leg. With a yelp of panic, he stumbled forward, catching himself on the windowsill, which bowed slightly.

Sam frowned.

'Sorry,' Olivier offered as Sam stood and approached.

'No…look.'

Sam gripped the apparently solid windowsill with his powerful hands, and with one impressive tug, his beam snapped open, revealing a hollow interior. Something rattled inside, and Corbin and Agard rushed over as Sam tipped the contents into his hand.

A locker key.

Agard's phone buzzed, and he pulled it from his

pocket. He lifted the receiver to his ear and frowned. Corbin looked up at him and he rolled his eyes.

'Vivier.'

Their boss. Corbin gestured for him to take the call, and Agard left the room. Sam hoped the man was reserving his manners for their commanding officer. Attached to the key in the palm of his hand was a metal coin, with the emblem of a storage facility on it.

'You know this place?' Corbin asked.

'Nope.' Sam shook his head. 'But let's go and check it out.'

Corbin turned on her heel and marched towards the door, and Olivier took a final puff and tossed the cigarette out of the window, sending it spiralling to the ground below. Agard met them at the door, muttering something in French to Corbin as she approached. Sam took one final look around the depressing, neglected room and thought of Etheridge.

'You never make things simple, do you, Paul?'

Chuckling to himself, Sam headed towards the rest of the group to continue their scavenger hunt.

———

The entire journey had been taken in silence.

Cissé's crew had been obliterated by Sam at the hotel, with the majority of them suffering from serious head wounds or gunshots to the leg. Or in the case of his good friend Emile Domi, they had been killed. Ducard had called in a few favours for his high-ranking government friends, and two assets who had been on UK soil were assigned to the meagre task force.

Cissé didn't know their names.

Didn't ask for them either.

Their instructions were clear: Sam Pope was his, and

141

his alone to kill. Both of them had little problem with it, and one of them seemed happy to be behind the wheel while the other would cover the door to the storage unit. As much as loathed to give the man credit, Cissé had been impressed with how swiftly Lascelles was able to turn the tide of events in their favour, and all that was left now was to wait until they arrived.

The storage unit was in the most non-descript business park on the outskirts of London, and as they had pulled off the motorway towards it, Cissé had seen a sign for a town called Farnham not too far away. It meant little to him, but it was worth remembering if an extraction point was needed.

But that would only happen if things went wrong.

And he had no intention of walking away with anything less than Sam's head.

In the back of the 4x4, Eva had sat silently, watching the world go by through the window. In the back of the vehicle was her suitcase, which carried her SPR300 Sniper Rifle, a USA-made killing machine that would make her deadly from over a hundred and fifty yards away. It wasn't the longest-range rifle, but over the years, she had found that urban targets were routine, with upper floor windows from buildings offering enough cover for a straight hit to someone stepping out from across the street. The sleek, black design was easy on the eye, but she loved the ease with which the rifle was quickly broken down for transport, allowing her to make a swift getaway once her deadly finger had pulled the trigger. The lighter rifle also meant she didn't need to rely on the tripod to align her shot, relying more on her own ability and nothing felt better than the stock pressing back into her shoulders as she let off a powerful .300 calibre round.

The other advantage to the rifle was the long suppressor, making it one of the quietest rifles on the market.

'Hollywood Sound'.

That's what she had called it when Ducard had asked to see the weapon, which had clearly been what the gun salesman had said to her. Either way, Cissé knew that the woman knew her guns, and when she assembled the gun as if she was playing with Lego, he understood what Ducard was paying for.

A guarantee.

The two of them had shared no words on the journey, but Eva had made no complaint when Ducard had told her that she was to only take out Olivier Chavet.

Pope was his.

Ideally, Ducard had stated, they want to leave the two DGSE agents alive, as one dead French traitor was something he could probably make go away.

Two dead agents would be significantly harder.

As soon as they had arrived at the storage centre, they had found it closed. Another business long since fallen to the impending recession, and Cissé looked around at the surrounding units and saw little life. There was a plumbing outlet store, a car parts factory and a furniture shipping unit. A few vans were in the parking spaces outside a few of them, and through the glass front doors, he saw little sign of life. As he did a little recon, Eva had left the vehicle, taken her rifle, and disappeared behind the buildings directly opposite the storage unit. Cissé didn't know if there were any fire escapes or outside stairwells, but he doubted she would have trouble finding higher ground. The storage unit was a vast, metal warehouse, with corrugated iron walls, and big, square windows that symmetrically broke through the metal. Along the far side, there was a metal walkway that wrapped around the side of the building and extended across to another small facility. The walkway was lined by two railings and it connected to a metal stairwell that ran down the side of the other building.

A fire exit, perhaps?

Cissé's phone buzzed, with an update that their targets were fifteen minutes out.

'*Very good.*' He uttered to himself, not sure if he was talking about the situation or Lascelles' espionage acumen. Either way, he wouldn't have too long to wait until he would have his revenge. Despite the positive changes in the world, racism was still writhe in most parts of Europe, and he had experienced an untold level of abuse when he had first moved to France with his family. Considering how he had served, killed for and would gladly die for the French flag now, it was remarkable just how alienated he had been when he had joined the armed forces at the age of just twenty. Back then, his hair was a thick, rich brown cap and his beard a wispy nonsense that hung from his chin.

A world away from his hairless scalp and the trim, grey beard that lined his face.

But it was Emile Domi who had been there with him. They had faced the hatred and the prejudice together, and when the Sergeants singled one of them out for punishment, the other would take his licks alongside him.

They'd done it together.

They'd fought, served and killed as a team, and now, knowing his dear friend was dead, had felt like Cissé had lost his right arm. But he hadn't.

For his right arm reached around to the base of his spine, and he touched his fingers to the PAMAS G1 that was snugly tucked into the waist band of his trousers, just to remind himself it was still there.

It would be a last resort.

Revenge would be his, but he wanted to savour every last moment of it, and feel Sam Pope's blood and life seep through his bare hands.

Less than fifteen minutes.

Cissé fastened the button of his blazer and strode back across the industrial estate towards the 4x4, that had been parked by the side of an abandoned warehouse and shielded from the entrance by a line of metal bins.

Somewhere above, The Bolivian was waiting, her expert eye and murderous reputation at the ready.

Cissé got back into the car. And waited.

CHAPTER SEVENTEEN

'And I think that, *if*, and it is an *if*, I become the President of France, then the relationship between our country and this great nation can be repaired. Not only that, improved.' Ducard paused for the applause and he gave the audience his best smile. 'Hopefully, that day comes, but until then, I must say thank you for your hospitality, and I hope the next time I am here in this wonderful city, I will be representing France as its next leader.'

A round of applause echoed through the auditorium, and McEwen rolled his eyes. He was seated in the first row, alongside prominent members of the British government including Mulgrave, who was slapping her hands together like a hungry seal. A well-respected news broadcaster was chairing the Q&A session, which McEwen saw as nothing more than a publicity stunt, and watching Dipti Patel, a woman he had come to respect, placating Ducard, which didn't sit too well with him. She was also at the front of the room, on the elevated stage, and she sat stoically in her chair, her eyes staring into space. There was no doubting that she had been put under excessive pressure by the

146

government to hold the event, and to wilfully allow Ducard his shot at propaganda.

McEwen had been warned, too.

Both Mulgrave and Admiral Wainwright had made it very clear to him that the relationship with France was a priority for the country and rolling out the red carpet to Ducard, regardless of his views and policies, was their best way of securing it. They didn't care what the man stood for.

They just wanted his handshake.

'Thank you, Mr Ducard.' The host said with polished panache, honed from years on the TV screen. 'Mayor, is there anything else you would like to add before we let these fine people go?'

Mayor Patel seems to startle awake, and as she leant forward to speak, Ducard held out his hand.

'Sorry to interrupt, Mayor, but I would also like to take this moment to apologise for the incident yesterday. It is unfortunate that such a situation has come to pass, and with Olivier Chavet wanted by the French government, we saw an opportunity to capture him.' Ducard looked deeply saddened. 'We didn't account for a rogue element to intervene, and we hope to not only work with the fine officers of the Metropolitan Police, but to draw a line under it as soon as possible.'

'Very commendable.' The host said. 'Mayor?'

Patel looked shellshocked and had clearly been manipulated into a position where there was only one response.

'We hope for the same.' Patel said curtly. 'Thank you for your help to resolve the matter.'

Ducard held Patel's gaze, a powerful move to tell her he had her when he wanted her. The host, oblivious to the tension, turned to the watching audience.

'That's all we have time for. Thank you all, and once again, a big thank you to Mr Ducard for his time.'

A rapturous applause erupted and Ducard stood, took a bow of acceptance, and then made his way to Patel and to the host to shake their hands. Then, he was down the steps to the front row, where the handshakes, back slapping and laughs were thrown around in abundance. McEwen watched from his seat, as Patel stood, hands on her hips and with a shake of her head, she marched from the stage. McEwen lifted himself from the seat and followed, his respect enough to command people to move from his path. Leaving the festivities behind, he pushed open the door to the side of the stage and stepped into the corridor.

Patel was gone.

'Damn it.' McEwen muttered under his breath. It had been an excruciating watch, and seeing someone he considered a friend have her integrity sacrificed for nothing more than a publicity stunt didn't sit well with him.

'Leaving without a goodbye?'

Ducard's voice came from behind McEwen, and it sent an uncomfortable twinge down his spine, like nails down a chalkboard. For the past few years, he had watched Ducard's rise in France with little interest, but always found the man to be a believable leader. Perhaps it was the extensive military background or the way he carried himself, but he seemed like the sort of leader any country would need. But since seeing the man up close and personal, McEwen realised he was another snake in the political garden. All fake smiles and firm handshakes, and to those of a similar ilk, he was someone to be revered.

But McEwen was different.

Ever since his tirade after the Munroe incident at the end of the last year, he had seen his role as the Commissioner of the Met in a different light. Gone were the pleasantries and the political moves to ensure support. It had been replaced with a steadfast need to do the right thing, and while it had undoubtedly put a time limit on his time in charge, it had given him more fulfilment than the years before.

'I have work to do.' McEwen said as he turned, towering over Ducard. 'A mess to clean up.'

With a wry grin, Ducard took a step closer.

Was it a challenge?

'I understand. Allowing a man to take the law into his own hands must leave a big mess.' Ducard shrugged. 'It certainly has this time.'

McEwen accepted the challenge and took a step closer too. Although he was taller, they were almost nose to nose, and Ducard's eyes twinkled with excitement.

'They might be clapping their hands for you, Ducard, but as far as I can see, you instigated an armed assault on a London building…'

'With your permission.'

'I didn't permit anything. Especially not with fucking guns.'

'Ah, but you looked the other way. Tell me, Bruce… wasn't it?' Ducard's disrespect was deliberate. 'Do you look the other way whenever Sam Pope is involved?'

'Careful, Pierre.' McEwen spat back, aware of his pettiness. 'You don't want to start making accusations. You're still a guest here, remember?'

'I am, indeed. And one, it would seem, more welcome than yourself. I'll remember this conversation when your government is begging me for a handout.'

Both men refused to break their stare, and McEwen could feel his knuckles whitening as he clenched his fist. With the palpable tension rising, it was broken when the door flew open and a lost-looking man in an expensive suit rushed through. He breathed a sigh of relief upon seeing Ducard, and strode towards the two of them.

'Sorry, sir. Our car is out the other way.'

'Thank you, Justin.'

The man nodded, glared at McEwen, then lifted his wrist to his mouth and told the rest of the security detail that he had located their boss. McEwen arched an eyebrow.

'Where is your head of security?'

Ducard's face twisted into a cruel smile.

'Let's just say he's handling the fallout.' Ducard reached out and slapped McEwen on the arm. The force was surprising. 'Good luck, Bruce. I feel you will need it.'

Ducard turned on the heel of his expensive shoes and then made his way back through the door, to another round of cheers and applause as he made his way towards the correct exit. McEwen watched the doors close behind him and then finally unclenched his hand. The sheer arrogance of the man hung in the corridor like a bad aroma, and McEwen understood exactly what he had meant.

Ducard had sent his men to clean up their mess.

Which meant Olivier Chavet was still in danger.

And if Chavet was still with Sam, then it meant things were only going to spiral further out of hand.

With his teeth clenched and his disdain for politics at an all-time high, McEwen stomped down the corridor, avoiding the other attendees, as he made his way to the exit to try and grasp some sort of control on the situation.

The drive through London had been punctuated by traffic, drawing out the journey and quashing the excitement of finding the locker key. As the four of them sat in the car, Corbin had done a search into the storage company, discovering that it had shut down within the last year. It didn't completely rule out that they would find anything, but it would make their task a little harder without any records or staff to assist.

Sam had kept an eye on Chavet, who had been sulking ever since Corbin denied him permission to smoke out of the back window. The young man was clearly dealing with the gravity of the mess he had made, and the fact that armed men in balaclavas had laid siege to his room.

Twenty four hours before, he was toasting himself for appearing on a major, international news channel and getting his message out there. Now, he was in the custody of the French Secret Service, being hunted by the future president with very clear intentions to silence him. The one time his eyes did meet Sam's, Sam offered him a reassuring nod which didn't seem to register. Chavet just turned and stared out of the window. Corbin was flicking through her phone, offering the odd announcement on traffic or a theory on what they could do next.

Beside her, with his hands on the wheel and his eyes on the road ahead, was Agard, who seemed distracted. The evening before, while Corbin had laid out the situation, the man had struck Sam as efficient and quietly effective, allowing his partner to get them up to speed while he watched with interest. At times, the man looked like the one in charge through his powerful body language, but ever since they had been to Etheridge's old flat, he had seemed hesitant.

Like he didn't trust the mission.

Sam had asked him a couple of times if he was okay, and each time, Agard had batted away the concern. But even now, as Sam looked through into the front of the car, he could see the man's mind was racing. Sam could understand – going up against the man likely to be in charge of the country was a big ask. Corbin seemed to revel in it, whereas perhaps the weight of their actions was beginning to take its toll.

Either way, the man said nothing for the entire journey, and even when he pulled into the empty car park in front of the storage facility, he just grunted to announce their arrival. All four of them stepped out.

The business park was pretty much abandoned, with the majority of the car park spaces vacant and the lack of movement jarring. It was as if the world had forgotten about it entirely, and as Sam and Corbin approached the front door to the storage unit, they could see it was closed.

No lights.

No sign of movement.

'We'll need to find a way in.' Sam said out loud, his eyes scanning the long, metal walkway that connected to the next warehouse. His focus was snapped back to the door by the sound of glass shattering and Corbin retracting her elbow from where the pane had once been. She reached through the broken window, turned the handle and popped the door. She turned back to Sam, and the two other men who were looking at her with their eyebrows raised.

'Oh come on. Breaking and entering is the least of our worries.'

Sam smirked, looked to Chavet who approved and then to Agard who looked around with caution. A low buzzing sound rumbled from his jacket, and he pulled out his phone. He glanced at the screen for a few seconds, then returned it and shook his head.

"Vivier." He shrugged. "He can wait."

The reception had been cleared out, the wooden desk empty of any equipment, and there were square patches on the wall where photo frames once hung. A few sturdy slams and Sam was able to push open the door to the main storage facility, which was a vast, open space across two floors. There were over five hundred storage units in this warehouse alone, and a further one hundred larger ones in the smaller annex connected via the walkway.

'We've got a number, right?' Corbin asked dryly,

looking into the gloom of the warehouse. The top of the walls were lined with murky windows, permitting a stingy amount of light. The place was like a derelict prison, with the tiny cells shrouded in darkness.

'Maybe we should turn back?' Agard suggested. 'Have this place locked down and searched properly…'

'Absolutely not.' Corbin snapped. 'Hold it together, will you?'

'Trust me, buddy. We've only got one shot at this.' Sam said, patting Agard on the shoulder. He dipped his hand into his pocket and pulled out the key. On the back of the fob, Etheridge had marked it.

Two lines. Followed underneath by another three, a two and a six.

'Upstairs. Lot three two six.'

Quickly, the four of them bound up the staircase that led to another seemingly endless number of gloomy, narrow corridor, lined with closed shutters. Each one was covered in a layer of dust, and as they walked single file, the space felt like it was shrinking. Finally, after meandering through the dark corridors, they found their shutter.

'What if it's been cleared out?' Olivier asked anxiously.

'Well, then we are up slack alley.' Sam said as he slotted the key in the padlock and turned.

It clicked open.

The metal lock hit the floor and echoed loudly through the warehouse. He reached down and with two hands, lifted the shutter which rolled satisfyingly into its bracket. Corbin activated the torch on her phone and engulfed the room with light. The dust swarmed throughout the confined space like smoke, and she and Sam stepped tentatively in. Agard had illuminated his phone too, providing further light. There wasn't much, beyond two suitcases and a filing cabinet. As Corbin fiddled with the zips on the suitcase, Sam tried the filing cabinet, but it was locked. He looked around until his eyes rested on a rusty, metal bracket affixed to the wall of the unit, and with one ferocious kick, he snapped some of it clean off. As he lifted it, he had a quick check in with Corbin.

'Anything?'

'Nope. Just some clothes. Cash.' Corbin sighed. 'No stick.'

'Check the lining.' Sam suggested. He then lodged the thin strip of metal into the groove of the filing cabinet, and with a tug that flexed every single muscle in his body, he snapped the locking mechanism and the filing cabinet sprung open. Agard handed Olivier his phone and rushed to Sam, and the two of them began opening the manilla folders that lined the drawer. All of them were empty.

All except one.

'Bingo.' Sam said, and Corbin rushed towards the two of them. Taped to the inside of the folder was a USB stick, and quickly, Corbin pulled a USB adapter from her pocket, connected it to the stick and then to her phone. As she tapped away on the screen, Sam's ears picked up.

He thought he heard the sound of a footstep.

'This is it.' Corbin said. 'There are thousands of files on here.'

'Search for Ducard.' Agard said, running an anxious hand through his hair.

'Guys…' Olivier said from corridor.

'Not now.' Barked Corbin.

'There's someone here.' Olivier's words hit all of them light a lightning bolt, and the three of them rushed back to him. Holding up the phone, Olivier was casting the entire corridor in a bright, manufactured glow.

Footsteps.

'You need to get him out of here.' Sam said firmly.

They grew louder.

Then, round the corner, stepped a man in a resplendent suit, the jacket open and beneath it, a black t-shirt clung to his impressive physique. His dark skin was smooth, and his strong jaw was coated in a trimmed, silver beard.

Corbin raised her gun.

'Stay where you are, Laurent!' She commanded, her voice betraying her confidence.

'You know him?' Sam asked, as the man casually walked forward, roughly fifty yards away.

'Laurent Cissé. He's head of Ducard's security.'

'Then you need to go.' Sam ordered. Corbin ignored him.

'One more step. I swear.'

'Your bullets are allocated to your weapon. You shoot him, then they will trace it back to you, the reason you're here and everything will be lost.' Sam spoke with conviction. 'So go, get out of here, and get Olivier to safety.'

'What are you going to do?'

Sam turned and looked straight at the approaching man, whose eyes were locked on him. Something told Sam it was personal.

'I'll buy you some time.'

Corbin grit her teeth and then reluctantly lowered her weapon. She turned to Agard and a terrified-looking Olivier, and signalled for them to move, and they scarpered towards the darkness and the labyrinth of the warehouse, with no idea of how many men Ducard had sent.

Sam watched them dart up the corridor and disappear into the darkness, and then turned back to the approaching Cissé, who dipped his hand to his spine and pulled out a handgun. Sam felt his muscles tighten. There was no way of avoiding a shot in the tightness of the walkway, and the storage unit would make him a sitting duck.

He'd just have to stand his ground.

Cissé lifted his hand that clutched the weapon, and then to Sam's shock, he slid the magazine from the grip, and tucked it into his pocket, along with the gun. Then, he pulled off his jacket, revealing his powerful arms that burst from the sleeves of his t-shirt. Calmly, he folded the jacket and placed it on the floor. He then cracked his knuckles, loosened his shoulders, and continued walking, eating up the distance between himself and Sam.

Sam clenched his fists, ready for the incoming fight.

CHAPTER EIGHTEEN

In the calmness of the early afternoon breeze, Eva had found her way to the edge of the opposing building and opened up her case. Quickly, she assembled her SPR300 and checked the bolt to ensure that one of .300 calibre bullets was ready and waiting. The golden instrument, with its piercing tip, had sent many a man to the afterlife, and as she snapped the bolt shut, she knew that today would be no different. She'd chosen the weapon due to its easy mobility, meaning she didn't need to lock it in one place, and potentially give away her position to anyone with a trained eye.

No barrel peeking over the edge.

The car journey over had been pleasant enough, despite the fact that Cissé hadn't been best pleased with her involvement. But Ducard had made assurances to him regarding a personal matter and that had seemed to have placated the man. He was familiar to her.

Not personally.

But for what he represented.

During her time in the Ejército de Bolivia, she was subjected to many men who lived and breathed conflict.

The type of men who spoke better with their fists than their mouths, and would measure their self-worth by the fear they could strike in others. They treated her with contempt, rationalising that a pretty girl such as herself shouldn't be messing in their world.

But they hadn't known what she had been through, or the pain that she channelled to make her name.

There were jealous eyes as she was promoted to the sniper division, using her mathematical brain to accompany her steady hand and her keen eye. She became a killing machine.

She became a legend.

When she finally deserted the army, it wasn't for her own self-gain. That would come later. It was because she was tired of being a pawn in a political game that saw many of her comrades, the ones who had come to respect her, killed. If she was going to put people in the ground, it would be on her terms, and so she carved out her name as one of the deadliest contract killers in existence.

She became a weapon to everyone, and her clientele was made up of world leaders and army generals. There had been regime changes and revolutions that had begun with her finger squeezing a trigger, and she was certain there was more to come. She hadn't particularly questioned Ducard any further, and in truth, she didn't care. The man was about to become the leader of one of the most powerful countries in the world, and having him as a paying customer would certainly be fruitful for her and her home village. Although she lived a life of luxury, she still took time to ensure most of her money was invested back into the village of Coroico, where she had been brought up by her doting father after the untimely death of her mother.

As she sat, thinking of them both, her hand clasped the

wedding ring that hung around her neck, like it had her father's for the years between their deaths.

Somewhere below, she heard the low rumble of an engine, and she peeked over the edge of the building to see a blue Mercedes turn into the vast parking area of the industrial estate. It slowed to a stop near the door to the facility, and four people stepped out. The woman looked like she was in charge, followed by a man that she found vaguely familiar.

Sam Pope.

Without warning, her brain sent her memories spiralling back to that moment on the cliff face may years ago, and the pain of having her shoulder ripped apart by a bullet and the terrifying fall into the Teles Pires below.

He'd aged well, and still had the build and stance of a soldier despite the reports of his crimes. There was a temptation to pull her rifle to her eye, place his skull in the crosshairs and eradicate that memory forever, but that wasn't the deal. Pope would be left to Cissé.

She identified the two agents pretty readily, which meant the anxious civilian was the target. She could have eliminated him then and there, as the three men watched the woman smash the window and enter the premises, but it would have given away her position. The remit was to let them enter the building, find what they were looking for, and then let Cissé confront them. The man was bloodthirsty, but a patriot, and it seemed unlikely he would hurt agents working for the government he served so diligently.

They'd have to smoke them out, and put Chavet in a place where the shot would come as a surprise.

The walkway.

Eva lifted her phone and sent a message to Cissé, telling him that they needed to direct the man to the walkway, where she would eliminate him.

A few moments later, Cissé confirmed that it was in motion.

Then, she heard a car door slam shut, and watched as Cissé strode across the concrete with purpose, followed by the man who had sat beside her the entire journey. They hadn't spoken a word, but he carried a FAMAS Assault Rifle, which had been the French Military standard for nearly half a century. Cissé pulled the door open and stepped in, while the gunman stood, rifle at the ready, covering the entrance and ready to fire.

Now all she had to do was wait.

It was something she was accustomed to, and she lifted her SPR300 with the care and adulation a mother would give to a new-born, and slipped it perfectly into her grip. At that moment, with her gun tucked into her shoulder and her laser focused through the sight, there was nobody more dangerous on the planet. She adjusted her foot, so she was steady and she drew the rifle up, locked onto the metal walkway, and waited for the door to open, and her next kill to rush unknowingly to his death.

Kovalenko. Bowker. Edinson. Kovac. Defoe. Mendoza. Hudson.

The list of men who had fought Sam one on one was endless, and as his mind rushed through those battles, reminding Sam of the echoes of pain that he had experienced, none of them had the same bloodlust in their eyes as the man that was walking towards him. Most of them were just hired guns, men looking to make some money, or those who were paid to keep others safe. To keep Sam away.

But Cissé's eyes betrayed the composure of his body, and Sam could see the anger within them. The man was clearly military bred, with a physique and stance that screamed special ops, and judging by the fear that had clearly rattled Corbin before she left, the man's reputation preceded him. Less than ten feet from Sam, Cissé stopped, the two of them shrouded in the dim light that tried to burst through the grime of the windows. With his piercing white eyes, Cissé pointed a finger at Sam.

'This is for my fallen brother.'

Whatever he had said, the words were laced with venom, and Sam removed his jacket and tossed it into the open storage unit. Like Cissé, his arms pulled the sleeves of his t-shirt to breaking point, and he raised his fists, adjusted his feet and set himself.

'I don't speak French.' Sam said curtly. 'So let's just get this over with shall we?'

Cissé didn't need a second invitation. For a man of his age, he shocked Sam with the pace with which he moved, letting out a roar of anger as he charged towards Sam, swinging his brutal fist down like a hammer. Sam got his arms up to absorb the first few blows in his biceps, but then Cissé snuck a left jab through, catching him on the side of the jaw. With no time to shake the blow, Sam felt Cissé's hands wrap around the back of his head, and then he drove forward, lifting vicious knees up into Sam's body. Sam held his arms across his chest, absorbing the impact that shook the bones of his forearms, before Cissé drew back and threw a violent right hook.

Sam ducked, threw a hard right of his own into the man's solid stomach, then rocked him with a snapping left. Cissé stumbled back a few steps, and then slowly lifted his hand to his lip. He tapped the blood with his fingers, smiled, and then he and Sam raised their fists again and slowly edged towards each other.

Throughout his years as a soldier, Sam had been a handy boxer, but it wasn't until he had joined Project Hailstorm that he became as deadly with his fists as he did with a rifle. Weeks of training, mandated by General Wallace, saw Sam suffer and inflict more pain than he thought imaginable, but it now made him a unique fighting machine. Krav Maga, Muay Thai – styles of fighting that had all amalgamated into a repertoire that had kept him alive for so long.

As Cissé edged closer, Sam knew he was going to need it.

Cissé unloaded with another barrage of blows, which Sam was able to deflect, before the man rocked Sam with an uppercut to his broken rib. As Sam arched in agony, Cissé swept his legs from the side, and at the same time, clubbed Sam in the face with a devastating elbow. Sam hit the ground hard, a cloud of dust erupting behind him, and instantly, Cissé dropped on top of him, his hands wrapping around Sam's throat. With murderous intent, Cissé loomed over Sam, pushing his entire body weight onto Sam's jugular. Gasping for air, Sam rocked his hips and then drove a knee into the man's spine, shunting him forward and Sam shoved him away. Cissé hit the metal shutter of a storage unit hard, but scampered back to his feet just as Sam was getting to his, and he charged, driving his shoulder into Sam's stomach and both of them slammed into another shutter, denting it and rocking it on its hinges. Sam drove hard elbows down into the man's back and skull, and then loosened Cissé's grip with a knee to the chest. Cissé stumbled back, and Sam drove his boot into his chest, lifting the Frenchman off his feet and he collapsed on his back with an impactful thud. The dust rose, illuminated by the smoke and Sam stretched his spine. The collision with the shutter had amplified the damage done by his trip through the door the day before, and he took a moment to block the pain from his mind. Cissé took advantage, lifting himself from the floor before unleashing a hurricane of blows, which Sam tried to evade before one of them caught him flush on the nose. The pain was instant and as his vision blurred, he was able to make out the fist as it cracked against his jaw and sent him spiralling into the open storage unit. He fell over one of the open suitcases and hit the floor, and as he struggled to his feet, he could hear the joy in the man's voice as he approached the open shutter.

'You are good.'

Sam didn't know if it was a compliment of not, but he found his footing and charged forward, catching the man off guard as he burst from the shadows. He drove his shoulder into the man's stomach, lifted him off his feet and then launched towards the shutter on the opposite side of the narrow walkway. The impact was sickening, the noise echoing like a clap of thunder throughout the warehouse, and both men hit the ground hard. The shutter rocked on its bracket, and as both men got to their feet, Cissé loosely swung a right hand, which Sam dodged, and he snatched the flailing arm and pulled it over his shoulder. Cissé left the ground, flipping over Sam and landed on the hard ground, the air driven from his lungs along with a groan of pain. Sam stumbled back a couple of steps, the blood trickling from his eyebrow and his nose and then sighed as Cissé began to push himself up again.

There was no respite.

Cissé turned to Sam, his mouth bathed in blood, and he grinned a claret smile. With the dust swirling around them like a tornado, they traded rights, both of them evenly matched enough to either evade or block, until Cissé drove a knee into Sam's stomach and then rocked him with an uppercut that sent his head snapping back and blood to splatter the surrounding storage units. Sensing an opening, Cissé launched forward and leapt, looking to drive a downward fist to finish Sam off, but Sam was ready. Pushing off his back foot, Sam caught Cissé by surprise and before the murderous Frenchman could react, Sam swung his arm with all his might, his forearm colliding expertly with the man's throat. The impact sent Cissé's head snapping back and he crumpled awkwardly to the ground, wheezing for air. Sam readied himself for another round, then a sound shook the building and his own self to its very core.

A gunshot.

But the unmistakable sound of a sniper rifle.

Drawn by the devastating noise, Sam glanced down at Cissé, who was coughing and spluttering, as blood dripped from his lip. There was no doubting that the man would try to stand, and would undoubtedly find a second wind. But for now, he was beaten, and Sam knew that somewhere outside, someone had his newly found acquaintances in their sights. With his back screaming in submission, his ribs cracked and his face smeared with blood, Sam began to jog down the corridor towards the harrowing sound of his past, ignoring the angry French screams behind him, hoping he wasn't too late.

CHAPTER NINETEEN

After leaving Sam to confront the terrifying Cissé, Corbin took control of the situation, leading both a panicked Olivier and an increasingly anxious Agard into the darkness of the warehouse. They moved swiftly, covering the ground quickly as they raced past identikit storage units. The light afforded to them was minimal, and Corbin relented from using the torch on their phones.

They didn't know who else was in there.

After racing through the claustrophobic walkways, they eventually looped back round to the staircase they had climbed earlier, and Corbin raised her fist as she approached the top step. The two men skidded to a halt behind her.

'*Behind me.*' Corbin ordered, the need to speak in English had gone in Sam's absence.

'*We should find a different way.*' Agard suggested. '*The walkway. We can exit through the other building.*'

Corbin shook her head and then, with her hands gripping her gun down by her waist, she slowly began to descend. With each step, she peered out into shadows of the lower floor, but saw nothing. Something sat uneasily in her stomach. There was no way a man such as Cissé was reckless enough to come on his own, yet there were no signs of backup. Somewhere in the warehouse, the thundering echo of two men colliding into a metal shutter pierced the air. Corbin had read up on Sam while he was resting and from what she had discovered, he was more than capable of handling himself.

Men like Sam Pope were built to survive. She stepped off the staircase and swept the walkways with her gun, clearing the pathway before beckoning the others to follow. Once they were behind her again, she pushed on, keeping her eyes peeled and her weapon ready. As the light of the reception grew, she kept herself pressed tight to the shutters, concealing herself in the shadows. Ten feet from the reception door, the entire room became clear to her and she stopped in her tracks.

Olivier and Agard did likewise.

There was a man guarding the door.

Non-descript, with a military hair cut, the brutish soldier was holding an assault rifle. The man seemed a little bored, and his eyes were wandering around the vacated office, looking for anything of interest. As far as Corbin could see, there was only man, but without giving her position away, she couldn't see any further. She turned back to both her partner and their cargo.

'It's covered.'

'Let's turn back.' Agard insisted. *'If we can make it to the other building, we can catch them by surprise.'*

'Last resort.' Corbin said. *'Keep out of sight and stay quiet.'*

Before Agard could contest her decision, Corbin turned and began to shuffle towards the door. Her thighs burnt as she squatted down and moved the next ten feet, until she was pressed against the door itself. The top half was a large, glass pane that gave a view into the room and likewise, back out into the warehouse. She was covered by the solid wooden bottom half, and as she set herself correctly, she tucked her gun into the holster on her belt. She then place one hand on the door handle, and with her teeth gritted and her fingers crossed, she slowly turned it, opening the latch. But she held the door in place, and then, with her other hand, she rapped her knuckles against the wood.

Knock. Knock.

Corbin held her breath, and through the wooden panel, she could hear the footsteps approaching. A looming figure began to appear in the window above her and trusting her judgement, she threw her entire body weight into the door and let go of the handle.

The door swung into the office, edge of the solid wood colliding sweetly with the soldier's nose, and sent him stumbling backwards. The rifle fell to the floor as his hands rushed to his obliterated nose, and Corbin's momentum sent her sprawling into the room. The soldier blinked through the pain, and his watering eyes were filled with fury as Corbin scrambled to her feet.

She reached for her weapon.

He charged.

Before she could draw it, the man barrelled into her, taking her clean off her feet and careening into the wall. The office shook as she collided, and she hit the ground gasping for air.

'You bitch.' The man spat in her native tongue, and then snatched a handful of her hair and hauled her to her feet. Holding her in place, he swung a gloved fist to her face, which she managed to spin away from, and then drove her knee into the man's genitals. He howled in agony, and as he hunched forward, Corbin swung a fist of her own, disconnecting the man's jaw on impact and sending him to the ground, motionless.

She stood, trying to catch her breath, as Agard and Olivier entered.

'*Thanks for your help, guys.*' She said dryly. As she smiled at Agard, she saw his expression turn to shock. '*Martin…*'

'*Look out!*' He yelled, and dived at both her and Olivier, pinning them to the floor as a burst of machine gun fire eviscerated the remaining glass fragments in the front door, and began ripping through the office wall. For what felt like ages, the gunfire erupted, but then stopped, as the shooter had clearly run out of ammo.

'*Let's move.*' Agard shouted and then led both Corbin and Olivier back into the warehouse, running at full pace as they made their way to the flight of stairs. Corbin yelled at Agard to stop, but he either didn't hear her or didn't listen, and once he got to the top, he turned and headed in the direction of the metal walkway. Olivier was close behind him, clearly shaken by the gunfire, and Corbin tried to keep pace. The impact of her collision with the wall had drawn all her breath from her and as she took a second to catch her breath, she looked back.

No one was following them.

There were no footsteps.

Something didn't feel right.

The silence was penetrated by the sound of feet slamming on metal, as Agard and Olivier made there way up the staircase towards the emergency exit, and Corbin pushed through the stitch that had formed in her side and sprinted to catch up with them.

'*Stop.*' She yelled up the staircase, just as Agard opened the door. The sun burst through the opening like an explosion, and Agard shielded his eyes. Corbin began to rush up the steps, just as Agard was guiding Olivier out of the warehouse. Corbin screamed one more time.

'*Wait!*'

But Olivier was out of the door, his feet pounded the

metal four times before he was out in the open, and the horrifying crack of a sniper rifle punctured the airwaves. The bullet ripped through the air and burrowed through the side of Olivier's skull, the impact blowing out the side of his head and sending him toppling over the side of the railing. He was dead before he plummeted to the ground.

Eva had watched, her body unflinching, as the driver left the 4x4 and appeared in the car park, storming towards the door where the rest of them had entered. Again, her eyesight was drawn to the commotion, as he unloaded a round from his assault rifle into the building, the bullets destroying the remaining glass and ripping holes through the front wall. The mission could have been over, she wouldn't know until someone gave her the order.

Until then, her focus remained razor sharp.

She pulled the rifle back to her shoulder, pressing it in tight, and then drew her eye to the scope. Carefully, she swung the weapon back towards the walkway.

She had already lined up the shot. There was minimal breeze, but at such a short distance, it would hardly impact the shot. The weather was good, a nice, cool afternoon with pockets of sun occasionally piercing through the clouds above.

There were no obstacles.

At such a range, the bullet would do some serious damage, and the only comfort she could offer the poor soul that it was intended for was that he wouldn't feel it. He might hear it, but before the realisation would register, his lights would go out as if someone cut a power cable. The shooter below hadn't re-engaged, meaning that whoever was the target had been turned around, and if their supposed plan was in place, then her target would be delivered to her like a gift-wrapped present.

It was almost too easy.

The knowledge that Sam Pope was in the building had opened up the archives of her mind, sending her rushing back to that fateful day in the Amazon. Back then, she was still making her name, and taking on a job from someone as revered and feared as General Ervin Wallace was what brought her to the top table. She had gone from word of mouth to legendary rumour with a snap of the man's fingers, and the job that day was easy as they would come. Positioned atop a cliff face with a clear view of the outpost, she had lain under the warm, relentless downpour, waiting for their arrival and thinking of her father. The instruction was to act as an insurance policy, to let the squadron of local militia take out the team. That way, there would be less of a trail back to Wallace and especially, Ducard.

But Sam and his team were equipped and more than capable, and she watched as they fought back, using clever tactics to draw fire to one direction while they attacked from another. One of the men, either brave or reckless, stepped into the doorway to engage, and after he killed a few of the militia, Eva had stepped in to the turn the tide.

She remembered the crunch of his skull as she obliterated it.

Then there was the woman, who had fought valiantly, but made the mistake of not keeping down, meaning Eva had the clearest of shots.

She was paid to take them.

The final kill was of the man who had led the team into the clearing, who poked his head above a wrecked vehicle which she now knew was a ploy to draw her shot from Sam, who darted into the trees.

They had been sitting ducks, and unfortunately for Chavet, he would be too.

When the door to the walkway flew open, it slammed against the corrugated iron so loudly, it echoed through the park. The noise kicked Eva's instincts into action and it felt to her like time slowed down. She took in a deep breath and steadied her arms, locking them in place as the crosshair of the scope stuck to the walkway.

The metal walkway shook.

Then, emerging from the edge of the building and into her sight, was a young man with floppy brown hair, striding as if his life depended on it. Little did he know that it truly did, and little did he know it was a pointless endeavour.

With the building no longer an obstruction, Eva's mind rushed through every detail in a millisecond and cleared the shot for her.

Her finger squeezed the trigger.

The bullet exploded from the weapon, with a clap that sounded like the roar of the gods themselves.

The rifle kicked back into her shoulder, and she lowered the weapon from her eye immediately.

The bullet hit Olivier Chavet in the side of his skull, reducing the bone to mulch as it ripped through his brain, and burst out the other side. The spray of blood was incredible, and the impact sent his already lifeless body over the railing, where it tumbled like a ragdoll until it shattered on the concrete below, his limbs askew.

A scream echoed from the doorway, but Eva couldn't see anyone. Then, the woman emerged, her gun in her hand, scouring the rooftops of the surrounding buildings, clearly desperate to take her shot. Eva could have reloaded, but Ducard had given her strict instructions.

Just Olivier.

Eva ducked down behind the ridge of the rooftop and dissembled her rifle with ease, slotting it back into her case before she stood and looked over the top once more. The two agents were rushing down the metal fire escape of the other building, before the woman rushed to admire Eva's handiwork. She dropped to her knees beside the broken corpse, as the other agent raised his hands in surrender. The driver, who had reloaded his assault rifle, was approaching, the PAMAS raised and he was barking something inaudible.

Another gunshot echoed out.

The driver dropped the weapon and collapsed to the floor, screaming in agony as he clutched the hole in leg, that was pumping blood. Eva's eyes were drawn away from her fallen comrade to the door of the building, where Sam Pope emerged, his face covered in blood, and the other soldier's PAMAS in his arms. He raced to the two agents, and he stopped in his tracks when he saw Olivier's corpse.

It was clear that he had got the better of Cissé, and Eva bit her lip, as the temptation for her own revenge grew rapidly.

Her right shoulder was a tribute to the bullet he had sent through her all those years ago, and with Cissé out of the picture, she could throw Ducard a freebie and fix another problem. As she peeked her head over the crest once more, a barrage of bullets hit the concrete, causing her to spin and drop for cover.

Sam had clocked her position, and she didn't move until she heard the sound of the car doors closing, the engine roaring, and when she looked over once more, she saw the blue Mercedes hurtling from the car park, counting three figures within the car.

Olivier's corpse lay in a puddle of blood, brain and broken bones beneath the walkway where he had been executed.

The other soldier finally emerged from the building, racing to his friend who was still groaning in agony as he clutched his wounded leg.

It was only when a bloodied and beaten Cissé emerged in a murderous rage did Eva make her way back to the car, ignoring the trials of the three men.

She had delivered on her contract.

She had killed Olivier Chavet.

CHAPTER TWENTY

Despite his years of service, and the countless people that Ducard had sent to their death, seeing the outcome was always a morbid moment. He had always squared off the guilt of his decision with the fact that it was for 'the greater good', but this time was different.

This wasn't to protect his country.

This was to protect himself.

Cissé had taken a photo of Chavet's obliterated body before the team had returned to the hotel, and now, while his head of security was being patched up by a private doctor who had been shuttled in from Harley Street, Ducard stared at the phone with a heavy heart. Sitting on the balcony of his hotel, a cigarette hanging from his fingers, he scolded himself for what had happened.

Olivier Chavet was a young man who, at his heart, was doing what he thought best. He'd become a serious threat to Ducard's leadership campaign, but in truth, he was just searching for answers about the death of his father. It had been a long time since Ducard had lost his own that he had forgotten the pain of it, but then his father had died of natural causes.

Didier Chavet had been murdered.

Ducard hadn't pulled the trigger, but he had basically aimed the gun, and all Olivier had done was hunt the truth with the same ferocity that Ducard knew he would have. But instead of the justice he sought, Olivier Chavet was now a crumpled heap of blood and bone, left for the world to discover and as a subtle message of Ducard's power.

The visceral nature of the photo had shown Ducard that there was no way that the young man would have known he was being killed, which provided him with at least some comfort. But unlike a decade ago, there was no way for Ducard to hide from the fact that he was the villain of the piece. He had sanctioned another murder, this time to protect his reputation, and now more blood had stained his hands.

Cissé emerged from the suite, his eyebrow stitched up and his left wrist wrapped in a thick bandage. Ducard knew that the only pain the man had suffered was to his ego, and reigning him in before they left that evening was going to be a job in itself. As he took his seat at the table, he glared at Ducard, then his eyes crossed the balcony to the railing, where Eva Marie Rojas stood, here eyes hidden behind her designer shades. Ducard tried to ease the tension with a smile, then slid the phone across to Cissé and turned to the killer.

'Nice shot.'

'I trust the payment has been made.' Eva ignored the praise.

'It has.' Ducard puffed his cigarette and then flicked the ash into the ashtray. 'However, I would be happy to double it if your calendar is free.'

'What are you doing?' Cissé demanded.

'This mess is far from cleaned up, Laurent. Francois is hoping to discover what they have within the next hour, and if it is what I fear, then we cannot let that information get out.'

'I can handle it.' Cissé said through his busted lips.

Ducard gave a dismissive wave and turned back to Eva, who looked bored.

'My men are depleted right now. This Sam Pope has been a problem we did not foresee…'

'You want me to kill him?' Eva asked, and Cissé clenched his fists in frustration. Ducard clocked it and lifted a hand to ease the tension.

'Not quite. I am a man of my word, and that man owes my dear friend here a pound of flesh for what he has taken from him.' Ducard nodded to Cissé, solidifying his promise. 'However, we do need to move quickly, as our plane is prepped for tonight and there will be eyebrows raised if we are not on it. The number of passengers is not of importance, so if yourself and three more were added to the flight, there will be no questions asked.'

Eva pulled her lips together in contemplation, and then nodded.

'Triple.' She stated firmly.

'That will not be a problem.' Ducard sat back in his chair and took a victorious pull on the cigarette, allowing the smoke to filter from the sides of his mouth. 'Like before, Laurent will lead the extraction, but if you can provide cover in the case of any interruptions, then that will be all I ask.'

As she took a seat, Eva raised a finely groomed eyebrow in confusion.

'You do not expect any resistance?'

A cruel smirk crept across Ducard's face as he stubbed out his cigarette.

'Not this time.'

Before the conversation could continue, Lascelles stepped through the patio door and blinked as the sunshine hit him. With his messy stubble and creased clothing, it was obvious the man hadn't slept or stepped from the laptop since the whole thing had begun. Once again, his eyes locked onto Eva, who rolled hers in response, before he shot a glance to Cissé.

'Whoa. Did it go well?'

Cissé slammed his bandaged fist onto the table and stood, and Lascelles stepped back, as Ducard raised his voice.

'Stop it, now!' Ducard waited for Cissé to take his seat and then turned to Lascelles, who looked a little too smug for his liking. *'What do you want? Is everything in place?'*

'Yes, I have had confirmation. Will get the go ahead when he's ready.'

'Fantastic. Anything else?'

'Yes, sir. The information they have…it's what you feared.' Lascelles said sheepishly. *'Apparently, enough to destroy you completely.'*

Lascelles looked around the table, as if expecting a reaction from the other attendees, but there was nothing. Both Cissé and Eva had been through war and knew the reality of the world. The cold, hard decisions that get made in the comfort of an office but are acted out in a blood-soaked battle elsewhere. Lascelles was different, an analyst with a gift for tracking information, and the past forty-eight hours had opened his eyes to just how bleak the world truly was. He'd been proud to serve Ducard, given the man's reputation and likely ascension to the presidency.

Now, his uncertainty was clearly etched across his face as Ducard stood and regarded him coldly.

'Have you seen the information?'

'No, sir.'

'Then you will do well to forget it exists, Francois. I like you, I think you are a vital cog in this machine. But do not mistake my kind-ness for weakness. Just like Agent Agard, you too have people that you care about. Understand?'

177

The message was crystal clear, and the colour drained from Lascelles' tired face.

'Yes, sir.'

'Good.' Ducard clasped his hands together. 'Tell Agard to do it now. If they have the information I think they have, I want them and the files retrieved immediately.'

Ducard turned to Cissé and Eva, who both stood, understanding their orders. Cissé's eyes twinkled with excitement and Ducard stopped him before he left.

'Remember what we discussed?' Ducard asked quietly. Cissé nodded. 'We will handle it after.'

'Yes, sir.'

Cissé stepped through, taking just a second to intimidate Lascelles, who looked as if he had fallen into a pit of despair. Ducard turned back to Eva, who began to follow Cissé, but before she left, she removed her glasses and looked him dead in the eye.

'Triple.' She reminded him, and then disappeared into the hotel, leaving Ducard to anxiously light another cigarette, and look out of a city that had caused him nothing but trouble for the past few days.

———

The drive back to Hertfordshire was excruciating.

Despite securing the information they needed to bring an end to Ducard's campaign, a morbid feeling had engulfed the car. Corbin was the most affected, having watched Olivier's head be blown apart as he ran for his life. The haunting image of his body flopping over the railings would stick with her until her dying day. Agard kept his eyes on the road the entire time, his arms straight and his lips drawn tight. He'd turned a deathly pale, which Sam considered odd. For a man who had given his life to the French Secret Service, he seemed to be taking the death pretty hard.

Sam was racked with guilt.

It wasn't his fault that Ducard had taken extreme measures to ensure Olivier's silence, but he had felt an element of responsibility for the man's safety. He was an outsider to their world, a young man who had lost his father in the worst way imaginable and was offered nothing more than an empty apology. It was admirable, how Olivier had gone against men of such power in a hunt for the truth, to connect the final dots to lay the blame at the feet of Ducard, despite the obvious ramifications. Men like Ducard do not stay in power for decades by playing by the rules, and most people knew that.

Olivier was just brave enough to try and prove it.

But as he travelled in the back of the car, Sam cast his gaze to the empty seat beside him and felt the familiar feeling of failure.

Another person he wasn't able to save.

Once they had returned to the cottage, Corbin immediately fired up her laptop, while Agard gave into his old habit and stepped outside for a cigarette. He needed to return the call to their superior, no doubt to relay the events of the day and to begin the clean up of the shit storm they had created. Sam watched from the kitchen window as Agard lit the cigarette and then began his conversation.

He seemed worried.

'Is he okay?' Sam asked Corbin, his eyes still peering through the window.

'He will be.' Corbin's inserted the USB stick into the laptop.

'I thought you were running things.'

'I am.' Corbin said defiantly. 'What makes you think otherwise?'

Sam shrugged.

'Just surprised that your boss isn't on the phone with you is all.' Sam took a seat next to Corbin. 'Let's see what we've got.'

A plethora of folders appeared on Corbin's screen, all of them titled with a number pattern or a familiar cover title like 'Family Holiday 2018'. Quickly she located the files pertaining to Ducard, and when she opened the folder, she blew out her cheeks at the sheer number of files pertaining to her future leader.

The man had been dealing with Wallace for years, building a partnership that seemed to have been beneficial for both men along the way. There were files of missions across the globe, and as Corbin opened each one and scanned through, Sam took himself to the bathroom to clean up. He took a moment to inspect the damage done to his face, with the blood now dried and crusted across his upper lip, as well as around his eyebrow. It looked bad, it hurt like hell, but it would heal quickly. Grunting in pain, he hoisted his bloodstained t-shirt up and over his head, and instantly winced at the thick, purple bruising around his ribs. With the adrenaline wearing off, the pain that had enveloped his body returned.

'Fuck.' Sam murmured as he leant forward and turned on the tap, cupping the water with both hands and splashing it against his face. He scrubbed away the dried blood and as he brought a towel to his face, he heard foot-steps approach and the door open.

'Oh, sorry.' Corbin said with embarrassment. But instead of diverting her eyes, they widened with astonish-ment at Sam's body. Not the impressive, chiselled muscles that adorned his frame, but the myriad of scars and burns that ran across it like a hideous tattoo. A sudden twinge of self-awareness hit Sam, and he turned back to the sink to lift his shirt.

'I'll get you're a fresh one.' Corbin nodded, and scurried out of the room. She returned swiftly and handed Sam a grey t-shirt. 'It's one of Martin's. I'm sure he won't mind.'

'Thanks.' Sam offered her a feeble smile and then eased his body into it, his body aching for him to stop.

'Why do you do it, Sam?'

'Do what?' Sam asked firmly, pulling the t-shirt down as it wrapped around his bulging arms.

'What you do.' Corbin gestured to his body. 'You've been through the wars, but never for yourself.'

'Because someone has to.' Sam sighed. 'Someone has to fight back.'

'But why you?'

'Because I can.' Sam stepped from the room and past Corbin, clearly ending a conversation that would undoubtedly lead him to a dark place. He'd made his peace with his son's death the year before, refusing to wear that guilt as a bullet proof vest, but it was still there. Lingering in the back of his mind.

Corbin followed him to the kitchen and took her seat in front of the laptop. Sam stood, stretching his back against the kitchen worktop and crossed his arms over his chest.

'We got him.' Corbin said with a smile.

'Right, I've held up my end of the bargain.'

'You have.' Corbin agreed. 'So here's what *we* have. Over the years, Olivier's claims against Ducard ranged from the absurd to the abusive, but throughout it all, there clung an element of doubt as to Ducard's innocence. So, my department launched an investigation into his international operations and…'

'You found something.' Sam interrupted and then immediately lifted his hand in apology.

'We did. Thirteen years ago, a deal was made between a sub-section of the French military and the Taliban, where our country would supply anti-aircraft weaponry in exchange for access to certain benefits.'

'Oil.'

'Correct.' Corbin shook her head in disgust. 'Now, a deal like that wouldn't have been made lightly, and Didier Chavet began asking all the right questions which turned out to be the wrong questions. He began to take his queries up the food chain until he arrived at Ducard's table, and well, from what we know, that's where they stopped. A few months later…'

'He was killed.' Sam finished the sentence. Suddenly, the dots that Olivier had been desperate to connect were aligning. As was always the case, the blood was shed for money, with Ducard prioritising the prosperity of his own country over those who were under the tyrannical rule of the Taliban. They weren't his concern, but when Olivier's father had began to make the case that they should be, he was silenced.

As was his colleague.

'We've never been able to substantiate those claims against Ducard, without evidence of a kill order.' Corbin tapped a few keys and then tapped the last one firmly. The screen filled with a document. 'Until now.'

Sam stepped forward to lean in and look at the screen, when Agard entered the room, clearly shaken and reeking of smoke. Corbin and Sam turned to him and he shook his head.

'Vivier wants us back in the morning.' Agard complained as he lifted the kettle and began to fill it with water. 'The death of Olivier Chavet needs to be quietly dealt with, he said. Disgusting. Tea?'

Corbin and Sam both nodded, and Sam kept his eye on the erratic Agard for just a second or so longer. Then it returned to the document, which was as damning as it was jarring. For all of his faults, Wallace had been meticulous when it came to protecting himself, and he had recorded every conversation with Ducard throughout their dealings. The file was a written transcript of the conversation that proved that Ducard had sentenced Chavet and Rabiot to their deaths. Wallace had staged a kidnapping on behalf of Ducard, where the two diplomats had been taken by the local rebel militia and then stored away in a remote location.

Then, a team including Sam, would be sent in to die, to provide a false narrative that Ducard had done what he could to bring them back. As Sam read through, he felt his fingers tighten on the back of Corbin's chair and his arms flex.

Good people dead.

All for a cover up.

To hide the deal between the French military and the Taliban, Sam had been sent to die. Agard stepped forward, handing both Sam and Corbin their mugs, before stepping back across the kitchen to retrieve his own. Corbin took a sip and then looked at Sam and raised her eyebrows.

'Like I said, we've got him.'

Sam nodded and took a sip of his own, and then watched as Corbin woozily tried to place her mug down on the table, but lost all control of her fingers. The mug fell to the ground, and Corbin slid from her chair, unconscious. Sam rushed forward to help, but felt his vision blur and his knees buckle, and as he slipped into unconsciousness, the last thought through his head was that Agard had drugged them.

CHAPTER TWENTY-ONE

As he entered the meeting room, Commissioner McEwen slammed the door with fury, startling the three people already sat down. It wasn't just a show of who was now in charge of the meeting, it was a genuine display of his rage at what had occurred that afternoon. He'd first been informed of it a little after four o'clock, when after reports of gunfire being heard in an industrial estate out towards Surrey, the local Police had gone to investigate along with the Armed Response. When they arrived, they found nothing but a building riddled with bullet holes and broken glass, and then, underneath a metal walkway, a crumpled body in a dark red pool of blood.

The crime scene was closed off, and once the body had been investigated the cause of death had been confirmed as a bullet to the skull. The fall had been academic, as the man was already dead due to the fact half of his skull had been blown to bits. Although they would need to properly inspect the body through an autopsy, the size of the bullet wound and the impact told them that it was likely a high calibre bullet, most likely from a sniper rifle.

The man had been assassinated.

Then, when the confirmation of the man's identity came through, and McEwen realised that Olivier Chavet had been murdered on British soil, he demanded an audience with Mulgrave. The Foreign Secretary, who earlier that morning, had been bootlicking the French President-in-waiting and his entourage reluctantly agreed, and as he stormed into the meeting room at Downing Street, she collapsed into herself.

Also in the room was Dipti Patel, the Mayor of London who sat with her arms folded, a look of sorrow across her face and the occasional glance of acknowledgement to McEwen. On the far side of the table sat Admiral Wainwright, who looked unimpressed by McEwen's show of aggression, and next to him, to McEwen's confusion, sat William Doyle, the Home Secretary. The man was a stereotypical politician, with his neat side parting, glasses and insincere smile, he was already scribbling notes on the pad in front of him. McEwen stomped to his seat, removed his hat and sat down.

'Before we begin…' Mulgrave began, but McEwen lifted his hand.

'Unless that sentence is to acknowledge the death of an innocent man, then I suggest you keep it.' McEwen spat, his Glaswegian accent heavy with anger. 'A man is dead. *Dead*. When you and the Admiral told me to turn a blind eye to their operation, I raised my concerns, and look where we are. Olivier Chavet, a man who just yesterday was on our fucking news channels talking about conspiracies, now killed. Do you have any idea how bad this looks?'

'Yes.' Mulgrave mustered feebly, unable to look McEwen in the eye. The Admiral cleared his throat.

'It looks as though you have failed to get this Sam Pope problem under control, Bruce?'

'Excuse me?' McEwen spun to look at Wainwright,

who had leant forward in his chair, his forearms resting on the table and his hands clasped.

'When you took this role, Bruce, we all thought you were the right man for the job. After the whole rigmarole with Ashton, you were the best person to follow Commissioner Stout. They were big shoes to fill, indeed, but we all thought you were the right man for it. And for a long time, you repaid that faith, but then Sam Pope rose from the dead.' Wainwright kept his eyes locked on McEwen. 'No one could have foreseen that, least of all yourself, but it has been a year since he re-emerged and still, he is running roughshod over this country.'

'Correct me if I'm wrong here, Admiral, but Sam was a problem before I was in situ.'

'Indeed.' Wainwright continued. 'But unlike yourself, there was never any indication from Commissioner Stout of possible collusion.'

The accusation snapped the whole room to attention, and McEwen's brow furrowed with fury. He glanced to Patel, who looked just as shocked, and then to Mulgrave, who stared at the table before her. The reality of the situation had dawned on McEwen.

It was a set up.

With a wry smile, McEwen brought his hands together in a slow, sarcastic clap. Wainwright scowled, and finally, for the first time in the meeting, Doyle spoke.

'It's hardly a laughing matter, Bruce.'

'No, I agree. For a second there, I thought there was a genuine grievance into the way I have gone about my job, but I see it clearly now.'

Doyle put down his pen and pursed his lips with arrogance.

'Please enlighten me.'

'Okay. Permission to speak freely?' McEwen looked around the room and took their silence as acceptance.

'Okay, well I know for a fact that, I've pissed a number of high profile people off over the past few months. People who were once untouchable have now got my people looking into them. Now, if I'm not mistaken, a great many of these rich and powerful people have generously donated to your government and…'

'Careful, Bruce.' Wainwright interrupted.

'Yes. Any slanderous accusations won't help your case.' Doyle added on, like a school kid hiding behind a bully. McEwen pointed a finger straight at him.

'How's this for an accusation? She's shit the bed…' McEwen pointed to Mulgrave. 'By allowing this government to bend over for Ducard, who has now had a man executed in our country. But instead of this government, for once in its pitiful leadership, taking the necessary responsibility for its inaction, you're deflecting it elsewhere. Tell me, William, am I on the money?'

The room fell silent, as Wainwright glared furiously at the commissioner, and the Home Secretary shifted his jaw from side to side with agitation. McEwen shook his head, chuckled and stood.

'We're not finished here.' Wainwright shouted, slamming his hand on the table. McEwen reached into his pocket, removed his police identity card and tossed it on the table.

'Aren't we?'

'Commissioner Bruce McEwen, you are suspended pending an investigation…' Doyle began, trying to take control of the narrative and assume authority. McEwen waved him off.

'Save it, William.' McEwen nodded a silent and respectful goodbye to Patel, and then headed towards the door. As he yanked it open, Wainwright stood, irritated by the man's defiance.

'You're out, Bruce. You hear me.'

'Loud and clear.' McEwen said calmly. 'Dipti, it's been a pleasure working with you. As for the rest of you, a man is dead. Just remember that, when you're working out how to spin my suspension as a positive.'

McEwen stepped through the door and let it slam shut behind him. He took a deep breath, composed himself, and then headed towards the famous black door with his shoulders straight and his head held high. He'd promised his wife that he would do the right thing, and as he stepped out into the cool, London evening, he knew that despite being relieved of his command, he had kept his word.

A large jolt sent Sam into the air, but his restraints slammed him back against the cold steel and startled him to consciousness. His brain felt like it had been melted down and then remoulded, and he tried his hardest to centralise himself physically. A loud, constant roar was piercing his ear drums, and at first he thought it was the after effects of the drugs, but then he realised it was something else.

An engine.

Another jolt took him off his seat again, but his shoulders wrenched back and he slammed back against the steel. He tried to move his arms, but they were locked in place, and the tightness of the metal cuffs around his wrists were digging into his skin. As his senses returned to him one by one, he blinked to try to restore his vision, which was shrouded in a black haze. With the engine roaring and shaking his aching brain, and the cold whipping his body with constant lashes, he soon understood that his eyes were wide open. His vision was obscured by the black bag over his head.

From what he could see, he was in a cargo hold, with a

number of bags, suitcases and trunks, all stacked to one side, and a metal ladder that led to the upper deck.

An airplane.

The gravity of the situation wasn't lost on Sam, which he found somewhat ironic considering their altitude. He'd been in restraints before and his mind raced back to three years previously when he had been strapped to a chair by Jose Vasquez, a dangerous drug dealer who had started a gang war in South Carolina. Back then, he'd been worked over by Vasquez's henchman, Edinson, who had pummelled Sam with sledgehammer-like fists until he spat up blood.

Both men were dead now.

Sam pulled against his restraints in frustration, but it was no use. Next to him, he heard a few groans of grogginess, and through the fabric of the sack over his head, he could make out the figure beside him.

Corbin.

As she slowly stirred, the panic set in, and Sam heard her begin to pull against the restraints, slamming her body forward, only for the cuffs to haul her back to her seat.

'It's no use.' Sam shouted, hoping his voice travelled over the relentless engine.

'Sam? Is that you?'

'Yeah.' He could hear the desperation in her voice. 'Looks like your friend made some new ones.'

Silence followed, and Sam understood that Corbin was processing the betrayal. For all intents and purposes, Agard seemed like a boy scout, and Corbin had mentioned that they had worked together for years. But at some point during the events of the last few days, something had changed in the man. Sam thought he had noticed it, but it clearly wasn't enough for him to outright confront him. Just something hadn't felt right, and now, with his head pounding, Sam knew that he'd been right.

Agard had been compromised, and now he and Corbin were shackled in the underbelly of a plane, going God knows where.

'That son of a bitch!' Corbin yelled.

But Sam didn't respond. She needed to grieve for a friendship and partnership that she had clearly trusted, and he didn't know her well enough to offer any comfort. It was a horrible feeling, when someone betrays your trust, and Sam remembered the overwhelming pain when he discovered the truth about Project Hailstorm and the depth of General Wallace's treachery. It had emptied the contents of his stomach and then fuelled him with nothing but revenge.

'Use it.' Sam yelled. 'Deal with it…then use it.'

For the next twenty minutes, they sat in silence, with nothing but the thundering of the engine for company. Sam tried testing the resistance of his restraints, but after a few unsuccessful wrenches, he gave up the ghost. There was no way out of the situation currently, which meant they needed to stay calm, keep their composure and assess what happened next.

Sam didn't believe in 'no-win situations', but his mind cast back to a conversation he had with his beloved mentor, Sgt. Carl Marsden. Years ago, in the heat of the Egyptian desert, Marsden had chastised Sam for his actions, explaining to him that battles weren't won by the squeeze of a trigger, but by the sharpness of the mind.

It had stayed with him, and after he had mourned his mentor's death, Sam had tried to apply that to his one-man war on crime.

But there was no way of avoiding what was to come. They were bound, stored away and most likely going to be delivered to their inevitable death. All Sam could do, was keep calm, stay focused, and *if* the opportunity arose to get Corbin out alive, then he had to be ready to take it.

His stomach did a forward roll as the plane dipped, making its final descent towards the ground, where the pilot guided them to a smooth landing. The wheels touched down seamlessly, and the plane eventually came to a stop. Above them, they could now hear the clear thumping of footsteps as the crew and passengers made their way to the doors, followed by a loud clunk of metal as the hatch to the storage unit was pulled open. A foot appeared on the metal ladder, and through the fuzz of the fabric, Sam watched as a muscular figure began to clamber down. Sam eased gently towards Corbin.

'Just stay calm,' he said out of the corner of his mouth, before a hand struck the side of his face with such venom, it snapped his head back against the metal. A chuckle echoed before them, and the man reached out and snatched the bags off their heads. Sam blinked away the blurred vision and looked up at Cissé, who glared at him with sickening pleasure. The man's eyebrow had fresh stitches running through it like a centipede, and his lip was swollen and lacerated.

Cissé looked at his prisoners, turned his attention to Sam and then shocked them both by speaking in English.

'Welcome to Paris.'

CHAPTER TWENTY-TWO

Martin Agard felt sick.

It wasn't due to the turbulence on the flight from London Heathrow to Paris, although being airborne was his least favourite part of the job. Over his eighteen years with the *Direction Générale de la Sécurité Extérieure*, he had been on more flights than he could remember, but his fear of flying never abated. Corbin often ribbed him about it, making the odd snide comment about how he had been involved in multiple gunfights, high speed chases and hand to hand fights during his time working for the DGSE, yet it was being strapped to a first-class seat thirty feet above the ground that scared him the most.

His heart ached just thinking about her.

Somewhere below the deck, she was currently being held, along with Sam Pope, whom he didn't care for, and it was his fault.

He had betrayed her.

It had all begun earlier in the day, when they had made their way to the old, decrepit building that Pope had once called home for a week. He had spun some story about lying low with an old friend who had sprung him from prison, but Agard hadn't paid it much attention. As far as he was concerned, Sam Pope was a criminal, despite his intervention that had saved Chavet's life. In his near two decades as an agent for the DGSE, Agard had proven himself an excellent judge of character, and while he didn't perceive Pope to be a bad man, he was still a criminal. It was easy to get caught up in his crusade, which had been built off the back of doing the right thing.

But there was a right way to do the right thing, and a wrong way, and leaving behind nearly a hundred bodies in your wake, didn't qualify for the first. After searching the abandoned apartment and finding a key within a hollow windowsill, Agard had received a call from a number he hadn't recognised. As he had answered it, an ominous message came through.

'Martin Agard. Pretend all is fine and move somewhere private.'

As he frowned, Corbin had sent a concerned look his way, and Agard had covered the received with his hand and announced to the room that it was their boss, Vivier. She motioned for him to take the call, and he stepped from the apartment, leaving Corbin and Sam to discuss the key's purpose and Chavet to smoke out of the window. When he was finally alone, his anger took over.

'*Who is this?*' He spat in his native tongue.

'Agent Agard, we currently believe that the two people that are currently within your protection have potentially damaging information regarding Pierre Ducard.'

'Listen here, you've made a big mistake. Once I hang up this call, I'm going to have this number traced and you'll be in a cell by dinner time. You understand?'

'I would implore you not to do that, Agent Agard. Am I right in thinking that both Louis and Marc are at school today? St. Clemin?'

The threat stopped Agard in his tracks. He tried to respond, but the caller continued.

'And your wife, Jeanette, she is at work in her salon, no?'

'If you even think about touching my family…'

'If you are unwilling to co-operate, Agent Agard, then we will see if they will.'

'Okay…okay.' Agard could feel his throat tightening with fear. *'Look, we've found some key that Pope thinks will take us to the information. I will find out where and send you the location.'*

'Good.' The voice hammered home the threat. *'Make sure Chavet and Pope are in attendance. Mr Ducard insists upon it.'*

The call hung up and the situation hit Agard like a slap to the face. Whatever information Pope was leading them to clearly had damning ramifications for their President elect, and he was willing to endanger the family of a DGSE agent to get to it. Every fibre of his being wanted to tell Corbin about the call, but he knew she wouldn't relent. She would demand they call Vivier, setting off a chain of events that Ducard could well see as a challenge to his threat.

As far as he was concerned, the lives of his family were more important than those of an activist and a foreign terrorist.

Before they made their way to the storage facility, Agard had sent the address to the number that had called him, and received a notification when they were there. As they made their way inside, he received another message.

'Bring Chavet to the walkway. Leave Pope for Cissé.'

Agard had already clocked the metal walkway on arrival, and after Cissé had located them, Pope had bravely stepped up to face the terrifying man. Despite Corbin's best efforts, Agard was able to eventually lead Chavet to the metal walkway, holding the door open for the terrified civilian and ushered him through.

What happened next would haunt Agard for the rest of his life.

The visceral explosion of the man's skull, as the bullet erupted through the bone was sickening, and the life left

Chavet instantly. As he flopped to the ground, dead, Agard did his best to lead Corbin back to the car and to safety. They had the information, Pope had entrusted the USB stick to Corbin, and all they needed to do was get out of there and he would be able to arrange the transfer. But Pope emerged, gun in hand, to tackle the rest of Ducard's men, having seemingly bested Cissé and Agard had to keep up appearances by bringing him with them.

The order came through to drug the two, and although Agard pleaded for Corbin's life outside the cottage, the ultimatum was either her life or the life of his kids.

So Agard had drugged them both, sent Ducard his location, and before he knew it, Cissé and a team of highly paid and highly trained soldiers arrived at the cottage. Now, he was sitting on the private plane belonging to Pierre Ducard, who busied himself at one of the tables, flicking through sheets of paper and murmuring to Cissé. The flight wasn't a long one, but it felt like an eternity, and Agard knew it was being prolonged by his guilt.

Corbin would understand. Although she had never had a family of her own, she had been a big part of his life for years and knew his kids and his adoration of them. And although he had betrayed her, scuppered the case being built by the DGSE and had directed Olivier Chavet to his death, he had done it under the direction of the next President of France. In some ways, it was patriotic.

Agard stared out of the plane's window as it landed on home soil, feeding himself a lie of patriotism to stop his inner turmoil from breaking him completely.

As soon as the plane touched down, Ducard nodded to Cissé, who needed little encouragement to collect their hostages. For a man who had lost his closest friend over the past few days, Ducard was impressed with Cissé's composure. Although he had been bested in his fight with Sam Pope, Ducard had seen the cuts and bruising on Pope's face, and he imagined that Cissé had relished every single moment of it. As the steps from the private jet were lowered, one of the cabin crew collected Ducard's papers from his table and he stood, thanked them all for their hard work and then made his way to the exit. Paris Charles de Gaulle Airport was a hive of activity, and from across the vast, concrete runways, he could see the commercial flights all lined up in a neat row, ready to whisk the natives away and take the tourists home. The Parisian spring had been relatively warm when the sun was out, but now, under the darkness of a moonless sky, a bitter chill slithered around Ducard, and a cold drizzle fell upon him. His assistant rushed up the steep steps of the plane and snapped open a black umbrella, which he held over Ducard who thanked him. Three black 4x4s were waiting in the hanger, along with a police escort of two cars and four armed officers. They were there to ensure Ducard's safe return to his estate, where he would no doubt have some pressing matters to attend to. Making his way into the hanger, Ducard made a point of shaking hands with every police officer and waiting member of staff, forever on the charm offensive. When the news broke about Chavet's death, he knew the spotlight would be on him, and it was important that he maintained the usual perception of confidence to mask his culpability. He glanced across to the vehicle at the back of the line, and watched as Cissé lead both Pope and Corbin to the back seat, a black bag over their heads and their hands bound to the base of their spines.

No one said a thing.

Such power was hard to attain, and Ducard afforded himself a wry smile as he dropped into the back of his ride, where Martin Agard sat, a broken shell of a man, in the passenger seat. Eva hadn't said a word on the plane ride over, and she slid into the back alongside Ducard, put in her earbuds and lost herself to her music.

Ducard admired her professionalism, which was less than he could say for the snivelling agent in the front of the car.

'Sir, can we talk…' Agard began, but Ducard held up his hand.

'Not now.'

That was all it took. Agard returned his vacant gaze to the window, and as they filtered out of the airport, Ducard pulled out his tablet and checked his emails. There was a stream of messages from his campaign team, with a number of them showing colourful graphs that acted as proof that his popularity had grown, both at home and overseas, thanks to his trip to the UK. When it came to the matter of Chavet and his interview, he was surprised to see that the split was fifty/fifty. His fist tightened with anger, that so many people would sympathise with the man, and it made his death easier to take. Chavet had been no true threat to Ducard, be it physically or politically, and Ducard knew that. But, like a wasp buzzing around a family picnic, sometimes you just wanted to swat away a problem for good. The man's death had been escalated due to Pope's intervention, as the original plan would have been to stage a mugging. There would be conspiracies surrounding it, but nothing that they could make stick. Unfortunately, now, due to the violent nature of Chavet's execution, there would most certainly be questions and Ducard knew that the Commissioner of the Met Police had him in his sights.

That wasn't a problem he foresaw, as after McEwen had confronted him at his final speaking event of the trip, Ducard had leant on the British Foreign Secretary with all his weight to ensure the man was out. She tried to reason with him for a few minutes, but Ducard squeezed tighter, threatening a very different outcome to their trade talks once he became President.

Again, the power he wielded filled him with a warmth he couldn't describe, and he flicked through the emails for the entire forty-mile journey to Theuville, a small commune to the north of Paris where Ducard's estate was situated. Surrounded by nothing but fields and a small, classic French village that looked like it had been built purely for a postcard, Ducard's estate sat behind a large wall that surrounded the vast, fifty acre property that he had acquired due to his immense wealth and standing within the French government. The entrance point to the Ducard estate was situated down a nondescript country road, lined by tall trees that shielded the wall, until a gap presented the cast iron gate that opened slowly. A gravel path, which stretch over a kilometre led down towards the mansion, lined by trees and ground level spotlights that illuminated the falling rain. Once all three vehicles had passed through the gates, the two police cars drove away, handing over the protection of Ducard to his own private security. After barrelling down the long pathway, the cars eventually pulled up in a row outside the front of the house, with its perfect brickwork and large bay windows that gave the building a sense of majesty. Although shrouded in darkness, the grounds were immaculate, with eight gardeners in Ducard's employ to ensure the upkeep. The rest of the house was staffed by a further twenty five people, ranging from cooks to maids, to his armed security who were trained and encouraged to do whatever was necessary. Although the security were employed by Ducard, they were loyal to Cissé, and news of Domi's death hadn't sat well with them. The eight men who were on duty that evening all welcomed Ducard with a salute, but then offered Cissé a handshake and even a hug to abate his grief. As Cissé and his men dealt with the hostages, Ducard made his way into one of the recreational rooms of the house, where leather sofas provided a crescent-shaped seating area, and large, well-kept plants sat in expensive pots. Everything was neat as a pin, expensive in cost, and Ducard directed Agard to one of the sofas before the waiting staff brought in some drinks for them. One of his security detail stood at the door, his hands linked and resting on his lap and a PAMAS G1 strapped to his hip. Eva dropped onto one of the sofa's and looked at the room with appreciation, while Agard sat, his eyes looking at nowhere in particular, waiting for the inevitable to happen.

Ducard spoke to his assistant, telling him to break the story of Olivier Chavet's death to the Parisian press machine before it was announced in the UK. It was the perfect opportunity for Ducard to spin it in his favour, and by being at the forefront of the news, and being the one to demand justice for the man who had tried to ruin him, it could paint him in an even more shining light.

The wheels of the political machine were spinning, and Ducard knew exactly how to direct them in his favour. With the doors closed, the errands attended to, the drinks poured and the trip to the UK finally over, Ducard clasped his hands together and rubbed them gently. Cissé stepped in, a firm nod to indicate things were as commanded.

A malicious grin spread across Ducard's face.

'I think it's time to welcome our guests.'

CHAPTER TWENTY-THREE

They'd driven in silence, with not so much of a word from Cissé or the driver. Before they'd left the plane, Cissé, who had the air of victory surrounding him, replaced the bags over their heads once more, before rattling Sam with a vicious punch to the stomach.

One for the road, and it made the first fifteen minutes of the journey particularly uncomfortable. Sam had occasionally turned to his right to Corbin, but with the natural light of outside non-existent, it was hard to see how she was doing. The air inside the bags had become stuffy, and the only thing he could ascertain was that they were heading to the countryside. He'd been to Paris once before, on a weekend break with Lucy in the halcyon days of their love, and one thing he remembered was how bright it was. The city reminded him of London, with its swathes of tall buildings and heavy footfall, interspersed with famous, historical buildings that acted as a magnet to tourists.

There was none of that.

Apart from the occasional burst of light from a car travelling in the opposite direction, they travelled in darkness, and the fabric obscuring his vision made it impossible for him to find his bearings. Eventually, they slowed, and the hum of a gate opening welcomed them onto a gravel path that filled the car with intermittent bursts of light.

Then they stopped.

The driver killed the engine and he and Cissé stepped from the vehicle. As their feet crunched on the stones, Sam leant in towards Corbin.

'I will find you, okay?'

His promise was empty, they both knew that, but he hoped it offered her a modicum of comfort as the door beside her swung open and she was hauled from the vehicle. She didn't fight, didn't make a sound. The woman was strong and Sam knew she would be resolute to whatever conclusion was coming. The door beside Sam opened, and as he turned his head, it was sent snapping backwards with a rock solid fist. Sam rocked on the seat, tasting the blood pooling in his mouth, before a hand grabbed the scruff of his t-shirt and hauled him out onto the stones. Sam stumbled and hit the sharp gravel, unable to block the fall, before two sets of hands clasped his arms and hauled him up. The bitter wind nipped at his naked forearms and the rain crashed against his body.

'Take him inside.'

Sam heard Cissé's voice, and although he didn't understand the words he understood the tone. The warmth of the house enveloped Sam, and as he was roughly pulled through a corridor, he was pushed through a door and he stumbled and hit the floor again, this time, greeted by a plush rug. The crackling of a fire echoed from the far side, and the bright lights burst through the fabric and blurred his vision slightly. He managed to rock back onto his knees, with his hands still pressed to the base of his spine, and he scanned the room.

Then, without warning, the bag was ripped from his head and the layout of the room became clear.

The room was impressive, with gigantic windows that fanned out in a loop, the glass covered with thick, expensive curtains. The sofas were all pristine, wrapped in expensive leather and arranged around a solid oak coffee table. Agard sat on one of the sofas, his eyes looking anywhere at Sam, and the back of a woman's head that Sam couldn't identify. Two armed guards were standing casually on either side of the room, and at the far end, Ducard was leaning over a table, discussing something with a man whom Sam assumed was his assistant.

The door opened again, and Corbin was shunted next to Sam, and Cissé stepped into view and removed the bag from her head to. Then, without provocation, Cissé swung his arm at Sam, and clouted him across the jaw with the back of his hand. The connection echoed loudly, and Sam rocked to the side. He spat a little blood onto the rug, and then turned back to an excited looking Cissé in defiance.

'Enough.' Ducard commanded, stepping across the room with a glass of wine in his hand. 'That's no way to treat our guests.'

Sam ignored the pain in his jaw and looked to Corbin, who hadn't taken her eyes from Agard.

'I see some of us are being treated better than others.' She spat. Agard refused to acknowledge her, and Ducard mockingly looked to the treacherous agent, and then back to Corbin.

'My dear, don't condemn the man for his patriotism.'

'Patriotism?' Corbin laughed. 'Olivier Chavet is dead because of him.'

'That is true.' Ducard agreed. 'How unfortunate? A young man, lost to his own conspiracy theories, finding out the hard way that his own government would have him killed.'

'Excuse me?' Corbin struggled slightly against her cuffs. Sam and Ducard were both impressed by her resolve.

'Well, that is how we will spin it. You see, unlike the pathetic government in the UK, we are in control of everything, and right now, they are keeping quiet on his death until we have our press release sorted.' Ducard sipped his wine. 'Unfortunately, it would appear that after spinning his little story on UK television, he alerted none other than Sam Pope, the protector of the truth, who wanted him silenced. You see, your files that your have thankfully delivered to us, gives us a direct link to Sam's past and Didier Chavet's death...'

'It links you, too.' Corbin spat.

'Not anymore.' Ducard waved dismissively. 'With this evidence, we will be able to build a narrative that you were just tying up loose ends, Sam. After that fateful afternoon in the jungle all those years ago. Do you remember?'

'Everyday.' Sam replied coldly.

'Oh, while we are on the subject of that dark day, say hello to an old friend.'

Sam's eyes diverted to the sofa, and Eva turned around. As she did, Sam's mind flashed back to the top of the cliff face, where he was screaming at the shooter to turn and face him. She had aged in the decade since, but her beauty was still as evident now as it was then, only her eyes emitted a confidence of a woman who had killed many and feared none.

Sam felt his arms bulge with anger, and without control, he tried to launch forward, only for Cissé to rock him with a right hook that could have won him a heavyweight championship.

'Sam.' Corbin yelped, as Sam hit the floor, groaning in pain.

'Well, enough of the reunion.' Ducard intervened. 'What we need to discuss is what happens next. Now, unlike your fine colleague here, I am going to assume that you have some misguided belief that taking me down will save this country? Well let me tell you something, Agent Corbin, you don't know the half of what it takes to keep this country safe. Do you think I took pleasure in having Chavet's father killed? Or sending Sam and his team into the jungle to die? Of course not, but I did it to keep this country safe.'

Before Corbin could react, everyone's attention was diverted to Sam, who had begun to chuckle. He eased himself back to his knees, blood dribbling down his stubbled chin and he laughed louder. Cissé took a step forward but Ducard stopped him with a hand on his shoulder.

'Safe?' Sam scoffed. 'You were dealing under the table with the Taliban. Providing them with funding and money in exchange for oil.'

Ducard's lip twitched with annoyance.

'A necessary move...'

'To line your pockets.' Sam interrupted. 'Years ago, a doctor in Afghanistan saved me from the Taliban. They were terrorising the village and radicalising the local kids, including the doctor's son. Terrorists. That's what they were and that's what you are.' Sam spat blood onto the rug. 'You. Wallace. All of you. Nothing more than terrorists.'

Ducard's smug façade had dropped, and he took a few steps forward.

'Your insults mean nothing. Any evidence you have to that effect, is gone.'

Sam returned the man's gaze, with hatred in his eyes.

'Do you know what I did to that Taliban cell? I burnt it to the fucking ground.'

Ducard lifted his hands in faux fear and then slapped Sam across the face. He had to admit, Sam Pope was an impressive man. Throughout his decades in the military, he had seen strong men. Brave men. Men who were skilled with a weapon, be it a blade or a gun. But beyond Cissé, he had never seen one who pulled it altogether. A man who had the steadfast resolve of a champion, married to the lethal skill of an elite soldier. But here was Sam Pope, a man who had been sent to die by his orders a decade ago, arms strapped behind him, body covered in scars and refusing to back down.

Refusing to accept defeat.

Throughout all of his long, distinguished career, Ducard had dished out orders, praise and contempt with ease and regularity. But he rarely offered respect and he found himself in a rare instance of respecting the person before him.

It was a shame he'd have to kill him.

He regarded Sam with intrigue, looking into the hate filled eyes of the man.

'Tell me, Sam. After all this. All that has happened. What exactly are you fighting for?'

Sam's back straightened, along with his broad shoulders, and he lifted his blood soaked chin with pride. Although he was kneeling, it looked like he was standing to attention.

A soldier. Forever and always.

'Sergeant Javier Vargas. Private Laurel Connell. Private Jason Bennett.' Sam stated coldly, his eyes drifting to Eva. 'All of them executed that day. Their deaths deserve the truth.'

Ducard took a long, solemn breath. He reached out and patted Sam on the shoulder.

'You may not see it now. And unfortunately, you will not live to see it in the future. But their deaths were a necessity. When I take my place in charge of this country, I will do my best to fix this world.' Ducard stepped back and shook his head. 'Your death, however, will be a little more personal.'

Ducard clicked his fingers, and the two armed guards fell upon Sam like vultures, and they hoisted him to his feet. Sam kept his eyes on Eva as he left, silently promising her revenge for the people she had taken from him. As he was dragged from the room, Corbin watched, her eyes watering, and she turned back to Ducard, who was gently swirling the wine in his glass.

'Where are you taking him?'

Before Ducard could answer her, Cissé marched to the door, following his men and he closed it behind them.

'Let's just say that he and Laurent have a few issues they need to iron out.' Ducard finished the wine and set the glass down on one of the side tables. 'As for you, Agent Corbin, I will offer you one last chance to rethink your options. There are two ways you leave this building tonight and I can tell you that only one of them is amicable.'

'*Go fuck yourself.*' She spat in their mother tongue, and she glared at the man, who began to chuckle.

'Forgive me for not reciprocating, but our guest here, she would rather we not speak French the entire time.' Ducard nodded to Eva, who ignored him. 'So, I take it you've made your decision, which I can accept. Unfortunately, it will lead to a series of events, where the evidence will be built that you not only aided Sam Pope in the assassination of Olivier Chavet, but you in fact went as far as to help him infiltrate my home with the express purpose of assassinating me.'

'That will never stick.' Corbin said in defiance. Ducard dismissed her and continued.

'Obviously, we will need to make the story believable enough. I'm sure our friend, Agent Agard here, will attest to the affair you and Sam were having, and how he was working a case against you under suspicion that you were working against the French government.'

Both Ducard and Corbin turned their attention to Agard, who tried his best not to look at them. When he sighed deeply and turned to face them finally, he saw the tears streaming down Corbin's cheeks.

'Martin?' She asked, her voice breaking.

'I'm sorry, Renée.' He shook his head. 'I had no other choice.'

Ducard clapped his hands, breaking the tension and he beamed with joy.

'Wonderful.' He walked back to his drinks cabinet and poured himself another glass of wine from the expensive bottle that had been taken from the extensive cellar that connected to his kitchen. He took a sip, smacked his lips and continued. 'Oh, and don't worry, Agent Agard will be presented with the highest honours for his bravery and his service to the President. Congratulations, Martin Agard. Not many people can say they killed for their President.'

Both Agard and Corbin snapped their necks in the direction of the fiendish Ducard, who was revelling in his victory. Agard looked to Corbin, and like her, his eyes began to water.

'Excuse me, sir?'

Ducard's face twisted into a cruel grin.

'You're the one who's going to kill her.'

CHAPTER TWENTY-FOUR

SEVEN YEARS AGO…

'I'm really proud of you.'

Lucy's voice carried all the love that Sam thought he would ever need, and he arched his neck to his wife and smiled. Her blonde, shoulder length hair, was pulled back into a loose ponytail, and he admired the striking features of her face. Her mint blue eyes, the immaculate cheek bones. There was being lucky in life and then there was this. He couldn't help but smile, and he readjusted himself on his elbows. They had picked their favourite spot in the park, under the large oak tree, and after fanning out their picnic blanket, Sam had sat down next to his wife, leant back and propped himself up on his elbow.

'Thanks.' Sam said, almost embarrassed. He turned his attention back to the incline of the hill, the trimmed grass dotted with dandelions that led all the way down to the small river that sliced through the bushes. The sun was blazing down on the park that was packed with families, all enjoying the weather before it took its usual British turn and subsequently disappeared. Through the mass of kids all exploring the stream, Sam's eyes rested on Jamie and his heart

pounded with pride. The boy had just turned five, and with his floppy blonde hair tucked under his cap, he was squatting down, ankle deep in the river, his head buzzing around with excitement.

'I'm serious.' Lucy continued. 'After what happened, after how close we came to losing you, I wasn't sure if you'd ever make it back.'

Sam nodded, trying not to let her words affect him, but she had a way of turning a phrase so it slipped between the cracks. It had been over a year since Sam had been moments from death, and the two scars that stained his chest were timely reminders of how close he came to never seeing his family again. On a raid of an outpost in Afghanistan, Sam had been blasted with two shots that had ripped through his back and out of his chest, somehow missing his heart and leaving him with the slimmest of chances of survival.

But that's what Sam was.

A survivor.

He'd made it through, and with his military career over, one that he had been immensely proud of, he had just begun his intake at the Metropolitan Police College in Hendon. There had been conversations of Sam re-joining the military as a trainer, with the Armed Forces keen to use his expertise to train the next batch of killers.

But Sam wanted something different.

The army had always been the plan, after a lifetime of following his father around the country after their mother had left when he was only young. His father, William Pope, was a respected Major within the British Military, and Sam always knew he'd follow his father's footsteps. But where is father was a force for good behind a desk, forming strategies and seeking solutions, Sam had grown to be a force of death.

It was time for a change.

His father had passed before Sam's eighteenth birthday, so had never witnessed the exemplary career Sam forged, but Sam often thought that his father would have been proud.

Now it was time to help in a different way.

He rolled over to his wife, and kissed her tenderly.

'Well, I had you and Jamie to come back to.'

Their eyes met, and Lucy blushed.

'You soppy sod.'

She nudged his elbow out from underneath him, causing him to lose his balance and drop. As he did, he landed on a packet of strawberries, that squished under his weight, splattering him with juice. Lucy howled with laughter, and in the throws of their joy, Sam reached up, wrapped his arms around her, and hauled her down with him. Both of them were giggling like teenagers, when Sam noticed the shadow looking over him.

Jamie.

'Dad. Come and see.'

'What is it, mate?' Sam said, pushing himself up. The shoulder of his white polo shirt was stained pink.

'I've found a toad.'

'A toad?' Sam faked the excitement. 'No way. Show me.'

Jamie turned and ran as enthusiastically as he could back down the hill, and Sam looked at his wife once more, smiled, and then pushed himself to his feet. As he made his way to his son, he watched as the young boy frantically looked around the stream, his eyes wide with panic. After a few moments of looking, he turned to his dad with a woeful look.

'It's gone.'

'Oh no. Never mind.' Sam squatted down on the edge of the water. His son, ankle deep in the cold stream, reached up for a hug. 'Maybe he went home for his tea?'

'But I wanted to show you.'

'You know what?' Sam said, clutching his boy to his chest. 'I've seen toads before. They're pretty gross.'

'I know.' Jamie chuckled and pulled away. 'This one was massive.'

'Tell you what, kiddo. You keep looking for him, and if you find him, give me a shout and I'll run down to you and we can take a picture of it. Deal?'

Sam lifted his hand, and as always, his son couldn't resist the high five.

'Deal.'

The boy had a sudden wave of resolution and began to pull apart the long weeds of the stream, adamant he would find the toad again. Sam stayed on his haunches for a few moments, watching his son with fascination. The compassion for every creature and thirst for knowledge were traits he had drawn down from his mother, and Sam was fascinated by how Jamie's mind worked. He was a bright kid, always investigating, whether it was rummaging through bushes or with his head in a book.

Every single move the boy took made Sam proud.

Sam stood and made his slow walk back up the slight incline to his wife, who was beaming. Sam raised his eyebrows.

'What?'

'Just you two.' She waved her hand in front of her eyes, trying to stem tears. 'I just love watching you together.'

'Don't be ridiculous.' Sam mocked as he assumed his position next to her. Secretly, he loved the bond with his son and how much his wife adored it. 'He's a complete mummy's boy.'

'True. All boys love their mumma.'

The two of them sat in silence for a few moments, their eyes locked on their son as he systematically scanned the canal, looking for his lost toad. All around them, the noise and joy of the park began to dim, and as Sam turned and looked at his wife, he could see the finer details of her face fading away. He became aware he was in a memory, one that he had clung to lovingly for years.

But as with all things, time had ebbed away at the clarity of it all, and as the surrounding beauty of the park began to blur, his wife turned to him, a vague image of a person he had loved so dearly who had now been pushed away by the cruelty of life.

As the scene began to blur and fade, he heard her blood curdling scream of grief, the same one that he heard the night Jamie died.

He turned to his left, and the last thing he saw before he awoke, was the lifeless body of his son, lying crooked in the grass, his eyes open but gone.

Begging his father for help.

He turned back to Lucy, who's face was shiny with tears and before the entire memory cut to black, she spoke.

'Fight for him.'

Darkness.

Lucy's words echoed in Sam's subconscious, stirring him awake. The ringing in his ears was faint but constant, gnawing at the thumping headache that had set up camp in his skull.

He'd been knocked unconscious. That much was clear, and as he tried to bring a hand to his head, he was reminded that his arms were bound. The reality of the situation began flooding back to him, and he recalled having his hands tied behind his back. However, now, his arms were directly above his head, and as he blinked his eyes open, he noticed that he wasn't the reason he was standing up. The shackles around his wrists had been looped over a clasp which hung from the ceiling by a tight chain, with the little give it had allowing him to swing ever so slightly. The tendons in his bulging shoulders were at breaking point, and he took a few breaths and then looked around the room.

It was empty.

The walls were painted a dull grey. There was no furniture at all and the only feature Sam could distinguish beyond the clasp that was hanging him from the roof, was the drain on the floor.

Presumably for the blood.

The room was a torture chamber, designed specifically for guests as welcome as he was, and Sam tried his best to apply his body weight onto the clasp to break free. He knew it was a useless endeavour, but being strung up to wait for his death wasn't something he was willing to accept. With the pale glow of the lights that were affixed to the separate corners of the room illuminating him, Sam heaved with all his might, gritting his teeth through the immense pain that hummed from his damaged rib cage.

It was no use.

The door flew open, and in stepped two armed men, both resplendent in their black suits, and they smirked at Sam as they entered. One of them, who had a thick, dark beard, muttered something in French, and the other scoffed.

'Gentleman.' Sam said. 'Fancy letting me down?

The joke maker chuckled, stepped forward, and then rocked Sam in the stomach with a hard right. Sam doubled over, the restraints snapped him up right, and he gasped for air.

'Enough.'

The booming voice of Cissé emerged from the doorway, and in stepped Ducard's attack dog, his eyes locked on Sam. The two men quickly scurried to the side of the room, and Cissé leant back through the doorway and then dragged a metal chair through. It's legs screeched as he approached Sam, the irritating sound elevated by the confined space, and Cissé slammed it down three feet from Sam. Without breaking his stare, Cissé took his seat and folded his muscular arms across his chest. He ordered something in French to the men, and moments later, Sam felt the chain loosen and he was able to lower his arms. The other guard hurried from the room and returned instantly with another chair, and he placed it behind Sam and then retreated back to the wall. Confused, Sam looked at Cissé, who sniffed, and then, to Sam's total shock, spoke in English.

'Sit.'

Obediently, Sam dropped down onto the metal, his hands given enough slack to rest in his lap, and he looked at the man before him. There was no doubt, in Sam's mind, that Cissé intended to kill him.

'Thanks.' Sam said. 'I imagine a glass of water is out of the question?'

'You have no fear.' Cissé said fiercely. 'It is one thing I have noticed over these past few days. The moment you got involved at Chavet's hotel, I have read everything that has been written about you. I know who you are, what you are, what you've done. It's all very impressive, but there are many people who are trained to do such things. But what I see now. And what I saw in that warehouse, is something that cannot be trained. That is something that comes from pain.'

'You have no idea what I come from.' Sam responded coldly.

'I know you lost your son.' Cissé spoke with little emotion. 'For that, I am truly sorry. But it is not enough to excuse you for the mistakes you have made or what I will have to do in response.'

'Don't talk about my son.'

'I do not intend to. The thing is, Sam, I also come from pain. I grew up in a village called Bargny on the coast of Senegal. It was a hard time, but I had family. But then, war blew the village to pieces and my father put me on a boat to France. That was the last I ever saw of him or my family. No doubt, they were killed. The last time I saw my father's face was on that beach.'

'Why are you telling me this?'

'On that boat, I met a young boy. I was fourteen at the time, and he was a few years younger. I looked after him. We became family. We joined the army together and Ducard looked after us both. We served him, for years, and that is why I am here now. My brother, he is not. His name was Emile Domi, and *you* killed him two nights ago.'

The penny dropped, and Sam understood the imminent danger. He was trapped, in a foreign country, in one of its most secret and guarded locations. He was unarmed. He was bound. And he was looking into the eyes of a dangerous man running on vengeance.

'It wasn't personal…' Sam began, but Cissé, who looked genuinely moved at the memory of his fallen friend, lifted his hand to cut him off.

'I would have offered you a soldiers death. Quick. Proud. But I'm afraid the retaliation must be as devastating as the loss. Which means, for you, this will be more pain than you ever thought possible. I will take my time. I will be creative.' Cissé leant in close, and the calm demeanour dissipated to reveal a scowl of fury. 'And by the time I am done with you, Sam Pope, you will understand what true pain is.'

Cissé leant forward and patted Sam on the side of the face. It was a show of comfort, knowing that it would be the last Sam would be offered and then he stood. He flashed a look across the room to the other two men, who were still lurking in the shadows. He called out to them in French. One of them remonstrated, but Cissé's voice rose and they backed down. Sam watched, confused, as Cissé walked back towards the door.

'This is Yohan and Hugo and I've told them they are not to kill you, Sam. But they served with Emile as well, and they want their pound of flesh.' Cissé nodded across to one of the guys, who then tossed a key that landed in Sam's lap. 'I told them to at least give you a fighting chance.'

Cissé stepped out of the door and slammed it firmly behind him. Sam glanced across to the two men, who were stretching their arms out and cracking their necks, a show of intimidation and intent. Sam bent his hands inward, uncomfortably found the lock with the key and snapped his restraints open. With his eyes on the two trained men who began to circle him, Lucy's voice, the same one that had called him back from the void minutes earlier, echoed once more.

'Fight for him.'

Rubbing the soreness of his wrists, Sam stood, stretched his back, and clenched his fists, ready to fight for his life.

CHAPTER TWENTY-FIVE

Sam understood the drive of revenge.

Over three years ago, the man who guided him through most of his military career had been killed, and Sam went through extreme lengths for his vengeance. He'd led an assault on a motorcade in the middle of London, abducted a high ranking military figure and although he didn't kill Wallace himself, it had burnt within him from the moment Marsden died.

So he understood the anger in the eyes of the two soldiers who had been locked in the room with him. Although they were now living a more charmed life as part of Ducard's private security, Sam was under no illusion as to how dangerous they were, and while they circled him like sharks, he'd have felt safer in the water.

The two men carefully removed their dark jackets, revealing impressive frames that stretched their white shirts, and the one with the beard, Yohan, made a show of rolling his sleeves up. Sam rolled his eyes.

'Can we get on with it?' Sam goaded, not knowing whether either man spoke English.

But it provoked the necessary reaction.

Yohan launched forward, roaring with fury as he swung a few punches, but Sam repelled them with his forearms, ducked a third, and then retaliated with a stiff jab that sent the man back a few steps. Hugo grabbed Sam from behind, wrapping his thick arm around Sam's throat and tried to wrench him off his feet. Sam let his feet lift a few inches, before he fell forward, dropping to his knees and wrenching the man over his shoulder. As the man's spine connected with the hard concrete, Sam rocked back onto his knees, only for the Yohan to drive a boot into his chest, sending him backwards. Sam rolled through, and Yohan charged, driving his shoulder into Sam's stomach and he kept moving. As they hurtled towards the wall, Sam drove his elbows as hard as he could into the man's spine, and inches from the wall, he was able to loosen his opponents grip, pivot on his foot, and send Yohan slamming into the wall. The impact was brutal, and Yohan woozily fell to the ground. Sam turned straight into a hard right, which re-opened the cut above his eye, and Hugo followed it up with a few more punches, before he leapt forward, trying to drive a knee into Sam's chest. Sam side-stepped, wrapped his hands around Hugo's leg and pulled as hard as he could, sending both of them to the ground. All three men took a moment, a joint collection of breath, and Sam and Hugo made their way to their feet at the same time. Sam ducked the errant punch and caught the man with a two punch combo, sending him back into the wall, and as the man rebounded off the brick, Sam drilled him with a hard elbow that took him clean off his feet.

Behind him, Sam heard Yohan scrambling to his feet, and as he turned, he saw the man fumbling with the PAMAS G1 handgun that he had pulled from his side holster. Sam ate up the space between them as fast as he could, and as Yohan drew the weapon up, Sam sent a clubbing blow into the man's forearm, knocking the weapon from his grip, but Yohan responded with an uppercut to Sam's damaged ribs, and then a hard left hook that sent Sam spinning to his right, straight into a rugby tackle by Hugo that send them both toppling over one of the metal chairs. The clatter of body and metal echoed like a clap of thunder, and Sam grunted with pain as he tried to clamber to his feet. Yohan drove a boot into his ribs, but Sam wrapped his arms around the man's ankle and twisted, dragging him down to the floor with him. His eyes searched the floor for the loose handgun, that had slithered across the room into the shadows, but Hugo pounced, mounting Sam like an MMA fighter and began driving his fist down like a judge's gavel. Sam managed to get his hands up, blocking the blows, and then on the fifth or sixth one, he managed to slide an elbow over the man's forearm and drive it upwards, breaking Hugo's nose and sending him rolling off to the side.

Again, the three men took a moment, the battle beginning to take its toll, and as Sam stood, Yohan leapt towards him, driving a knee into Sam's hip, and then rocked Sam with a right hook. Sam nearly hit the ground again, but managed to steady himself, and in one swift movement, lifted the metal chair with his hands and swung it.

The collision with Yohan's cheek was sickening, shattering the bone and sending the murderous Frenchman howling to the ground. Still holding the metal chair, Sam turned towards Hugo, who launched forward and snuck his punch in before Sam could swing, and he followed it up with another punch that Sam took flush on the jaw. With the room spinning, Sam dropped the chair, and all he saw was a blur as Hugo launched into him, striking him with a shoulder barge that lifted Sam up into the air and crashing back first into the wall. Hugo grunted, the adrenaline surging through him, and he glanced at his fallen comrade and then marched menacingly at Sam. He lifted

Sam up by his throat and began to push against Sam's windpipe, cutting off the air and grinning maniacally as he stared into Sam's eyes. He was bulkier than Sam, and despite his best efforts to fight him off, Sam was unable to relinquish the man's grip. As he tried to fight the man off, Sam felt the man's tie scrape across his hand, and Sam clutched it and pulled with all his might. The man's head surged forward and as his face connected with the wall, he let go of Sam's throat. Hugo's head snapped back, but Sam grabbed the man's hair and then slammed him as hard as he could into the brick wall, cracking open the man's eyebrow and sending blood gushing down to the ground. One more forceful slam, and Hugo was out, and Sam let the man's limp body slide down the stone wall, face first, and then turned to Yohan, who was stumbling to his feet.

Sam edged forward.

Beaten.

Bloodied.

Breathless.

But still fighting.

Yohan's face was disfigured, and the bruising from his shattered cheek was already visible beneath the beard. The eyes that were filled with such murderous rage were now filled with desperation, and as Sam inched towards him with his fists raised, the man shot to his left and dived to the ground. As he hit the concrete, his fingers wrapped around the handgun, and he spun onto his back and raised his arms to fire.

But Sam's boot connected with his jaw, sending him flopping backwards, the gun limp in his feeble grasp. With considerable pain, Sam leant down and relieved him of the weapon, and then stood over him with the weapon in his hand. Blood had painted half of Sam's face red, and his hair was slick with it. His dark t-shirt was ripped, stained with blood and sweat, and his entire rib cage felt like it was connected by string.

But he was standing.

'Stay down.' Sam managed, taking deep, pain stricken breaths. Yohan glanced across the room to Hugo, who was out cold, and then back to Sam.

He spat.

The phlegm missed, veering off to the right, but the act of defiance was clear.

Sam moved the gun, squeezed the trigger, and sent a bullet into the ground that shattered Yohan's shin on the way through. The man howled in anguish, and as he clutched at his devastated leg, he hurled abuse that couldn't be heard from the echo of the gunshot. With his ears ringing, Sam ignored the French tirade and stumbled across the room, relieving the motionless Hugo of his handgun and then headed to the door. He had no idea what was waiting for him on the other side, where Cissé was or how many more men wanted their revenge.

But with a PAMAS G1 handgun in each hand, Sam pushed open the door and stepped out, ready to give himself a fighting chance.

———

With a long and considered pull, Ducard drew the smoke into his lungs and it almost trumped the taste of victory. With the rain lashing down against the grand windows of his mansion, he had decided to enjoy his cigarette in his study, the room lined with thick, wooden shelves that homed copies of every book of relevance. He cast his eyes over the leatherbound spines of them all, knowing that most of them had never been opened, and wondered when he would ever get the chance. With Sam Pope dead and Agent Corbin having made her choice, the pathway was clear. There would be an inquest into the death of Olivier Chavet, especially after the failed attempt by Domi that had resulted in death and panic. But Ducard had already spoken to his assistant, who was in the process of forming a believable narrative.

What if Domi and his team were acting on intelligence of Sam's attack?

They were already pinning the death on Sam, in some long-winded conspiracy that he was trying to silence the truth from emerging. With both Sam and Chavet in the dirt, and Corbin to follow, there was enough doubt in their actions for it to feel believable, and at the end of it all, it would be Ducard who not only stopped a known vigilante, but also uncovered corruption within the DGSE. Agard was on the hook for life, having been compromised, and Ducard had made it crystal clear that the man's role was to keep the DGSE off his case until he made appropriate changes when he came to power.

When he became President.

It should have been an overwhelming thought, to become the most powerful man in the country, but it was a role Ducard had played for years from the shadows. Now, with his slick grey hair and his handsome, seasoned looks, he would be able to play it in the limelight. There would be too many things to do, and he looked at the books with regret and wondered about donating them. A knock echoed from across the room, and in stepped Cissé.

'Laurent. My friend.' Ducard stubbed out his cigarette out of respect for his visitor. *'Is it done?'*

'Two of my men are having a go first.' Cissé spoke as if they were playing a video game. *'They mourned Emile like I did.'*

'Very well. Just make sure it's done soon.'

Cissé glanced across the study to the seating area in the far corner, where luxurious leather chairs surrounded a small, round coffee table that was adorned with a fake plant. Sitting in the corner seat, giving her the perfect view of the whole room, was Eva. Looking uninterested, she nodded to Cissé who responded in kind before he turned back to Ducard.

'Is she really necessary anymore?'

'Laurent, you're not jealous are you?' Ducard smirked, but instantly regretted it.

'No, I am just careful. Her purpose has been fulfilled. Perhaps now would be the best time for her to leave, before she becomes a problem.'

'Once we are out of the woods, then we will be done. It pays to have someone like her on hand. Just in case.'

Cissé nodded, clearly not in agreement, and then turned and made his way to the door once again. He shot a glance towards Eva as he approached the threshold, and she returned it lazily.

There was no fear.

Agitated, Cissé stepped out of the room and closed the door behind him. Ducard perched on the edge of his desk and sighed, tapping another cigarette out of the box and lighting it.

'He can be...difficult at times.' Ducard offered through a plume of smoke.

'He's just cautious. It's understandable.' Eva shrugged. 'But he has a point. Perhaps our deal is done.'

'Not quite.' Ducard smiled, reached back onto his desk, and then tossed a file across the space between them. It slapped onto the coffee table, and Eva whipped it up instantly. As it fell open, her eyes scanned the photos.

'Who is this man?'

'Jean-Pierre Vivier.' Ducard said with grimace. 'He is the *Direction générale de la sécurité extérieure.'*

'The head of DGSE?' Eva's eyebrow arched upwards. 'That wasn't the deal.'

'No, but considering you were charging me triple I

figured I'd get my monies worth.' Ducard's veil dropped. 'I am many things, Eva, but I am not a weak man. I do not allow my assets or my connections to take advantage of me. The moment one does, then more will, so I act. Right now, your weapons are in *my* armoury and you are sitting in *my* home. I have nothing but respect for the work you have done and the skills you possess, but you are not in a position to refuse.'

'Or what? You will kill me?' Ducard smiled and let the notion float in the room along with his cancerous smoke. Eva sighed. 'When?'

'Preferably within the next week. The panic it would cause the public will be palpable and then when I swoop in and take control, I can promise to restore order and bring his killer to justice.'

'Agard?' Eva had already connected the dots, and Ducard grinned. The final few loose ends would be tied up, and the idea that anyone would believe Agard's defence was farcical. Yes, the man had children, but Ducard would see that they were looked after. Then he could appoint a new director, one who was loyal and would bend to his every whim, and Ducard would have added another string to his bow of power. Eva contemplated the offer and then nodded her acceptance. 'I'm impressed.'

'Why thank you.' Ducard lifted his drink to her.

'I will need my rifle.'

'It's in the armoury. You can take it when you go.' Ducard looked out of the window, as the thunder storm erupted. 'But perhaps best to wait until morning. When the rain is finished and everyone is dead.'

CHAPTER TWENTY-SIX

As she was hauled from the room and down the stairs to the more clinical rooms of Ducard's mansion, Corbin had felt sick. The fear of her imminent death had begun to bubble in her stomach, threatening to empty its contents. But it wasn't just the impending end of her life that was causing the room to spin, but the betrayal.

She had worked with Martin Agard for over a decade. Over that time, they had become close friends, having worked hundreds of cases together and built a trust and bond that can only be forged in loyalty. Although it had threatened to spill over into something far more damaging on one occasion, the two of them had promised they would never cross that threshold. Corbin had met Agard's wife, Jeanette, a number of times, knocking back glasses of expensive wine in the sun and regaling her with funny stories of her loving husband. His two handsome sons, Louis and Marc, even referred to her as *Auntie Renée*, such was her closeness with the family.

It had almost been a surrogate for her own, as she had never quite been able to distance herself enough from the job to ever let someone in quite like Agard had.

Years had passed.

Trust built.

Love, in some ways.

And now, as she was marched through a sparse and empty corridor to a room where she would be executed, the man she had spent more time with than anyone in her life, was traipsing behind, with the strict order to end hers. Two men walked beside her, their firm grips locked around her muscular arms but they weren't necessary. Her hands were bound behind her back. Corbin knew a game of chess when she saw one, and Ducard, thanks to Agard's betrayal, had managed to move his pieces into place where there was only one outcome. The door to the room opened, and one of the men let go. The other roughly shoved her through the door to her knees, and she turned to her side to take the impact of the floor on her shoulder. The room was as empty as the corridor, with the halogen lights hanging from the corner, bathing most of the room in an inauthentic glow. The shadows clung to the spaces the light couldn't reach, and embedded in the floor was a drain, no doubt for the amount of blood that Ducard had spilled over the years. Defiantly, Corbin turned back and looked at the door as Agard stepped through, his head low and the gun in his hand.

'Tell me why, Martin.' She demanded, her eyes locked on him with hatred. He didn't respond, and as he shuffled to the other side of the room, he refused to look at her. *'After everything we have worked for. All these years, this is how it ends? For God's sake, look at me. You at least owe me that much.'*

Sitting on her knees, Corbin could feel her muscles bulging with anger. She wouldn't beg, she already knew that much, and she bored a hole through her treacherous partner with eyes that were burning with tears of rage. Behind her, the door closed, and she could see the shadow of the other man who had stayed in the room with them, undoubtedly to ensure the deed was done.

'*Please.*' Agard begged. '*Just close your eyes and know that I am sorry.*'

'*No. You motherfucker, you look me in the eye and kill me. Look me in the eye and do it.*'

Corbin shook with adrenaline, surprised at how willing she was to accept her death in the face of such betrayal. She had served her country with pride for two decades, and she was willing to die for it. If she was heading to the afterlife, she would do so with her head held high. Eventually, Agard raised his, and for a split second, Corbin felt pity for the man. The rugged, world-weary face was locked in a broken gaze, his cheeks drenched by the tears that slid from his pained eyes.

'*I have no other choice.*' Agard muttered, wiping away the tears with his free hand.

'*You do have a choice.*' Corbin stated. '*There is always a choice.*'

'*I'm sorry. If I don't, they'll go after the boys. I have to do what's right.*' Agard took a deep breath, composed himself and then stepped forward. '*I love you, Renée.*'

The confession of love broke through Corbin's resolve, piercing her cold defiance and pulling forward her tears. The heartbreak of the treachery flooded forward, and she understood her friend's predicament.

It was for his boys. His family.

He'd die and kill for them.

She met his gaze, both of them weeping, and she nodded her acceptance. With the final grains of sand falling through her hourglass, Corbin took a deep breath, straightened herself and nodded once more.

'*I love you, too.*' She closed her eyes for him and braced herself. '*I understand.*'

'*I have to do the right thing.*' Agard repeated, and he lifted the gun and pulled the trigger.

The gunshot seemed to reverberate off every wall at once, deafening with its fearsome power, and it took Corbin a few seconds to realise she hadn't been hit. She opened her eyes to her partner, who still held the gun at arm's length, only it was aimed above her head. She spun on her knees, to see the security officer falling back against the wall, his white shirt stained red, as he gasped for air and some sense of the situation. Realising his time was fading, the man's eyes widened with rage and his hand fell to his hip, his fingers grasping the handgun of his own.

Agard fired twice more.

He made sure.

With the man dead, Agard rushed towards the man to locate the keys to her cuffs. He found them in the man's pocket, and he hurried back to her, fumbling with the lock.

'*I'm sorry, Renée.*' He said as he found the lock. '*I had to do something.*'

'*But your family…*'

They both heard the lock open, and with a click, Corbin's hands were free. Her wrists were red raw, and as Agard helped her to her feet, she rubbed them tenderly. A silent moment of thanks was shared between them, and then Agard lifted the gun.

'*Let's go take this piece of shit down.*' Agard's resolve was contagious, but before they could move, the door behind Agard flew open. A gunshot rang out as Agard spun, and the bullet hit him in the chest, sending him crashing backwards into Corbin and a splatter of blood to erupt into the air. As they fell to the ground, Agard tried to lift the gun, but another bullet rang out, and the cracked him between the eyes, instantly ending his life.

The guard who had stood watch in the corridor moved

into the room with his orders clear, and crushed under her partner's lifeless body, Corbin frantically clawed at his lifeless grip to retrieve the gun.

The man's eyes locked onto her.

She grabbed the gun and fired.

The bullet caught the man in the side of his neck, blowing out the artery and sending a wave of blood crashing to the floor. He stumbled, slapping a hand to the wound and then foolishly tried to retaliate. But as he stepped forward and tried to raise his own weapon, the loss of blood and life took over and he crashed to the ground, his eyes wide with fear as he gurgled the final seconds of his life away.

He soon stopped.

Blood was trickling across the room, from the three dead men, a steady stream to the drainage unit. Corbin managed to sit up, and Agard's heavy, lifeless body slumped in her lap. For a few seconds, she cradled him, her tears splashing onto his blood stained face and then she let out a guttural roar of pain and vengeance.

Then she carefully laid her friends corpse to the ground, stood, cocked her handgun, and headed to the door for some payback.

Sam had edged his way out of the room that was supposed to have been his last, and he held the guns out in both directions. The corridors were dimly lit, with nothing lining the bare walls except the halogen bulbs. For all the expense and decadence that had gone into Ducard's mansion, the money didn't filter down below. Whereas the rooms above ground were for show, the corridors and chambers beneath were not for public consumption.

If people were brought down here, they weren't being brought back.

Sam took careful steps, treading lightly as possible, with one gun held out in front, and his other arm by his side, ready to aim backwards at a moments notice. He had no idea where he was heading or how many people he might come across, but he needed to move. He had made a promise to Corbin that he would find her, and he didn't doubt she could look after herself, but the odds weren't so much as stacked against them but had completely passed them by. As Sam approached a corner, he heard footsteps approaching, and he pressed himself against the wall. As the guard rounded the corner, Sam drove the harsh metal of the gun into the man's temple, shutting his lights out and watched as the man swerved to the other wall, hit the metal door with a sickening thud and then slumped into unconsciousness.

A gunshot echoed.

A bullet ripped past and into the wall.

Sam fell back against the wall, the guns drawn up, and he heard at least two different voices, barking instructions in French. As the footsteps began to approach, Sam took a breath, and then arched his shoulder around the corner and fired blindly, the gun kicking wildly in his hand as he unloaded four shots into the narrow corridor.

The response was instant.

A barrage of bullets ripped into the corner, sprinkling Sam with dust and debris. The corridor shook from the noise, which pinballed off every surface and rattled his eardrums. He hadn't heard anyone hit the ground or any cries of pain. Another bullet hit the corner, and Sam ducked down and then pushed himself off the wall, sliding onto the floor and out into the adjoining corridor.

He heard the cries of shock from the guards.

Sam pulled both triggers.

He lit both men up with bullets, with the first man taking two in the chest before his legs buckled, and the other one in the gut and then one in the shoulder, that spun him round and to the floor.

More gunshots penetrated the corridor, and Sam could see further down into the murky tunnel, two more guards rushing towards him, their weapons trained on his location. He shuffled onto his knees, and then darted forward, keeping as low as he could. He covered the distance to the fallen men in two paces, and then dived forward, just as a bullet hit the corpse he had slid behind. One of his guns was empty, and Sam tossed it in frustration. More bullets hit the dead body, splatting Sam with blood, and the two guards made the mistake of unloading their guns at the same time.

They stopped to reload.

Sam had seconds.

Instinctively, he spun up, balancing on one knee and he drew the gun up with both hands and through the smoke and the carnage, he brought it up to his expert eye.

He squeezed the trigger.

The first man's head snapped back and his legs buckled, and he hit the ground, spilling blood and brain out of the back of his skull.

Sam squeezed again.

The bullet hit the man in top of his chest, knocking him off balance. He hit the wall but stayed up right, and then, in a final act of defiance, roared angrily and lifted his gun, shooting aimlessly in Sam's direction. Sam fired again, this time hitting the man in the dead centre of his chest and obliterating his heart.

He was dead before he hit the ground.

Sam pulled the mag from the bottom of the gun. He

already knew it was empty due to its weight, but he confirmed it and tossed it anyway. As he stood, the effects of the last few days scurried across his body like a swarm of ants, and he leant against the wall to steady himself. From his ribs and his spine, to the cuts that were dribbling blood down his face, Sam felt like he'd fallen down a flight of stairs. But he had to push on.

Corbin was somewhere.

A gunshot echoed loudly from somewhere in the labyrinth of corridors beneath the estate, and Sam focused in on the sound, limping slightly as he hurried as fast as he could. Each dark, dingy hallway was lined with metal doors, and Sam could only imagine how many enemies of the state had been taken into one of these for their hard goodbye.

Another gunshot echoed.

Sam turned a corner, and collided with an armed guard, who already looked shaken by the carnage he had heard. The man was young, not even out of his twenties, and his youthful face was framed by a patchy beard that seemed like a pointless endeavour.

The man's eyes bulged, as if he had just downloaded his job description, and he lunged at Sam, wrapping both hands around Sam's throat as they collided into the wall. The young man was well built, but the rage had made him sloppy, and Sam held onto the man's wrists, and then drove a boot as hard as he could into the side of the man's knee. He buckled, and Sam twisted the arms to the side, pulled the man to his knees, and then, while holding his arms out, drove a sickening knee into the man's face.

His nose let out an audible squelch as it disintegrated into his skull, and the man flopped back helplessly onto the ground. The door a few feet away from them was open, and Sam edged towards it.

It was a staircase.

With a final look back at the broken bodies behind him, Sam shoved the door open fully with his shoulder, stumbled into the stairwell, and with his bloodied hand gripping the banister, made his way back up into the house.

CHAPTER TWENTY-SEVEN

The doors flew open and Cissé barged into Ducard's study with purpose, not even acknowledging the hired killer in the corner who looked on with interest. Like Ducard, she had heard the eruption of chaos from the catacombs beneath the house, but unlike Ducard, she hadn't shown even a flicker of worry. Ducard, however, looked to his Head of Security for answers, his eyes wild with panic.

'What the fuck is going on?' He demanded, his hands gesturing wildly.

'You need to leave, sir.' Cissé spoke calmly. He looked over to Eva. *'You, drive him out of here.'*

'Do I look like a driver?'

Cissé took a step toward her, his eyes widening with anger. Unlike Ducard, he hadn't spent the last decade getting soft behind a desk, and with a war breaking out below them, he didn't have time for insolence. Eva stood, accepting the challenge, but before Cissé could take another step, Ducard stepped forward and placed an arm across his chest.

'Enough, Laurent.'

'Your things are being packed and are in the hallway.' Cissé spoke to Ducard, but kept his eyes on Eva. She smirked.

'Mine, too?' Her mind raced to her rifle.

'Oui.' Cissé turned to Ducard and placed his hand on the back of the man's neck. *'I will come to you once I am finished.'*

Throughout it all, the bloodshed, the rank, the orders, they had become firm friends, and Ducard knew that Cissé struggled with displaying emotion. It was why he had assaulted Lascelles after the death of his friend, Domi, and why he had made it a personal mission of his to kill Sam Pope himself. But through it all, he still served Ducard, and as his Head of Security, he had made getting Ducard out of the building the priority over his own vengeance.

'See you on the other side, my friend.'

Ducard shook Cissé's hand, and then, the terrifying man turned and stomped across the room, flashing one more threatening glance to Eva, before he disappeared through the door, closing it behind him. Ducard realised he had held his breath and let it go, inhaling the fresh air greedily.

'He's an asshole.' Eva offered.

'That may be, but he is also a loyal friend.' Ducard clasped his hands together. 'We need to go.'

'Say the word, and I will handle this problem for you.' Eva said, checking her nail. 'I'm an expensive driver.'

Ducard looked at her with a frown.

'This hardly seems like the time for jokes. Let's move.'

Ducard slipped his arms into his jacket and made a move towards the door, and Eva reluctantly followed. A few feet behind him, she watched as he opened the door and saw the gun barrel pushed against his forehead. Eva fell back against the wall, biding her time.

With his eyebrows raised, Ducard lifted both hands.

'Agent Corbin.' He smiled his best smile. 'This seems excessive.'

'Does it?' Corbin fixed him with a stare, that through the tears, told him she wasn't joking. 'You're under arrest…'

'What for?' Ducard asked smugly, taking a step backwards. Then another.

'For the murder of Olivier Chavet. Sam Pope. And my friend…' Corbin stepped forward, the gun and her hand passing through into the room. 'Agent Martin Alg…'

Eva reached out, dug her fingers into Corbin's pressure point and relinquished her grip on the gun instantly. As it fell loosely in her hand, Corbin stepped in to try and combat the move, but Eva dropped to her knee, shifted her body weight into Corbin's hip and flipped her over her shoulder. Corbin hit the ground hard, the gun spinning from her hand but she rolled over and pushed herself to her knees, just in time to deflect the vicious kick that Eva swung at her. Fluidly, Eva swung the other foot as that one hit the ground, and she caught Corbin in the face, sending her into the side of the leather chair. Eva took a few steps into the room, looking down at Corbin with an expression of disappointment. Corbin spat blood onto the wooden floor and then stood, her fists clenched, and she met Eva halfway. Corbin swung a few punches that Eva evaded, but then caught the Bolivian with a left jab to the ribs, and then a straight right that knocked her back a few steps. Eva reset herself, absorbed the next right, and then drove her knee into Corbin's ribs, drilled her in the jaw with an elbow, and then sent her sprawling across Ducard's desk with a right hook. Relentless, Eva grabbed Corbin by the hair, lifted her up, and then slammed her face against the oak, pressing down with all her weight on the side of her skull. Through bloodstained teeth, Corbin yelled in agony, her hand rapidly roaming the desk before her fingers found a paperweight, which she promptly swung upwards.

The edge of it caught Eva on the eyebrow, slicing it open and causing her to fall back a few steps. Corbin pushed herself up, charged forward and took both herself and Eva to the ground with a hard tackle. She rained down on Chavet's killer with right hooks, but on the fourth, Ducard swooped in, locked her arm under his and lifted her off. For a man of his age, he was still in incredible physical condition, and he shifted his whole body weight as he hurled Corbin over his desk. She hit the wood, bounced, rolled and then collapsed on the other side. She groaned groggily, stirring slightly as she tried, but failed, to push herself up onto her knees.

Eva stood, wiping the blood away from her lip and her eyebrow, and then stomped towards Corbin's fallen body.

'Leave her.' Ducard ordered, but Eva ignored the man. She rounded the desk and hauled the bloodied and battered Corbin to her feet, and then rocked her with a sickening right hook that sent her flopping back against the desk. With the fight beaten out of her, Corbin slumped to the floor again.

'Hand me the gun.' Eva demanded, but Ducard shook his head.

'Leave her to Laurent.' Ducard demanded. 'We need to leave. Now.'

With a furious huff, Eva turned and followed the politician out of the room. They rushed towards the front door, ignoring the luggage that had been packed and piled nearby, and stepped out into the rain. One of the 4x4s was still parked out the front, and as Eva jumped into the front seat, she demanded the key that Ducard, in his haste, hadn't collected. As the man who had once waged many wars anxiously waited in his seat, Eva yanked open the panel beneath the steering wheel, exposing the wires beneath. With Ducard's panicked commands for speed echoing in her ears, she began to pull at the wires, trying to bring the engine to life.

———

Cissé had been alerted to the situation below as soon as the first duo had made contact with Sam. One of the men had hit their emergency button that was strapped to their belts, and it had set off the internal alarm in the house. Although it made no sound, it did lock down the exits of the building, beyond the front door. It had been installed for years, but never been used, as Cissé was certain no one would ever have been foolish enough to launch a raid on the premises. The alarm had buzzed Cissé's phone, and he had made his way to the CCTV office, where Lascelles had been posted up since they had returned from the UK. The bruising around the man's eyes brought a smile to Cissé's face, as did the lack of eye contact when he burst into the room. There was limited camera coverage of the corridors below the house, purposely so to ensure the multiple assassinations or tortures of years gone by was never documented, but it at least offered some views of the carnage.

Sam Pope had escaped.

Although Cissé had doubted leaving Yohan and Hugo alone with the man, he knew that they wanted their revenge for Domi's death just as much as he did, and seeing as how he would be the one to snatch the life out of Pope, it was only fair they got their licks in beforehand. But again, just like in the warehouse, Sam Pope had impressed him.

Had shown him a proclivity for survival.

A few dead bodies littered the corridor, and one of the other cameras was showing Sam brawling with another man in the narrow, dark walkway.

Cissé walked away before seeing the outcome, already knowing that Sam would prevail. The man was cut from the same cloth as himself, and Cissé knew that Sam's victory was assured.

He'd soon make his way into the house.

As ever, his duty was to Ducard, the man who had given him a purpose in life, and he had hurried back to the man's office to instruct him to leave the building immediately. The woman, as deadly as her reputation had claimed, had given him some unhelpful comments, but Cissé had maintained his control. He had found her involvement needless, but also knew that his failure to kill Sam and her efficiency in eliminating Chavet told a different story. There would be ramifications, for sure, but Cissé knew that his friend would always stand on his side of the line.

If anything, Ducard would allow Cissé to eliminate Eva, just to tie up the last of the loose ends.

With his message delivered, Cissé strode from Ducard's office and back into the immaculate stately home. The grand hallway opened up onto a wide staircase, that swept around to the walkways that overlooked the reception area. There were countless guest rooms, along with entertainment rooms. It was too much property for one man, but Ducard was a man of perceptions. The estate was just another tool within his arsenal, as those who came to visit couldn't help but be impressed, and those who came to die would quiver at the sheer size of the man's wealth and power. But now, because of one man, Ducard, who was on the cusp of officially becoming the most powerful man in the country, was having to flee for his life.

Because of one man, their mission to take Chavet off the map had become a snowball of mishaps, with blood shed and international relationships frayed.

Because of one man, they had agents of the DGSE locked below, ready to be slaughtered.

And because of one man, Cissé had lost his younger brother. When the bullet hit the wheel two nights ago, Domi's car had flipped and spiralled into a lamppost. The resulting crash had snapped his neck, and due to not wearing his seat belt, his face had been torn to shreds via the shattered glass and unforgiving concrete. The two of them had often joked about their own demise, and how they would want nothing more than a respectable, soldiers death.

To go out fighting.

Instead, Domi was dragged across the ground like a dog under a car wheel. It boiled Cissé's blood, and as he took his steps towards the chaos, he knew that there would be no restraint.

There would be no mercy.

In the warehouse, he had wanted to hurt Pope. Beat him severely so he had felt every ounce of the pain that he had caused him. But this time, he would execute the man.

This time, Cissé would hold nothing back, and he would summon all of the rage that three decades of warfare stored in a man.

He had already done his job. Ducard was safely out of the house, which meant this was no longer professional. It was one hundred percent personal, and Cissé marched down the hallway towards the high, heavy, double doors that led to the impressive kitchen facility within the house. Inside, there would be a team of five chefs, all scrambling around the noisy room, preparing a meal for their boss and his staff. Judging from Sam's position on the CCTV, he was near the stairwell on the other side of the house, which meant Sam would be making his way up the building and through the kitchen.

Cissé pulled the PAMAS G1 from his spine, slid the mag and then snapped it shut again. A force of habit.

He wanted to execute Sam, and stepping into the room and putting a bullet between the man's eyes would do it.

But it wouldn't be enough.

The grief and guilt of Domi's death pulsed through Cissé like a second heartbeat, and he placed the gun on the hallway table.

He removed his jacket, folded it, and placed it next to the gun.

Then, with his fists clenched, and the unrelenting desire to maim coursing through his body, he pushed open the kitchen door and stepped inside.

CHAPTER TWENTY-EIGHT

The difference between the main house and the tomb beneath was startling, and Sam appreciated just how luxurious the house was. The walls were quilted in the finest of wallpaper, the panelling that ran halfway up the wall was flawless. On the few hallway tables he passed, the decorative ornaments looked expensive. He followed the noise he could here, which was growing with every step. It started off as muffled voices, but as he cautiously rounded a corner, it grew loudly into a chorus of yells and laughs.

The crack and sizzle of cooking.

A smell wafted out from the door ahead, which was sheeted in frosted glass, and behind it, he saw the odd blur of white as a chef walked past. Sam stumbled forward. His face was smeared with blood, and his skeleton felt like it was stuck together with Sellotape. He pushed open the door and stepped into the kitchen, bringing the whole operation to a halt.

Four chefs, all of various seniority stopped and turned, their faces shocked at the bloodied man who had stumbled into their domain. The kitchen was restaurant quality, painted a sheer white without one speck of mess anywhere.

In the middle of the wide room was a massive, metallic island, which was lined with dishes and utensils, spread between hobs and other cooking appliances.

The far wall was lined with large ovens, fridges and whatever else was needed to prepare a banquet, and some of them were whirring with life. In the far-left corner was a walk-in wine cellar, sectioned off with a glass partition that still afforded a view of the expensive collection that hung in racks that reached to the ceiling.

But Sam's attention was pulled to the opposite side of the room, across the island and the boiling pots, where Cissé stood, his hands clasped in front of him, waiting patiently. The two men couldn't break their stare, and the head chef, reading the situation, quickly ushered his work force to the door. Sam stepped aside, letting them past, and then carefully, he shuffled into the room, doing his best to hide his injuries.

It was pointless.

Cissé had already sized him up, noted the pain points and was no doubt forging a plan of attack. There were no words spoken this time. After the arrogance at the warehouse, Cissé hadn't moved a muscle, letting his eyes tell Sam that there was only one way out of the room. Their chat in the interrogation room earlier that evening had already laid bare his motivation, and Sam knew, considering he had disposed of his other men, that Cissé wouldn't make the same mistakes. As he shuffled around the edge of the island to the vacant floor between Cissé and the wine cellar, Sam came to a stop.

Cissé pushed himself away from the metal work top and took a step forward. Like Sam, he was dressed in a black shirt, only his wasn't smeared with the evidence of war.

Not yet, anyway.

The silence spread through the room, only interrupted

by the bubbling of water and then both men lunged forward.

Cissé threw a barrage of punches at Sam, which he did well to deflect, before he pushed Cissé away and both men stopped again.

Sam lifted his fists.

Cissé's eyes glistened with excitement.

Again, they lunged forward, this time Sam went on the offensive, swinging some hard fists that Cissé dodged with the agility of a boxer, before he caught Sam with a blow to his damaged ribs. Sam hunched slightly, and Cissé clamped both hands on the back of his head and began to viciously lift his knees. Sam crossed his forearms across his face, absorbed the first few blows against the bone, and then he snatched Cissé's leg, lifted it and hurled him onto the island. Cissé hit the metal hard, rolled across and clattered the floor among a number of metal trays that clanged loudly. As Sam moved to meet him, Cissé swung one of the trays. Sam got an arm up to block it, but Cissé followed up with a right hook that snapped Sam back, followed by a hard boot to Sam's thigh, and then an elbow to the chest that took Sam off his feet. The air exploded from Sam's lungs as he hit the tiles, and Cissé ran and jumped, driving his boot down as hard as he could to Sam's chest. Sam rolled to the side, Cissé planted his foot hard, wobbled, and Sam swung a boot up and caught the man on the jaw, driving him head first into the side of the metal unit. The impact dented the metal, and both men pulled themselves up, both weary and Cissé charged at Sam, ignoring the blows that Sam rained down, slammed into him and lifted him up and onto the island. With all his strength, Cissé hauled Sam across the metal, clattering into the pots and pans, as Sam wildly tried to break his hold. As they got to the hob, Cissé pressed down on Sam's neck, trying to push his head back towards the naked flame that was currently boiling the water that frothed in the pan beside him. He could feel the heat and smelt the tips of hair as they began to singe. Sam managed to reach his arm back and he lifted the lid off the piping hot water and pressed it to the side of Cissé's face.

The skin sizzled and Ducard's right hand man howled in anger and relinquished his grip. Still laying on the counter top, Sam drove his boot into Cissé's chest, sending him stumbling backwards into the glass partition of the wine cellar. The man was roaring with agony, clutching the scorched cheek that was as pink as a rare steak. Sam slid off the counter, and charged forward. Cissé swung a punch, Sam ducked and drove his fist into the man's stomach, then lifted his knee to crack the man in the face as he hunched over. Cissé rocked back against the glass and Sam took a step back and then burst forward, slamming his shoulder into Cissé's midsection and sending them both crashing through the partition, which dropped into thousands of shards around them. They both collapsed among the wreckage, the broken embers of the partition slicing away at their skin. Their breathing was heavy, and as they pulled themselves to their feet, they knew they were beating each other to death.

It was just a matter of who got there first.

In desperation, Cissé pulled a wine bottle from the rack and brought it down like a sledgehammer to Sam's skull. Sam managed to lift his elbow, shattering the bottle and possibly his arm, and as the wine flowed over his arm, Cissé slashed at him with the jagged remains of the bottle neck. Sam dodged a few slices, before the enraged Frenchman slashed the jagged glass across his cheek. Sam roared with pain as his cheek sliced open, and as he turned in pain, he felt another slash across the top of his back, before Cissé drove his boot into the base of Sam's spine, sending him tumbling back out into the kitchen and sliding across the other shards of glass.

The floor, which had been an immaculate white, was now splashed with blood.

Sam tried to lift himself, but his back gave out, keeping him pressed on the tiles, and behind him, he heard Cissé's boots crunch the glass as he approached. Sam managed to roll over onto his back, just as Cissé lunged towards him, bringing down the razor sharp bottle neck to Sam's throat. Sam got his arms up, the bottle slicing across his forearm before Cissé pressed down further, aiming for Sam's throat a mere inch or so away. Sam struggled, flailing his legs for any kind of leverage, and Cissé adjusted, pushing more of his body weight down onto his arms and driving the broken shard closer and closer to Sam's death.

His face was soaked in blood, with various cuts accompanying the scorched cheek that hung from his bone in tatters. His eyes were wide, the notion of Sam's death all consuming, and he roared in Sam's face as he drove down harder.

The bottle nicked Sam's skin, drawing a little blood, but Sam's other hand slapped recklessly in the surrounding glass, slashing his palm to pieces before he felt the large shard beside him. He wrapped his fingers around it, ignored the lacerations it caused, and then drove it into Cissé's side. The warmth of Cissé's blood instantly flowed over his hands, and Cissé jolted in agony, and then Sam twisted the shard with all his might, slicing open the man's side and mincing whatever organ he had hit. As Sam pulled the blood-stained glass from his body, Cissé rocked back onto his knees, the life flowing from him, and with his guard down, he looked to Sam, a flicker of respect passed his eyes, which then quickly morphed into adrenaline fuelled fury.

Fight or flight had kicked in, and Cissé lunged at Sam

once more, only this time, Sam drove the shard as hard as he could into the centre of Cissé's chest. The air and life seemed to shoot out of Cissé in one horrid, blood curdling gasp, and he rocked backwards, falling off Sam who quickly rolled out of the way. Looking like a living example of a death by a thousand cuts, Sam gripped onto the metal island and hauled himself up.

He could feel the blood trickling down his spine. His face stung, as the skin on his cheek flapped open. His arms, hands and legs were covered in lacerations and his spine felt like it had been compressed like an accordion.

But he was standing.

With his boots crunching the glass beneath his feet, he rounded the island to Cissé, who was laid out on his back, his eyes open and vacant, with the shard of glass protruding from his chest like an iceberg. He was taking short, sharp breaths, as the blood gurgled in his throat, and he looked at Sam one last time.

Then, Sam lifted his boot and drove it down on the glass shard, thrusting it deeper into the man's chest and shattering within him, obliterating his heart and lungs, and killing him instantly.

The room was silent.

Sam took a few deep breaths, then turned and shuffled painfully towards the door of the kitchen, which he pushed open and stepped through, letting it swing back with a bloody handprint smeared across the glass and the carnage locked behind him.

Stumbling through the hallway, Sam passed through the reception area and was hit by a gust of cold wind that swept through the open front door, splashing the floor with the rain that had been pounding the world with malice. A pile of luggage bags had been stacked nearby, including a case that Sam recognised as a rifle carrier.

He ignored it and carried on, passing the living area where Ducard had met them earlier, promising their deaths with the arrogance of a man who had thought himself untouchable.

Sam had been happy to prove him wrong.

The tall, wooden doors to the study were ajar, and Sam headed towards the opening, his eyes drawn to the rows of books that reached from wall to wall, crammed together like they were passengers on the London Underground. His mind wandered to Jamie, his head in a book, and Sam always felt a twinge of guilt when he realised he hadn't been keeping his promise.

He'd told his son he wouldn't kill anymore, but the injustice of his son's death, and the broken world that had necessitated his intervention, had shattered that promise.

But he told his son he would read more, and as he fell against the door for support, he told himself he'd pick up a new book if he survived the evening.

He stumbled in.

He'd half expected to find Ducard sitting behind the desk, a cigar in hand, and the woman who had killed his comrades to be waiting with a gun.

But there was no-one.

A pained groan reached up from behind the desk, and as Sam limped around it, he saw the crumpled body of Corbin. She was beginning to stir, and he knelt to help her sit. Her face was badly bruised, with one of her eyes swollen shut and her lips were split open.

She was a fighter, and Sam helped her to her feet. She blinked away the cobwebs, the situation returning to her swiftly, and then she turned and looked at Sam.

'Fucking hell.' She exclaimed. 'You look like shit.'

'It's nice to see you, too.' Sam smiled through the pain,

and then staggered against the desk. Corbin quickly slid his shoulder over her own and propped him up, and together, the two of them headed towards the door. She stopped halfway, bent down, and picked up the handgun that had been knocked from her grasp earlier.

She had a feeling she might need it.

As they approached, Corbin cast her eye over Sam, who had clearly walked through hell to find her.

He'd promised he would.

As she was debating offering a kind word of gratitude, they heard an engine roar to life beyond the open front door. Whoever it was, was trying to make a break for it, and Corbin left Sam leant against the door frame of the study and she raced along the hallway to the door, as the car pulled away.

Ducard was in the passenger seat.

'Fuck. It's Ducard.'

Sam waved his arm for her to go, and without a moment's hesitation, Corbin launched through the door and out into the rain. The car surged forward, before it veered sharply to the right, skipping gravel up into the air as it turned and headed towards the long, open road towards the exit. Corbin sent a few bullets into the back of it, blowing out the window, before instinct pushed her forward, and she began to sprint across the grass, ripping through the darkness in a hopeless attempt to stop them.

In the house, Sam gritted his teeth as he tried to follow, but his eyes fell upon the rifle carrier, and he realised he needed to hurry.

CHAPTER TWENTY-NINE

With every squelch of mud beneath her shoe, Corbin sprinted through the rain. The immaculately kept grass was tearing up beneath her feet, and mud splattered her legs as she propelled forward. Her body ached, and her lungs were burning as she pushed herself forward.

She knew there was no way of catching the car, as it sped beyond through the trees, its visibility illuminated with every light it passed.

But she couldn't stop.

If Ducard escaped, then it was all over.

Olivier Chavet, and the historical death of his father, would be washed away, and their murders would be lost to a narrative that nobody would be able to unpick. Her friend, Martin Agard, would be tarnished as a traitor, and his legacy and family would live in the darkness of it forever.

She had to keep going.

The rain crashed against her, washing the blood from her face, and she knew she was crying. The desperation in every move she made was overwhelming, and as she saw the lights of the car speed further and further away, she felt her hope fading with it.

Her body begged her to stop.

Her lungs cried for air.

Despite her best efforts, Corbin felt herself tumble forward, the gun dropping from her hands as she crashed into the mud. She inhaled two deep breathes and pushed herself to her knees. Above her head, a rumble of thunder rolled through the sky and she watched as the car and any hope of redemption sped away.

Then the sky filled with another sound, and everything changed.

Ducard was breathing heavily in the front seat, turning every few seconds to look back through the broken window. The wind swept into the car, and the back seat was drenched with the intruding rain. Peering into the darkness, he could make out the figure of Corbin as she sprinted across the grass, and a smile spread across his face as the woman became smaller and smaller.

Beside him, Eva put her foot down, the car racing through the intermittent light and ripping the gravel path to shreds. The woman showed no emotion, her hands were clamped onto the steering wheel and her eyes were locked on the minimal view of the road ahead. They shot past the trees, putting enough distance between themselves and the truth, and Ducard afforded himself a smile.

As he collapsed back into his chair, he silently toasted his victory. He had no idea what the aftermath would hold, or whether he would see his friend, Laurent, again. But the most important thing was they had the information.

All of the evidence that existed of his deals with the

Taliban, his collusions with General Ervin Wallace and his orders of death for Didier Chavet and Simone Rabiot, were all gone. Lascelles was working through it all, cobbling a narrative that would implicate the likes of Corbin and Agard if need be. Sam Pope provided him with the perfect scapegoat, and while the man was an impressive force for good, the trail of bodies and carnage he had left in his wake would damage any credibility he had.

Ducard had won.

In less than two weeks time, he would become the President of France, would assume total control and rebuild the country in the way he saw fit. They would take back the power within Europe, and then become a global power that would make their neighbours quiver with fear. He had seen war. Been through it. And he knew what it took to win.

He turned to Eva, as a clap of thunder shook the heavens above and he chuckled.

'What a night.'

Then came a different sound, and his eyes widened with fear as the 4x4 swerved off the road, and flipped towards a tree.

Sam practically collapsed through the metal door and sprawled onto the hard slate that lined the roof of the mansion. The rain was relentless, the sound of it hitting the stone sounding like chattering teeth and Sam slowly pulled himself across the wet tiles towards the concrete wall that ran the length of the rooftop. Just climbing the stairs had taken it out of him, as the impact of his fight through the building had begun to take its toll.

He'd leant against the wall of the stairwell and forced himself to climb, leaving a smear of blood against the brickwork.

The weight of the rifle felt like it had doubled.

As he pulled himself across the cold tiles, his hand grasped the case, until finally he made it to the wall. He leant against it, gritting his teeth and pushing away the pain as he opened the case. The SPR300 was a clean rifle, one that he had used a couple of times in his career, and through sheer muscle memory alone, he began to assemble it, connecting the pieces of a puzzle to forge a killing machine.

Beyond him, he could hear the sound of tyres tearing through gravel, and somewhere below, he knew Corbin was running for her life.

For her career.

For the justice of everyone that Ducard had stepped on to get to where he was. Sam tried to push himself up, but the pain in his back felt like a weight and he collapsed once more. If Ducard made it out of his estate, then it would all be over.

The police would swarm the premises, find the blood soaked chaos of Sam's fight, and then haul him away for a lifetime of pain and darkness. That was always a risk, but the same thing would happen to Corbin.

The crimes of Ducard would be washed away by a PR machine more powerful than the rainfall and the deaths of everyone who deserved better would be forgotten.

'Get up old man.' Sam yelled at himself, and with a cry of anguish, he spun onto his knees and pushed himself to his feet. Looking over the edge, the impressive grounds of the estate came into view, although the rain was pulverising the rows of flowers and immaculately trimmed bushes and trees that stretched beyond the darkness that swallowed them. Mustering all the power he could, Sam lifted his slashed arms, which dripped with blood, and drew the rifle up. The weight of it felt like it was increasing with every second, and he grunted as he pulled it to his shoulder. As he pressed against his clavicle, he felt his shoulder blades squeeze, and the wound at the top of his back ripped open further.

The pain was numbing and he could feel his head spinning.

Thunder echoed above his head, like a warning from the gods, and Sam took a deep breath.

He planted his feet.

He saw Corbin sprawl into the mud. Defeated.

Beyond, through the gaps in the trees, he saw Ducard slipping away into the distance, to an underserved victory and a life of tyrannical power.

He brought the scope to his eye, the metal pressing against the slash across his cheek.

He ignored the pain.

The last time he'd looked down the scope of a rifle, he had seen Andrei Kovalenko, a gun pressed to Amara's head.

Sam took a deep breath.

Sergeant Javier Vargas.

Corporal Laurel Connell.

Corporal Jason Bennett.

With the memories of their deaths echoing through his mind, Sam kept his body still and then squeezed the trigger.

The rifle, despite its design, still kicked back with enough force to take his fading body to the ground. The crack of the shot echoed back at the thunder like a challenge, and before Sam could get back to his feet, he heard the sound of a car swerving, rolling across the gravel and the sickening collision of metal and tree.

As the rain fell upon him, Sam lay on the roof, ready for it to be over. But he hauled himself up and headed to the stairwell.

It wasn't over.

Not yet.

———

Corbin watched the carnage unfold before her, as the back tyre of the 4x4 exploded, ripped apart by a bullet from above, and the car lost all control. As the wheel arch hit the gravel, sparks shimmering into the darkness, before the vehicle's momentum became unhinged, and as it swerved, its speed caused it to topple and then flip, and it rolled twice before it slammed into the trunk of one of the trees. The impact shook the earth, and glass erupted like a grenade had gone off. Smoke billowed out from the wreckage, and Corbin retrieved her weapon and picked up the pace, speeding through the darkness towards the destruction. As she stepped off the grass onto the gravel path, her boots crunched on a combination of stone and glass, and the vehicle was upside down, its windows completely obliterated. Corbin raised her weapon and as she approached the driver's side door, she watched as the woman who had efficiently beaten her minutes before began to crawl through the shattered window. The woman's strikingly beautiful face was a confusion of blood, bruising and matted hair, and by the limp, uselessness of her left arm, had clearly broken her collar bone.

Yet, impressively, as she hauled herself across the jagged surface, she made not one sound. Just as her legs wriggled free, Corbin raised the weapon.

'Don't move.' Corbin yelled, the gun trained on the Bolivian. 'Show me your hands.'

Eva rolled onto her back, her hands free of any

weapons, and her head rocked back as she tried to deal with the pain. Her right foot was twisted at an unnatural angle, and Corbin could tell there was little chance of the woman going anywhere. As Corbin made her way around the wreckage, she heard the feeble cries from within.

'Help me.' Ducard begged, and Corbin pulled open the passenger door. Ducard slumped out, his face a mangled mess from his impact with the dashboard. One of his legs was obliterated, a blood-soaked bone had ripped through the skin and his trouser leg, while both his arms were hanging loose and shattered. The man had been pulverised by the crash, and now, the only mercy Corbin could afford him was a bullet through the skull. With little care for his pain, Corbin reached under his arms and pulled him a sufficient distance from the car, and then dropped him on his back on the grass verge of the track. Ducard writhed in agony, his body crumpled to such a state that he was unlikely to fully recover.

'I can't feel my leg.' He moaned.

The sound of footsteps crept up on Corbin, and she spun, gun drawn and then lowered it with a smile.

Sam approached.

Lashed by the rain, the man was a walking tapestry of pain, with blood staining any exposed skin, and a limp that told her he was on his last legs. She stepped towards him, wrapped her arms him and hugged him.

'It's over.' She said.

'Not yet.'

Sam took the gun from her hand, and despite her desperate remonstrations, he shuffled towards Eva, who was beginning to stir. As she pushed herself to a seating position, she looked up and directly down the barrel of the gun that Sam pointed at her.

'Don't do it, Sam.' Corbin begged. 'She's finished.'

'She killed my team.' Sam barked, his arm shaking with fury and his eyes watering. 'Good people.'

Corbin shook her head, disgusted by the truth of the words that were about to come out of her mouth.

'She was just following orders.' She stepped beside Sam, placed her hand over the gun and pushed it downwards. 'Killing her won't bring them back.'

Sam shook his head, furious that Corbin was speaking the truth. He looked down at Eva once more, their eyes locking, and he didn't detect one modicum of regret in her eyes. But Corbin was right, and Sam finally lowered the gun, knowing that hers and Ducard's capture was justice enough.

Corbin gently rubbed the base of Sam's spine to comfort him, when a gurgling noise punctuated the moment.

'Please, just kill me.'

Ducard was staring up at the sky, unable to move. Tears were flowing down his broken face, and Corbin stood over him with the gun.

'Pierre Ducard, you are under arrest for the murders of Olivier Chavet, Didier Chavet, Simone Rabiot and of DGSE Agent Martin Agard.' She stepped forward and looked over at the man's fallen, broken body. 'I hope you rot in hell for the rest of your life.'

As Ducard wept at the idea of his future, Corbin called it in, requesting the full force of the Parisian police service, as well as several ambulances for the body count. Then she turned to Sam.

'Before I contact my boss, you'd better get out of here.'

She gave Sam an address, and the two of them nodded their thanks to each other.

A spark ignited the petrol that had been flowing from the engine of the destroyed vehicle, and what remained of it exploded, lifting the entire frame off the ground a few inches before it crashed back down on the stone, ablaze with a mighty fire. Sam and Corbin had turned to shield themselves from the blast, but when they returned their gaze to the flames, their eyes widened in horror.

Eva was gone.

CHAPTER THIRTY

It was all Morgana Daily could do but smile when her co-workers made their comments.

'Wow. You really fucked up France.'

'That news story really blew up.'

'Nobody will take an interview with you now.'

It would all be harmlessly passed off as workplace banter, and while it probably did come from a good place, she had often found herself where she was right now.

In a bathroom stall, wiping away tears.

It had been ten days since her interview with Olivier Chavet had hit the airwaves, her first foray into live broadcasting and for all intents and purposes, it had been a smash hit. The viewing figures, not just on the day, but on social media sites since, had been the highest that British News Network had ever received, and every story that spun off from that fateful morning would link back to the video.

Morgana herself had become a sensation, with her social media profiles more than quadrupling in followers, most of whom made lewd comments about her appearance.

Her bosses were keen to get her front and centre, seeing her as a potential rival to BBC's Lynsey Beckett, a woman that Morgana fiercely respected. They said she was the right side of pretty to not be intimidating, and had the cachet with the younger viewers to draw them in. Never had she felt like a commodity in the world of journalism, but that was the reality since Chavet's death.

Nobody actually wondered if she felt any guilt.

She did. It was overwhelming.

If you peeled back all of the bells and whistles, and the dramatic flair that Olivier had seasoned his story with, there was a travesty behind it. The man had lost his father, and had been relentless in his quest for justice. By giving him the platform to tell his story, Morgana had been more interested in the impact it would have on her career. She hadn't realised she was putting the man in the firing line.

Now, with the man being killed a day later, she had found sleep difficult in the week since and her love and passion for journalism had taken a hit.

But it had set off a chain reaction that had seen the man ultimately responsible, Pierre Ducard, who had seemed certain to become one of the most powerful men in the world, brought to justice.

Not just for Chavet's assassination, but for the executions of Didier Chavet and Simone Rabiot. There were countless other crimes, and after a discussion with their French correspondent, Ducard was facing the full force of the law back home.

It was a small comfort, and one she clung to as she wiped away her tears and composed herself.

The world was a messed up place. That much was obvious and the further she went down the journalistic rabbit hole, the more true that would likely ring. But without her intervention, there was a good chance that nothing would have come to light, and a murderous dictator would have assumed power.

Silver linings were rare in life, and she knew she needed to cling to one when she found it.

With a deep breath, she stood, left the stall and reapplied her eyeliner in the mirror. The last thing she wanted was for her colleagues to see her suffering. It would raise eyebrows on whether or not she had the stomach to become a lynchpin at BNN.

With one last re-affirming nod to her reflection, Morgana stepped back out of the restroom and headed back to her office, ready to tackle the next story.

Hoping to make a difference.

'Is that it, then?'

Leanne McEwen looked to her husband with a comforting smile. One filled with love that had only grown in the decades which they had spent together. She sat on the garden decking, overlooking the freshly mowed lawn and the neat, obsessively-tended flower beds. She held a glass of ice-cold water in her hand, and nodded to the pitcher on the table beside her. Bruce McEwen strode across the decking, his long legs half covered by his shorts and he kissed her on the top of the head before he sat down on the seat opposite and helped himself to the jug.

'Yup,' he said firmly. The spring sun was a warm and welcoming feeling after such a bitter winter, and McEwen lifted his face to it. He could feel the stress melting from his mind.

'Well, it's about time, if you ask me,' Leanne said. 'You were too good for them, Bruce. Way too good.'

'I at least tried, didn't I?'

'Tried?' Leanne's immaculate eyebrows raised in anger.

'You gave that force everything you had. Sure, you missed time with our boys, but they understood. But now, you have all the time to make it up to them. Especially as…'

'As?' McEwen turned to his wife with intrigue, and he could tell she was bursting with excitement.

'Jenny's pregnant.'

McEwen fell back in his chair, his mouth open with shock. Glee trembled through his body like an earthquake. Jenny had been their son Max's high school sweetheart, and after they had finished university, they had reconnected, fallen in love and now lived an hour away in Sutton. Now that Max had reached his thirties and was holding down a senior position in a law firm, Bruce and Leanne had been predicting when the baby was coming.

Even if he had tried, McEwen couldn't peel the smile from his face.

'Well how about that?' He finally said.

'I know. You're going to be a Gramps. Or a Grumps.'

'Fuck off.' McEwen joked, and he and his wife chuckled. As the fun died down, a silence crept in. McEwen gazed out over his garden, contemplating how much he had sacrificed for the life that was now waiting for him. The investigation had been quick, and clearly corrupt, especially as he was offered a golden handshake to step down as Commissioner of the Metropolitan Police, as well as his generous pension.

It felt like a major chapter in his life had come to an end, and he wasn't sure how to write the rest of it.

'I'm proud of you.' Leanne's voice cut through the thought process. As ever, she knew where his mind was. It must have been written across his face and he turned to her, reached across the table and gripped her hand. His thumb ran across her wedding ring.

'I couldn't have done any of it without you.'

'Oh, I know that.' She joked. 'Now, you get to do the rest *with* me.'

'Sounds good.'

McEwen sat back in his chair and smiled once more. He knew he had given the country his all, had tried to make a difference and had tried to do it the right way. There had been bumps along the way, and brick walls he had run into, but he had never lost himself.

Never lost his reason.

It was ironic that the most wanted man in the country had inspired him to stick to his convictions, and even though they had resulted in him making the enemies who had forced him out, he had left with his head held high.

Bruce McEwen was no longer an officer of the law.

But he would still remain a good man.

As he sipped his ice-cold water, a wave of satisfaction passed over him. His predecessor, the now Sir Michael Stout, had given him one warning.

'Prepare yourself for a myriad of shit.'

McEwen placed his glass down on the table, and peered out at the sun that was glistening above the trees and imagined his grandchild playing in the garden.

It was someone else's myriad now.

───────

What should have been a proud day for Agent Renée Corbin was shrouded in regret. The presentation of her bravery award was at the *Direction Générale de la Sécurité Extérieure* headquarters, codenamed CAT, in the centre of Paris. The government building was a magnificent struc-ture, made up of three buildings that looped round like a crescent. The space between was a man-made garden of well-kept trees and grass, with picnic benches scattered irregularly under the branches. The entrance was heavily guarded, and all those who were in attendance for her award would have had to go through multiple metal detectors and bag searches.

But the reason for them being there wasn't one that she wanted to celebrate.

Pierre Ducard had been charged with over twenty counts of conspiracy to commit murder, with his name visibly on the sign-off sheet for a number of killings made over the years, both international and domestic. The DGSI had been involved, and once one of Ducard's men, Francois Lascelles, had negotiated immunity in exchange for his co-operation, the hammer fell on Ducard from the greatest of heights. The young man, who was no more a soldier than he was an acrobat, spoke of being physically bullied by Ducard's security staff and that resentment had led him to back up the files that the former presidential candidate had ordered destroyed. There were gigabytes of evidence that proved Ducard's shady dealings over the years, along with the clear link to General Ervin Wallace, who had been outed as a global terrorist three years before.

The deaths of Olivier and Didier Chavet, along with Simone Rabiot were laid squarely at the feet of the man.

As was the death of Martin Agard.

That was why a dark cloud hung over the day's ceremony, and when Corbin took to the podium to accept the award that Director Vivier proudly handed her way, she dedicated it to her fallen comrade. In the crowd was Jeanette Agard, along with her sons, Louis and Marc, to accept the tribute to her departed husband.

He was buried a kilometre north of where they were in the Père Lachaise Cemetery.

He had died a hero, and Corbin had ensured he had been buried as one.

After the presentation, and the small talk surrounding the visual injuries that were fading on her face, Corbin had spent the half hour celebration with Jeanette and her boys, treating the boys to stories of their father's bravery. She promised Jeanette that she would be on hand to help with anything she ever needed, and that she owed her life to Martin giving up his own.

The two parted ways with tears in their eyes.

Vivier took her to one side, rolling out the potential promotion to a more senior position and giving Corbin her own department to investigate the elite players in France. She said she'd consider it and then left, driving glumly through the streets of the capital with her award stuffed somewhere in the boot of her car.

It was never about the glory.

It was about justice.

And with Ducard detained behind bars, his murderous henchman in the ground and the deaths of the innocent now accounted for, she felt that she had at least managed that.

Closure would come at some point, but until she was ready, she would grieve not only for Martin Agard and his family, but also for the damage that had been done to her country. The presidential election had been suspended, with the serving president accepting the need to stay on for another six months.

Her phone was buzzing with an international number once again, and she had already been grilled by the UK's Foreign Secretary about the whereabouts of Sam Pope. The desperation in the women's voice was clear, especially as she had hitched her wagon to the 'Ducard Charm Offensive' and now found her credibility and career circling the drain.

But Corbin had refused to answer then, and now refused to even pick up the call.

Her house was situated in a quiet, residential street a forty-minute drive from town, and as she pulled into the driveway, she left the car without taking her award in with her. As she stepped into her house, she made her way to the kitchen and smiled.

'You're up.'

Sam turned and looked at her, his face still a dull shade of purple from the bruising and the scars now a dark, rusty red. They littered his face and forearms, and the stitching job she had done on the slash that ran the width of his cheek had begun to close fully. It would leave a brutal scar, but at least it would hold.

Sam smiled back, winced at the pain and nodded.

'How was it?'

'Rough.' She said as she opened the fridge. She pulled out a beer, offered one to Sam, and then closed the door when he politely declined. 'But it's done now.'

'On to the next one.'

Corbin twisted off the cap, scoffed at his comment, and then emptied half the bottle in one gulp.

'What about you?' She asked as she took a seat. 'Any thoughts?'

Sam shrugged. There had always been a fight, even if it meant he needed to go looking for one. But this one had hit harder than others. Perhaps it was the reminder of the pain and horror of being in that rainforest all those years ago, and watching his friends die for no reason.

When he had saved the likes of Jasmine Hill or Hayley Baker, he knew that had been the right thing to do.

This one had been personal, and while he had been haunted for years by the ghost of his son and the promise of a life he could never have, the ghosts of those who had fallen lingered in the background.

Sergeant Javier Vargas.

Corporal Laurel Connell.

Corporal Jason Bennett.

Their deaths had been laid to rest. Acknowledged for their bravery and respected for giving their lives.

Sam hadn't saved them. But he had honoured them at least.

Finally, he met Corbin's gaze with clarity.

'I'm going to get better,' he said firmly. 'And then I'm going to keep fighting.'

EPILOGUE

The spring was morphing into the summer, and in the month that had passed since Ducard's arrest, life had been a whirlwind for Renée Corbin. Her promotion was in the works, the final details regarding her remit were being ironed out, but the paperwork and salary had already been confirmed. The bruising on her face had disappeared, although a neat little scar sliced through her eyebrow as a reminder of her battle with the now absent Bolivian.

There had been no trace of the woman since she disappeared after the car exploded, a fact that had niggled at Sam ever since.

He'd been staying with her ever since the battle at Ducard's estate, and the superficial injuries had healed up. Most of the cuts had disappeared without much of a trace, but a scar now dominated his cheek, as well as the top of his back. When he had removed his shirt for her to inspect the stitches, she was shocked at how it just felt like another one to add to his collection. The man was a walking memorial to war, and his body was littered with reminders of how close he had been to death.

Drunkenly, one night, she had made a pass at him,

their bond and friendship had given her the incorrect notion that something more could be shared between them. In his sober state, Sam had politely declined and told her he wasn't what she was looking for, and despite his protests that she shouldn't be, she was mortified by her actions.

He explained it was just her grief for her friend that had made her seek comfort, and while the two of them would have made a beautiful couple, their bond was forged in blood, not lust.

Sam had made it clear he would be leaving tomorrow, and Corbin had made her way to the local market to source some fresh ingredients for a farewell meal. She wasn't much of a cook, but Sam had joked that it was in her French blood to be able to construct a delicious meal.

As she foraged through the stalls of the marketplace and collected her ingredients, she glanced up a few times, clocking the well groomed man that was clearly following her.

It wasn't one of Ducard's men.

His entire stranglehold over the military and French politics had crumbled, with the damning evidence against him all but ensuring he would die in prison. It was the least he deserved, and when the day came that he received his sentence, Corbin would be in the courtroom, along with Jeanette Agard, to revel in the man's punishment.

As she headed back through the streets of Paris to the car park, with two bags of fresh groceries hanging from each hand, she clocked the man again, about twenty yards behind her. Nonchalantly, she stepped into a small coffee shop, the rich aroma of fine coffee and fresh pastries filled her nose instantly. A couple of young, fashionable students, with dyed hair and more piercings than Corbin could count, looked up from their conversation and returned to it immediately. Corbin ordered herself a coffee, and then felt the presence of the man behind her.

'Shall I get you one, too?' She asked, without turning around.

'How did you know I was English?'

Corbin turned to face the man.

'The suit. It doesn't fit properly.' The man smiled at the insult and then stood proudly. His dark hair was neatly trimmed into a side parting, with the sides showing signs of grey. His clean shaven jaw was powerful, and under the ill-fitting suit, he had a physique that screamed military.

Or something similar.

'Agent Corbin. How's the promotion going? Has it gone through yet?'

She regarded him with a raised eyebrow. Internal information for the DGSE was strictly confidential, and the man had already played a fascinating hand. Judging from the excitement twinkling in his dark eyes, he knew he had her attention.

'Who are you?' She finally asked. The woman behind the till handed Corbin her coffee, and then asked the man for his order. He waved her off, and the two of them stepped to the side to let the woman behind them approach the counter. The man handed her a card.

'My name is Dominic Blake. Director of Directive One.'

'Never heard of it.'

'Quite right.' Blake smiled, enjoying his clearly rehearsed routine. 'We deal with matters that the British Government don't want people to know about.'

'Right.' Corbin handed him back the card. 'Am I an issue, Dom?'

The man chuckled, refusing to rise to the bait of her using his first name.

'No. But the man staying at your residence is.'

'I don't know what you're talking about…' Corbin began but Blake held up his hand to cut her off.

'Please, Agent Corbin. Don't insult either of our intelligence. We know you have offered Sam Pope a place to hide since the fallout of the Ducard situation.'

'Well, if you knew he was there, why haven't you arrested him?'

'Because we don't want to arrest him.' Blake said with a smile. 'But let's just say he wasn't too fond of me the last time I offered him a job.'

Corbin's eyebrows dropped in confusion. The man spoke so eloquently and was clearly high on himself. But he held a certain authority that made him very good at his job.

'Well, what makes you think he will listen to you this time?' Corbin asked, trying to figure the whole situation out.

Blake smiled.

'Because I won't be the one asking him.'

The man looked beyond Corbin, and she spun round. The woman behind her thanked the barista for her coffee and turned to face them. Her brown skin shimmered in the Parisian heat, and her exposed arms revealed tight, powerful muscles. Her striking face, with its sharp features, was framed by a bob of jet-black hair.

'Who are you?' Corbin asked, feeling she'd been ambushed. The woman confidently sipped her coffee and smiled.

'Amara Singh.'

GET EXCLUSIVE ROBERT ENRIGHT MATERIAL

Hey there,

I really hope you enjoyed the book and hopefully, you will want to continue following Sam Pope's war on crime. If so, then why not sign up to my reader group? I send out regular updates, polls and special offers as well as some cool free stuff. Sound good?

Well, if you do sign up to the reader group I'll send you FREE copies of THE RIGHT REASON and RAIN-FALL, two thrilling Sam Pope prequel novellas. (RRP: 1.99)

You can get your FREE books by signing up at www.robertenright.co.uk

SAM POPE NOVELS

For more information about the Sam Pope series, please visit:

www.robertenright.co.uk

ABOUT THE AUTHOR

Robert lives in Buckinghamshire with his family, writing books and dreaming of getting a dog.

For more information:
www.robertenright.co.uk
robert@robertenright.co.uk

You can also connect with Robert on Social Media:

facebook.com/robenrightauthor

instagram.com/robenrightauthor

Printed in Great Britain
by Amazon